I0736245

SINISTER STAGE

A WICKS HOLLOW BOOK

COLLEEN GLEASON

Published by Avid Press

Copyright © 2020 by Colleen Gleason, Inc.

All rights reserved.

No part of this book may be reproduced in any form or by any electronic or mechanical means, including information storage and retrieval systems, without written permission from the author, except for the use of brief quotations in a book review.

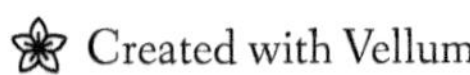 Created with Vellum

For my own group of Tuesday Ladies, the #12TRT gals. Can't wait for our next road trip!
(Can I be Maxine?)

CHAPTER ONE

Welcome to Wicks Hollow
Established 1889
Population 8,201

HER FIRST SIGHT of the familiar sign made her chest swell and her eyes sting.

Home.

She was home.

As Vivien Leigh Savage navigated her snazzy new Honda Accord around a sweeping curve, she caught a glimpse of Lake Michigan beyond a fringe of pines, maples, and elms, sparkling cerulean and sapphire in the late July sun.

We're home, Liv.

Her eyes stung a little more, and she blinked rapidly before they teared up so she couldn't see.

Home was a relative term, with layers and layers of

meaning and emotion. But Wicks Hollow—which held few but potent and enduring memories, and where she'd only lived for hardly more than four short years more than a decade ago—was truly her home.

There's no place like home.

She smiled and sang "Over the Rainbow" as she drove into town.

Beyond the long curve was a little hill, and when she reached the top of it, the village sprawled before her: compact, colorful, and busy. The town was all quaint shops, charming restaurants and cafés, Victorian-era houses, neat sidewalks with flowerpots every few feet cascading with blooms, and *lots* of cars and people—although "lots" was relative to someone like Vivien, who'd just come from New York City, her new car filled with boxes.

Wicks Hollow was a tourist haven, and June through July were the busiest, most crowded months of the year—as evidenced by the way the traffic slowed to a crawl as Vivien drove into the village. But once Labor Day came along, most of the tourists and summer-home owners abandoned the place, leaving the town mostly to itself.

Small bungalows and little Victorians, along with a few ranches and condos, clustered together on those shady residential streets far from the tourist areas. That was where the locals lived and where Vivien had rented a small house for the time being.

Things had changed radically since she'd left after high school—almost thirteen years ago—but at the same time, so many things had stayed the same.

Orbra's Tea House, owned by the grandmother of Vivien's

close friend Helga, sat downtown, precisely where it had been for nearly thirty years. The Roost, the biggest dive in the area, still perched on the corner of Pamela Boulevard (which didn't resemble a boulevard at all) and Lacey Street. The new and used bookstore was in its same location—a rambling old Victorian set back from the street a little. Vivien remembered a warren of rooms and tottering stacks of books *everywhere*. It was a place where a book lover could easily get lost and spend buckets of money. There was a sign in the window:

Author Event
New York Times Bestselling Author
TJ Mack
July 31 3pm

That was just over a week, and Vivien made a mental note to add it to her calendar, because now this was *her* town and she wanted to be part of it. Besides, she loved the Sargent Blue thrillers. She'd finished listening to the latest TJ Mack audiobook about the time she crossed into Ohio, then rapped, bee-bopped, and sang along with the *Hamilton* cast for the rest of the trip.

Trib's, a trendy artisan restaurant, was relatively new, but Vivien had been there several times over the years when she'd come back for visits. She knew the owner very well and had helped him get talented, chef-in-training summer interns through her contacts in New York.

Hot Toddy, a darling coffee shop in a cottage with hot-pink shutters and mint-green siding, was relatively new—two or three years ago—and she was disappointed to see that

Gilda's Goodies, a fantastic vintage clothing shop, was still closed while in search of a new owner.

Although Vivien had visited Wicks Hollow since she went off to NYU, just visiting wasn't enough. Now she was *home*, permanently (she hoped).

There is no hope—you are *home permanently,* she told herself, paraphrasing Yoda.

Even if the bank didn't come through with the loan, she was going to figure something out. It would just take longer than she planned. But she was going to open the theater for Liv no matter what.

She hoped.

There is no hope, dumbass, Yoda told her. *There is only* do.

Right.

Vivien navigated around tourists both on foot and in vehicle through the five blocks of the main route into town. She drove along Elizabeth Street, which eventually curved away from the nucleus of shops taking her less than a mile west to the small cove of Lake Michigan. A tiny marina there hosted no more than two dozen boats, and there were several small cafés along the water with bright umbrellas and perky flowers on the tables.

She passed a charming little alley called Violet Way on the right and noticed that the old antiques shop down there seemed to have had a facelift and was fresh and sparkling— must be a new owner. Vivien smiled to herself, for *she* was now a business owner in the town. The excitement fluttering in her belly settled into a little queasiness.

I hope I can pull this off.

There is no hope, there is—

"Yeah, I know, I know," she said, unsure whether it was her own thoughts or Liv who kept lecturing her in the voice of Yoda.

The winding two-lane road hugged the shoreline north, with a public beach, two small inns, a kayak, canoe, and bicycle livery on the left, and more small shops and a few private cottages on the right.

It was a little bit of a detour to go this route, but Vivien needed to take in all of Wicks Hollow, *all* of her town, her home, her memories on this important day—this *commencement* of the rest of her life.

Remember the time we had ice cream sitting on the pier and you had a double scoop of strawberry chunk and I had a double of chocolate and we tried to trade one scoop each?

Her eyes stung and her mouth twitched sadly as she remembered how hers and Liv's ice cream scoops had all ended up in the lake with four decided *plops*, leaving them with empty cones.

"We can buy new ones," Mom had said, her eyes bright and shining. "Now that the two of you are off and running! Just this once, though...we can't have our little actresses getting chubby."

"Now, Josey, let's not put that sort of pressure on them," said Gran, shaking her hat-bedecked head. The brim was so broad that it offered enough shade for both of the girls if they stood close to her, which they did whenever they could. "They're only children." She wrapped her arms around each of the twins and hugged them close. "Very talented, but children nonetheless."

So the second time, Vivien and Olivia had each ordered one strawberry and one chocolate scoop each—*and* sprinkles

—and they ate them on sugar cones while sitting on swings in the park across from the lake. They both had tummy aches after, but it had been worth it.

That was one of the two most vivid memories Vivien had of Wicks Hollow from when Liv was alive—likely because that had been a monumental day for the Savage twins. At age eight, Vivien Leigh and Olivia Dee Savage had just been cast as Oliver in a national touring revival of the musical. After playing smaller parts in *Annie* and *The Sound of Music*, it was their biggest, most demanding role yet, and Mom was over the moon.

Now, Vivien cruised along the lakeshore and thanked her grandmother for the millionth time for being such a stabilizing influence during those early years...and beyond. Gran had helped to balance the pell-mell, frenetic drive of the twins' mother with reality, and that, Vivien knew, was surely the only reason she was still alive, relatively sane, and not an addict—except when it came to ordering carry-out.

I miss you, Gran.

Gran had died nearly a year ago, having been in an assisted living center just outside of Wicks Hollow for about seven years. Vivien had visited her as often as she could get away from New York, and called regularly when she couldn't. Which was probably more than her mother had done. Not that she was judging—she truly wasn't. Mom was actually doing pretty well right now.

Vivien could almost hear Liv: *Don't think about Mom right now...don't ruin your homecoming.*

"*Our* homecoming, Liv," Vivien said. "*We're* home."

So Vivien put aside thoughts of their mother and continued driving just out of town on the north side, where the road curved away from the big lake. Her moonroof was open and the windows were down, and she could smell the distinct scent of lake from the breeze coming off the water as it mingled with the soft humidity of a Michigan summer.

Home.

If she kept going straight, she'd drive a couple more miles until she reached the southern tip of Wicks Lake—a long, narrow inland lake that attracted just as many summer visitors as the big lake.

Instead, she turned east onto Blueberry Road—barely two miles out of town—and that was when her heart really began to squeeze and her chest felt tight and anxious, and the butterflies went crazy in her stomach. Her palms slicked damp over the steering wheel and she had to start taking the long, deep, slow breaths (in-two-three-four, out-two-three-four-five-six-seven) her yoga teacher had taught her to help stave off an anxiety attack.

She breathed and refocused her attention above the road at the bluff that overlooked Lake Michigan. Several houses dotted the tree-studded, rolling hill, all spread out and partially obstructed by more trees. There was a tiny bungalow, a newer-looking mansion, a white clapboard farmhouse. But one stood out because it was an anomaly: a slant-roofed ranch that had been built in what she thought of as Brady Bunch style. It didn't fit the otherwise contiguous look of the hill, but it must have one hell of a view.

The thoughts and the distraction had calmed her, so by the time she turned into the parking lot near the end of the dead-end road, Vivien wasn't feeling quite so ill.

But now she was in the parking lot, facing the building, and there it sat: the Wicks Hollow Stage.

The theater had been closed since the early nineties, and the parking lot was strewn with broken glass and grass growing between cracks in the concrete. The building itself, made from brick and constructed around 1900, was in excellent shape—Vivien had made certain of that.

Back when they visited Wicks Hollow as young actors, she and Liv had been fascinated by the idea of a cute little stage plopped down in the middle of their grandmother's tiny town.

They were used to performing all of their shows in large, imposing, thousand-seat theaters in busy, loud cities. This minuscule venue was strange to them, their young minds imagining how different it would be to arrive at and leave a place like the Wicks Hollow Stage. But they both loved coming to visit their grandmother, and for obvious reasons, the theater that lived there captured their attention and imagination.

The building had been for sale at the time (in fact, it had never been taken off the market for as long as Vivien had known about it, with the same weathered sign hanging crookedly from the front for decades), and on a whim, Mom had insisted they take a look at it.

"Just for kicks," she'd said, her eyes bright with promise and prospect, and probably dollar signs as well, but Vivien had been too young to notice that part. The girls were nine by then and had just been cast as Young Cosette in *Les Misérables*, had sung live at the Tonys, and the world was the Savage Sisters's oyster.

Gran got the key from the realtor, so it was just the four of them walking into the dim old theater.

"Kinda creepy," Mom said, rubbing her arms, looking around in disappointment. "And it's a dismal mess."

Her daughters didn't notice. Vivien remembered running down the main aisle and up onto the stage without hesitation, Liv right on her heels. Without any communication, they immediately launched into "I'd Do Anything," then went on to "Tomorrow" and then "Be Our Guest," including the dance routines they knew and ones they made up on the spot.

Giggling, laughing, dancing around, singing at the tops of their lungs so their voices filled the space, echoing into every corner, the two of them owned that stage in the dark, empty theater in a way they'd never done in front of hundreds of spectators.

Then they sat on the edge of the stage, panting happily, and chattered to each other.

When we're rich and famous, we're going to come here and do free shows for all our friends, Viv said. *I'll play Nancy in* Oliver! *and you'll play Belle, and we'll have so much fun.*

We'll make the theater big and bright and beautiful and everyone will come even from New York to see us! And Gran can sit in the front row for every show, Liv added with shining eyes.

The idea flourished and became an anchoring sort of fantasy, something that gave her and Liv roots and a sort of mooring to cling to—a stable, harmless dream—during the crazy days of performing, traveling, touring, rehearsals, auditions, fittings...

They were at the top of their game, their mother was fond of saying, and in the twins' heyday, Josey Savage believed the sky was the limit.

And then Liv had died and everything changed.

Vivien never told Gran about her dream to return to Wicks Hollow and reopen the theater in honor of Liv and their shared dream, but it was Gran who unwittingly made it possible when she bequeathed Viv a small chunk of money.

It didn't make her rich by any stretch, but it was enough for Vivien to outright buy the abandoned stage...which would soon be known as the Olivia Dee Theater. She was picking up the keys from the realtor tomorrow, whom she'd known back in high school.

Tomorrow, tomorrow, she hummed.

And if—*when*—she got the loan from the bank, she'd be able to put it back to rights for performances.

As Vivien looked at the building that was now hers, the culmination of years of wishes and dreams now at hand, she smiled through her tears and pushed away her nerves.

We're gonna do this, Liv.

Welcome home.

CHAPTER TWO

"I AM *NOT* GOING to play a dead body in the window seat," said Helga van Hest. "Whoever plays Mortimer would break his back lifting out my giant self. He'd collapse there right onstage, die from a heart attack, and that would be the end of Wicks Hollow Stage's—I mean Olivia Dee Theater's—production of *Arsenic and Old Lace*.

"You'd have to refund tickets, and all those renovations on the old place would be for nothing. You'd file for bankruptcy and move back to New York in shame, and I'd never see my best friend again."

Vivien chuckled at her friend's rant as she snatched the last lemon blueberry scone from right beneath Maxine Took's greedy fingers.

The foiled eighty-one-year-old Maxine snarled under her breath, but Vivien ignored her. You had to if you wanted to get anything accomplished when you were sitting at Orbra van Hest's tea shop, where Maxine and her posse—known as the Tuesday Ladies—reigned supreme.

It was barely eight in the morning on a Tuesday in mid-

July, so the glut of tourists who filled Wicks Hollow to bursting were still sleeping in at their bed-and-breakfasts, boutique inns, RVs, or lakeside cottages...which meant Orbra's Tea House was nearly empty.

This morning, only Maxine Took, her best partner-in-crime Juanita Acerita, and Orbra herself were present from the Tuesday Ladies group. Helga, the granddaughter of the tea shop proprietress, and Vivien were the only other people in the café at the moment.

She had an appointment at ten to finally get her keys for the theater (she'd done the closing remotely while packing up in New York), and had been too antsy and excited to wait at her rental home until then. Plus, she was also expecting a call from the bank, and she needed a distraction to calm her nerves.

"You're six feet, two inches of gorgeousness, not a giant, Helga, and I'm pretty sure Baxter could handle wrangling you out of the window seat. Have you *seen* him lately? He's not the skinny dork he was back in high school." Vivien grinned.

"Baxter James is playing Mortimer Brewster?" Maxine exclaimed, spraying moist crumbs from the scone she was still eating. The greedy old crone clearly hadn't needed the one Vivien had swiped. "And you didn't tell me?"

"I didn't think you'd care," replied Vivien slyly. She knew *exactly* how Maxine Took worked. "You said you were too busy to do the show—"

"Well, I *just* cleared my calendar," said Maxine, thumping her cane for emphasis. Her brown eyes blazed from behind thick bottle-bottom glasses, and not one of her iron-gray hairs fluttered with her movement. Vivien suspected it was because it was a wig, although she (and everyone else) didn't know for sure. It could just be an entire can of hairspray. "Can't make a damned decision if you don't give a person all-a the information right out front, can I?"

"Certainly not," replied Vivien, exchanging glances with Helga. "Does this mean you'll take the role of Abby Brewster?"

"Is she the bossy sister or the fluttery one?" asked Maxine, narrowing her eyes.

"For pity's sake, they're both murderers," said Helga. "What does it matter?"

"Of course she's the bossy one," said Vivien at the same time, then broke off a large piece of the scone she'd swiped and wagged it in front of Maxine's face. "Typecasting, you know." She popped the crumbly pastry into her mouth and grinned. "And if we ever do *Wizard of Oz*, you know what role you'll be playing." She hummed the Wicked Witch of the West's theme song.

Maxine barked a laugh, her eyes gleaming with humor and appreciation. "I'd play the hell out of that role, and you know it. All right, then, Vivien Leigh. I'll be the bossy sister." She thumped her cane again. "And they're not technically murderers, you know, Helga."

"What do you call feeding lonely old gentlemen arsenic in elderberry wine—without them knowing about it—if not a murder?" Helga said. Which wasn't a surprise, as most of the time she was Officer van Hest of the Wicks Hollow Police Department.

The joy of watching their interplay was so comfortable and familiar that Vivien couldn't hold back a huge grin. She was just so glad to be back in Wicks Hollow—even though there was a dearth of carry-out options and no delivery service except for pizza. (She'd asked about DoorDash and whether she could get an Uber home from the Roost, and Helga had gone into fits of laughter. "The only ride home you might get from the bar is if you get your pal the cop to pick you up," Helga had hooted.)

Nonetheless, Vivien hoped, hoped, *hoped* everything was going to work out with the theater so she could stay. At least with her temporary rental—off the beaten tourist path and a deal, since the lease went through the end of the year and not just for summer; plus it belonged to a friend of Orbra's who'd done her a favor—Vivien's cost of living would be less than a third of what it had been in Manhattan.

"Why can't I play Elaine Harper?" grumbled Maxine. "I'd be perfect as Mortimer's love interest. That boy Baxter is *fine.*"

Helga choked on her chai latte. "But you're *fifty* years older than he is—"

"Typecasting, remember?" Vivien interrupted swiftly and soothingly. "Even though it's not spoken, we just *know* Abby Brewster is the mastermind behind the whole scheme, and—"

"That's age discrimination, you know," Maxine shot back at Helga, her voice rising into a familiar screech. "And I've had enough discrimination in my life being a Black female scientist—you know, I was thinking, they coulda made that *Hidden Figures* movie about me—"

"You're *loco*, Maxine. You're a chemical engineer, not a computer whiz, and that movie was about space and mathematics," said Juanita, but her friend just talked right over her as usual.

"—and why can't Vivien be creative like that Lynda-Miranda Miguel person? He didn't care about no ages or skin color or—"

"Maxine, you're going to be absolutely *brilliant* as Abby Brewster," said Vivien, using her firm, capable PR/handler voice—the one she'd perfected dealing with some of the biggest Broadway stars back in New York, including Louise London. "And besides, Abby's a much larger part than Elaine Harper. Everyone in Wicks Hollow is going to love seeing the town matriarch in one of the lead roles, you know."

Maxine pursed her lips and considered the (figurative) carrot Vivien was dangling in front of her.

And so Vivien decided to put a little butter and brown sugar glaze on that carrot. "You know, you might be the oldest person to ever play Abby Brewster—that would probably get a lot of coverage for our little semi-amateur theater production here in Wicks Hollow. I'll make sure to include that in the press releases." One thing Vivien knew was that Maxine was not only open about her advanced age, she was proud of it.

"And besides...as Mortimer's aunt, you probably get to give him at least one kiss on the cheek—that's more than Elaine gets to do," Vivien said with a sly grin.

"That's more like it," said Maxine. "All right, then, you've got yourself an Abby—she's the bossy one, right?"

"*Yes,*" Juanita snapped. "Vivien said it was typecasting—didn't you hear her?" She wiped her dimpled fingers on a napkin, showing off the screaming red fingernail polish that matched her lipstick—both of which clashed wildly with her flame-orange hair, which poofed into a mushroom-cloud-like shape over the crown of her head. She was wearing her normal attire of a flowing maxi-dress—this one tie-dyed in countless shades of blue. At least that didn't clash.

Vivien was itching to cast Juanita as Mrs. Potts—it would be a different take, with her being Latina instead of properly British, but that was the joy of being in charge. Unfortunately, the rights to *Beauty and the Beast* were a little out of reach for the first year of her production schedule. Maybe the Fairy Godmother in Rodgers and Hammerstein's *Cinderella*?

So many possibilities, but her plan was to have at least one production per season include locals from the town acting alongside whatever celebrities she could bring in for a short run. It would be a fun way to involve the community while keeping the productions high-quality.

"I get to be the other sister. Martha," Juanita said.

"Martha—the fluttery one," said Maxine dismissively. "Definite typecasting."

"And what about the rest of the characters?" asked Orbra before Juanita could retort. The tea shop proprietress was a tall, large-boned Dutch woman of seventy who could still manage a tray with four teapots and a three-tier sandwich server balanced on one hand without breaking a sweat. Or a teapot. Hmm. Orbra would be an interesting Mrs. Potts too... or even the Witch in *Into the Woods*.

"Doug Horner's going to play Teddy Brewster. And Vivien said Ricky could be in it, too," said Juanita, eyeing a thumb-sized currant tart. "Just a small role, but since Clara died a few months back, you know he's been a little lost with nothing to do."

"Clara? Why, it's been over a year since she died—" Of course Maxine had to argue.

Before Juanita could jump in and bicker back, Vivien spoke up. "That's right—Ricky is going to be Mr. Gibbs. The Presbyterian who runs away before he drinks the elderberry wine." She grinned. "I'll have to get his full name for the program and press releases, but anyway, Orbra, it's a semi-professional, semi-amateur production. I wanted Maxine and Juanita to be the Brewster sisters because everyone in town knows them—"

"Being expert murder-solvers and all," Maxine said.

"Murder-solvers? I don't think I've heard about this," said Vivien, giving her friend the cop a curious look.

"Please don't encourage them," Helga replied under her breath, then went on, loud enough to drown out Maxine, "Do tell us about the rest of the cast—not that I care, because I'm not going to be playing a dead body. I don't care *who*'s going to be pulling me—it—out of the window seat."

"Not even if it's Roger Hatchard?" Vivien said with a smirk.

"Did you say *Roger Hatchard*?" Helga clapped a hand to her chest, her blue-brown eyes going wide. "Roger Hatchard? For real?"

"The one and only." Vivien sat back, folding her arms over her middle.

"Wait—I thought you said Baxter is playing Mortimer." Helga looked skeptical but also slyly interested.

"He is. But in act two, the character of Jonathan Brewster—the villain—also has to help move Mr. Spinalzo—the *other* dead body—*into* the window seat."

"That's a lot of dead bodies being schlepped around," said Orbra, watching them with her hands on her hips.

"Jonathan Brewster—that's the role Boris Karloff played,"

announced Maxine. "Not that any of you young chickens even know who Boris Karloff—"

"Of course I know who Boris Karloff is. I watched *The Grinch*, didn't I? *Anyway*...Roger Hatchard?" Helga repeated. "He's going to be in your show? VL, how could you *not* have—"

"*Who* is Roger Hatchard?" asked Juanita in a prim voice. "Some of us older ladies don't know all of the newfangled stars—"

"He was only the best center for the Pistons in the early aughts," said Helga with a dreamy sigh. "Six foot eight inches of deliciousness, not to mention being brilliant on the court. His footwork in that playoff game against the Lakers... mmhmm." She did a French-chef sort of kissy thing to express her appreciation for either the man's playing or his so-called deliciousness; Vivien wasn't sure which. "Even *I* could have worn heels if I wanted to date him—and would still have to look up to kiss the guy."

"He was a little old for you at ten, Helga," Vivien teased.

"So how did you manage *that*?" asked Helga, still moony-eyed. "Getting a basketball player to *act*?"

"Well," Vivien replied slyly, "it could have something to do with the fact that I've been sort of seeing his son..."

"*What?*" Helga was nearly out of her seat. "VL, I swear I'd kill you if I didn't want to make sure this production goes off! How could you not tell me?"

Vivien gave a little snort-laugh. "Well, I'm telling you now, aren't I?"

Helga swatted her with a napkin and called her an unflattering name.

Maxine had pursed her lips so they stuck out in a massive

pout. "What're you *talking* about? You got a *baseball guy* playing in the show? Why, I ain't ever *heard* of anything so ridi—"

"Basketball," said Orbra firmly. "He played for the Detroit Pistons. He's originally from Lansing, so he's kind of a local boy. Now he's an ESPN sportscaster, isn't he?"

"He is. And yes, he can act—at least enough to play Jonathan Brewster—which isn't a very demanding role. He's just sort of hulking and mean," Vivien said, looking at Maxine. "I wanted to—er—support the hometown actors in the cast by having some local celebrities to round things out. It'll help create a draw for the show and we'll raise more money for the renovations."

"Celebri*ties*?" said Helga.

"Yes...well, Dr. Einstein is going to be played by Michael Wold—you know, the actor who did LeFou from *Beauty and the Beast* in the national tour last year, and—"

Vivien's cell phone chose that moment to buzz from its place on the table. It was the bank. Her stomach dropped to the floor as she snatched up her phone. "Sorry, ladies, I have to take this—it's the bank about the loan. More info to come, I promise. Rehearsals start next week, Maxine and Juanita."

I hope.

She answered the phone as she hurried out of the tea shop, knowing Helga not only wouldn't arrest her for dining and dashing, but would cover her tab.

Of course, then Helga would make her friend pay her back—and insist Vivien do so by going to Trib's, the trendiest and therefore most expensive restaurant in the county.

The phone call with her small business loan officer was brief and successful, culminating in the very best news: the loan she'd applied for had been approved—and at the highest amount she'd hoped for. She did a little pirouette in the street, feeling like she was back in ballet class at age five. The only thing that kept her from doing a cartwheel was the fact that she was wearing a sundress.

She was here in Wicks Hollow and was one step closer to fulfilling her dream and making a life in this sweet, quaint town.

So different from New York! She'd loved the big city when she first moved there, when she'd been dying to get out of tiny Wicks Hollow right after high school graduation. It helped to get away from memories and gave her a chance to spread her wings. Which she'd done, but not in the way she'd expected.

But sometime over the last ten years, her desire to live in the frenetic, energetic, demanding city had waned. She wanted to be in a place where she felt at home, where she belonged, where—yes, all right—everybody knew her name. And she wanted to honor Liv and the memories Vivien had with her.

Not that she didn't have people who knew her in New York. She did. Maybe too many of them. At least two or three times a month, she'd get contacted from someone in the business on either coast about doing a show or taking an audition or performing somewhere. As she no longer had an agent—she didn't need or want one—Vivien fielded all of those contacts with a simple but firm "No thank you, I don't perform anymore."

Still, her name and reputation had helped build her marketing and PR business in the Broadway world, and it was partly because of that that Vivien was right where she was now: walking down the main street in the town she'd only lived in for five years—but it felt like the only home she'd ever had.

In a way, it was.

Vivien always thought George Wicks (who, in her mind, would have been Henry Higgins in *My Fair Lady*) must have been the optimistic sort, naming the two main roads that intersected in the center of the village after his daughters— and giving them lofty names like Pamela Boulevard and Faith Avenue. Neither could be considered hardly more than a street, let alone a boulevard or avenue, and when there were cars parked on either side, like there would be by noon today, there was barely enough space for two vehicles to pass each other.

But that was part of what made Wicks Hollow so charming—its quiet, tidy streets studded by urns spilling with bright geraniums, gerberas, and lush, dangling vines.

There were shops and establishments—very limited compared to what she'd passed every day in New York, but Vivien certainly didn't miss the alleys smelling of urine, the constant blare of sirens and horns, the throngs of people everywhere all the time, and the perpetual odor of rotting garbage (every day was trash day *somewhere* in the city).

Vivien paused outside the window of the small florist to admire a springy, airy fern that she coveted for the kitchen in her tiny rental. But she'd probably kill it like she did the tomato plant she'd had on her windowsill one summer, and so she continued on down Pamela, heading toward Elizabeth Street—better known as B&B Row.

Vivien could have returned to the café and finished her scone (and paid her bill), but during the conversation with her banker, she'd automatically walked three blocks. Now she realized she'd almost arrived at the office of her realtor, whom she'd known a hundred years ago in high school. Though she was early, she decided to go inside in hopes of getting the keys sooner.

Twenty minutes later (hurray for a canceled appointment that had left her realtor free), Vivien was on her way to the theater—*her* theater.

She could finally go inside, knowing it was hers. She had seen it twice during the buying process, which had taken over five months, because although she was determined, she wasn't foolish enough to waste the money Gran had left her, and she'd negotiated the crap out of the deal.

But she'd always been with someone when inside. Never alone.

Never just her...and Liv.

The Wicks Hollow Stage had struggled with a few short-lived seasons in the late 1980s into 1990 before being shuttered permanently. Prior to that, it had been quite successful in turns as a vaudeville theater, a venue for silent films with an orchestra pit for live music accompaniment, and then the talkies that came out in the 1930s. But eventually, the old building had been abandoned sometime during the Second World War.

Whoever reopened it in the eighties had done a stellar job of updating and restoring the place, so fortunately for Vivien, she mainly had to clean it up and fix a few damaged areas, as well as update the lighting system and install new seats in the house. Her loan (she squealed happily inside) would more than cover those improvements, and she wouldn't have to dip into her savings...which meant she might even be able to buy a house next year.

It was a short drive to the six-hundred-seat theater she intended to make a tourist destination during every season—not just the summer. She suspected part of the reason it hadn't been successful in the past was because it wasn't in the downtown area, nor was it near Lake Michigan—both locations being the main draws for tourists. Instead, it was on a residential side street that ended in a cul-de-sac just off the two-lane state route that angled led outside of Wicks Hollow to Wicks Lake.

The location didn't worry her; it was only two miles from town, and tourists drove to and from activities in the area all the time. And Vivien didn't have a solid track record in publicity and advertising for nothing. The bank agreed: Wicks Hollow needed a live entertainment venue other than the small outdoor music stage and a movie theater ten miles away.

And now, Vivien thought as she pulled into the side parking lot of the Olivia Dee Theater, she was going to make it happen.

The original red velvet seats had long decayed and been removed, but Vivien would replace the rows of folding wooden seats from three decades ago with something like the original. The interior was dusty, dark, and very dingy, but there wasn't any indication of leaks or mold. The stage itself remained solid, and the catwalk above was stable and would be usable, with little need for repair.

However, the traditional red velvet curtains were a tattered mess (and would be the first thing Vivien would tear away once she got inside), and the dressing rooms and costume wardrobes needed a lot of work. She'd already ordered two fifty-yard Dumpsters to be placed in the parking lot, and they should arrive tomorrow. She'd have her work cut out for her, filling them up.

Vivien let herself in through the front door, the main entrance the theatergoers would be using hopefully six weeks from now, when *Arsenic and Old Lace* opened.

It was important for her to envision what it would be like when the place was illuminated and filled with chattering people milling about and filing down the aisles to their seats. She wanted to picture what the audience would see when they first walked in to the new, clean, renovated theater. Six weeks was an aggressive schedule, but Vivien had planned everything out and was optimistic it would work. She'd already had measurements taken for the new curtains, and had priced out audience seats and was ready to place the order. She would open the weekend after Labor Day.

She flipped on a row of light switches—*flick, flick, flick*—and a few stubborn bulbs sizzled to life, casting an uneven ochre glow in the small, gallerylike lobby. The place smelled of age, and dust motes glittered in the yellow light. Something moved in the corner, and Vivien turned just as she heard the rustle of old papers.

"I'd better get a cat," she said. "We can't have mice disturbing our show."

Not that she thought Maxine Took or Juanita Acerita would be the least bit put off if a mouse ran across the stage during rehearsal. She suspected neither of them would bat an eyelash. Hell, Maxine would probably adopt the rodent as her good-luck charm. Or familiar.

Vivien pushed through the double doors that opened into

the house. With no windows, it was even darker in here, and only a smattering of light bulbs worked when she flipped the switches. The main aisle projected like a shadowy ribbon straight in front of her, dipping on a gentle incline and ending at the great, dark maw of the stage.

The stage. The empty, open expanse standing proudly and expectantly in a shadowy building that had been abandoned to dust, cases of deteriorating playbills, sagging, creaking seats, and a small cache of rodents.

But the memories—the witty dialogue, the heartbreaking songs, the dramatic soliloquies, the energetic dances—all reverberated in the vast, dark space. For a moment, Vivien fancied she could hear them...

"The hills are alive..."

"To be or not to be..."

"I'm hopelessly devoted...to you..."

"I can do anything better than you can..."

"Consider yourself...at home...!"

She imagined the surrey with the fringe on top, the long table where twelve angry men had debated, the hotel room that was visited the same time every year, the telephone on which M had been dialed for murder...

A sudden chill caught her by surprise, and had her pausing there, halfway down the main aisle. She stilled, the hair prickling along her arms and over the back of her neck, and looked around. But there was nothing to see—no open door, nothing to cause a draft. Yet the chill was there, frosting her breath into a light cloud.

She waited, wondering if the ghosts of shows past recognized a fellow actor...someone who understood them.

"I'm here," she called out quietly. "I'm here to bring it back."

The chill remained, buffeting her, but it wasn't unpleasant. Noticeable, but not unpleasant.

She walked further. The emptiness above the stage loomed high and black before her, melding into the infinite space behind the proscenium, up into the hidden expanse of the catwalk trails, rows of light cans, and a jungle of frayed, looping ropes—all swathed by rows of tattered, faded curtains.

The air was still and quiet. The shadows sat heavy and long, their shapes dark and solid and unending. The scents of mustiness and age filled her nose, reminding her of death and rot.

"How morbid I am," Vivien said because, suddenly, she needed to hear something besides her own heartbeat thudding in her ears. "There's hope here, not just death and rot, Liv," she said, taking another step forward. "There will be laughter and singing and dancing again, and yes, there will be tears and death and drama...but that's life. That's the two masks of drama isn't it? Comedy and Tragedy."

The air moved, chill and sharp.

The phantoms of the theater were agreeing with her—a gentle nod, a soft affirmation, a nudge.

The slightest of breeze lifted her hair—she *swore* it lifted her hair, ruffled it—and it was shockingly cold.

And smelled dank.

Felt heavy.

She heard the soft skitter, a little rustle, and caught sight of a bit of crumpled paper as it danced on the floor near one of the dingy footlights by her sandal-bared toes. The floor felt soft under her foot, giving away a little as she stepped forward—

Just then, suddenly, there was light.

It came in a shocking, strident blaze from the empty stage: cold and blue and bright.

The illumination vibrated angrily in a swirl of shadow and light...and then suddenly it was gone.

The theater was silent.

And then she saw the words—green, vibrant, *glowing*—were emblazoned on the back wall of the stage:

GO OR DIE.

CHAPTER THREE

VIVIEN DIDN'T REMEMBER LEAVING the theater. She assumed she ran. She could have stumbled and staggered, tripping over her own two feet. She might have simply turned and walked—very quickly, without breathing—out of the building.

Regardless, she got *out*.

Quickly and soundlessly. That part she was sure of. She didn't scream or shriek or even gasp...because she couldn't catch her breath.

She just got *out*.

Then she launched herself into her car, locked the doors, and started the engine with an ugly grind—all in one nonstop movement.

She was just about to throw the car into reverse and get the hell out of there when she stopped.

"What the hell was that?" she asked herself. Out loud, of course—she was always talking to herself. It was a habit from when she'd had to learn lines. "What. The. *Hell. Was.* That?"

Her fingers were shaking, and she gripped the steering

wheel in an effort to give them something purposeful to do. Her stomach was tight, and she still felt a little clammy beneath her linen sundress.

"Okay. Deep breath. Calm down, step back, think about what happened, VL."

Easier said than done, because when she thought about what happened, how suddenly a light burst over the stage and how when the light went out there were *words*—a warning!—seeming to float in midair, shivering like ghostly words...she wanted to freak out all over again.

Cold sweat still trickled down her spine. That was the creepiest, most unsettling thing she'd ever experienced—other than when thirteen-year-old Tad Hunter had backed her into a corner and tried to shove his hand up her shirt when she was *ten.*

Nothing like that had happened during any of the other visits.

But she'd never been inside alone, either. Had the ghost—or whatever it was—simply waited for her (or someone) to be in there alone?

Vivien sighed and turned off the ignition with a frustrated *snap.* If she was going to reopen the theater and make it a success, she had to actually go inside the freaking building.

After all, as of today, she was on the hook for a six-figure loan. Her stomach wobbled a little at the thought. She had savings, and had kept a good number of her actor clients, but still...

Vivien was determined, but she wasn't a fool—so she dug out the can of pepper spray she used to carry when she took the subway but didn't think she'd need in Wicks Hollow, and primed it for use.

After all, *GO OR DIE* was a clear threat, wasn't it?

A shiver skittered over her shoulders. Maybe she should call Helga.

But it wasn't even noon; she'd only just got the keys herself. No one else had been in the theater at the time—she was sure of it.

She hadn't *sensed* anyone, hadn't heard anyone, and there weren't any cars around. The building, located on a dead-end road with a cul-de-sac, had its own parking lot—which was bordered on three sides by a butt-ugly chain-link fence. Beyond that were trees and bushes lining the perimeter, offering some privacy for the residences that abutted the stage's property, and above was the bluff with the row of homes, including the Brady Bunch house and its to-die-for view.

If someone had been inside the theater, they would have had to have walked or come from one of the few houses nearby—climbing over the fence.

Still holding the pepper spray, Vivien got out of her car. It was a sunny day, and even from several miles away, the breeze from Lake Michigan stirred the air. She considered whether she wanted to lock the door of her Accord—if she didn't, it would be easier to dive into if she had to leave in a hurry; but that would also leave the vehicle open and unsecured, which made her nervous as well.

She locked the car.

Then, holding the spray canister in one hand and her phone in the other, she decided to walk around the outside of the building to see if there was any sign of disturbance.

Maybe someone had broken in and painted graffiti on the wall.

Besides the south-facing front doors that led into the lobby where the ticket windows and a small refreshment counter were located, there was an entrance on the west side for the cast and crew and a huge, roll-up door next to it in order to accommodate the delivery of large set pieces or props. There was also an emergency exit on the east side, and two more doors in the rear.

The west side and back of the building were shady from the thick growth of trees on the other side of the fence, but there were no vehicles or bicycles parked back there. Nor did Vivien see any indication of recent tire tracks—although it had rained lightly last night, so if there had been any, they'd probably be gone.

She wasn't a detective by any stretch, but she felt better after having walked around the entire perimeter and finding nothing to indicate someone was lurking about inside.

At the same time, however, that left her with the knowledge that if no one had been inside...then...

Well.

Yeah, sure, theater people were wildly suspicious and believed the strangest things...

And yes, she conversed with her own dead sister on a regular basis, but...

No, she wasn't going to go down that path yet.

First, she was walking right back inside. *Yes*, she was. As soon as she calmed down a little more.

This time, though, she was going to enter through the side door. A less obvious way...just in case someone or some*thing* was lurking.

Vivien was just fitting her key into the cast and crew door's lock when a shadow fell over her from behind.

She managed to swallow a shriek—just barely—and swung around, pepper spray at the ready.

"What—" The words died in her throat when she recognized the man standing there, and for a moment she simply couldn't get her mind to work properly.

"V-Vivien?" The man standing there—the very familiar, selfish, immature *dickwad* she'd known eleven years ago at NYU—sounded just as gobsmacked as she felt.

"Jake." In her shock, she'd dropped the stupid key, but the can of pepper spray felt damned solid in her hand. She didn't bother to lower it as she lifted her chin and sneered. "I, uh, didn't know you were in town."

Understatement of the year. Like, what was he even doing in the *state*, let alone Wicks Hollow?

"Likewise." He looked pointedly at the metal canister in her hand. "You, uh, going to use that?"

"I'm thinking about it," she replied, but lowered her hand.

"Still holding a grudge eleven years later, are you?" he said in that maddeningly calm voice that she *used* to find wildly sexy on the telephone. Back when she was young and foolish and easily swayed by such things.

"Still lurking about trying to get lucky, are you?" she retorted, itching to raise the canister again. Why oh why did *he* of all people have to be here? Right now?

And how?

He snorted and planted his hands on his hips. "I don't have to slink around to—as you put it—get lucky."

His words were offhand and filled with bravado, but he

was definitely checking her out, sweeping over her with his dark eyes.

She couldn't help but do the same. Elwood DeRiccio, the bastard, looked just as good—*better*, dammit—than he had the last time she'd seen him. He was dressed in tight black running shorts (*just kill me now*) and his dusky olive skin glistened with a fine sheen of sweat, indicating he'd been in the process of actually putting the shorts and his Nikes to use. Fortunately for her hormones and their apparently eidetic memory, he wasn't shirtless but was wearing an athletic top—but that modesty didn't matter all that much, because its stretchy, shiny material clung to shoulders that seemed to have grown broader in the last decade. His walnut-colored hair was just long enough that he'd pulled it back into a ponytail to keep it out of his face, and his legs...well, it was obvious he was no stranger to regular exercise.

Though he didn't have overtly handsome features—his nose was a little too big and his jaw a tad too square—Jake was still attractive to women, as Vivien well knew—and not just because he was a doctor. At least, she assumed he was a doctor, since the last time they spoke they'd broken up because he'd decided to do his residency five hundred miles away from New York.

She still couldn't believe he was standing there in front of her. It was just so completely *random*. And shocking. Maybe whatever happened in the theater was still happening...some weird, surreal anxiety attack...?

But why would she imagine Jake DeRiccio, of all people?

Maybe a vacation? His parents lived in Grand Rapids, after all...but that was over an hour away.

"Is everything all right?" he asked once he'd finished that arrogant sweep of eyes over her.

"Yes, of course. Why wouldn't it be?" If she asked what he was doing here, it might sound like she cared. Which she *didn't*.

He tilted his head and looked at her. "Because when I was going by, I saw you running to your car like a bat out of hell was chasing you, and then you sat there for a few minutes, and now you seem to be...uh...having trouble getting inside this building."

Oh, great. Not only had there been a witness to her flight, but it just had to be an old flame. Wow. *Thanks a lot, Universe.*

"You just happened to be standing around watching me while I sat in my car?" she snapped. "Really?"

"No, Vivien," he replied ever so reasonably. "I was running by and saw you tear out the door here and practically leap into your car, and then on my way back from the end of the road just now, I saw that you hadn't left and instead were getting out of the car and seemed to be trying to find a way inside the theater here."

By now, any normal person would have taken the hint that everything was fine and that he should move on. Especially since *he'd* moved on eleven years ago and left her —well, not completely heartbroken, but definitely scarred. The lying, cheating bastard.

"Everything's fine," she said. "I was just trying all the doors to make sure the key worked. I'm the new owner of the theater."

The corner of his mouth tightened. It was a familiar

expression. He knew she was lying, dammit. "All right, then. Nice running into you."

"Same here," she lied again, and stooped to pick up the dropped key ring. "Bye, Jake."

He started to take off, but turned around, jogging lightly backward as he said, "I guess I'll be seeing you around, Vivien Leigh."

"Not if I can help it," she muttered, turning to fit the key back into the lock.

"I heard that," he called, then, pivoting away to run off, added over his shoulder, "See you at rehearsal!"

Wait, *what?*

She spun around, but he was already halfway across the parking lot. What the hell was he talking about, seeing her at rehearsal?

Whatever. He was probably just yanking her chain. Jerk. Some things never changed. She shook her head, blew out a frustrated breath, and put Elwood "Jake" DeRiccio out of her mind.

This time, she got the key properly inserted into the lock and opened the side door. At least there was one benefit to that unexpected encounter—her thoughts had gone from jittery and scattered about the creepy light on the stage to annoyed and disarrayed at seeing Jake again. It was too bad he still had the ability to affect her that way; you'd think after eleven years she'd be past that.

Over him.

She *was* over him.

It was just so unexpected, seeing him again—and here, in Wicks Hollow. What was he even doing here? Probably on vacation—the doctor with his lovely wife and maybe a kid or two. She'd be happy for him if he was. She really would.

Inside, the theater seemed darker than before—mainly because there were no windows in the backstage area. Vivien turned on her cell phone's flashlight and used it to scan the space until she found the light switch. The ceiling back here was two and a half stories high to accommodate large set pieces, all of the flies—the scenery backdrops—and the rows of spotlights.

Everything was still and quiet and dark. There was no indication that anything crazy had happened only a few minutes ago—maybe ten? *Only* ten? It felt like hours.

Just a few light bulbs in the wings and back area were working, of course, but it was enough illumination for her to make her way onto the stage without bumping into or tripping over anything. Her heart was beating faster and her hands felt clammy as she gripped the phone/flashlight and her pepper spray.

As she stood in the wings, the stage yawned before her: a large, open space ahead—empty and ready for anything; filled with promise and expectation.

To the left was the back wall, deep and dark in shadow, and to the right was the house with its rows of empty seats, almost equally as dark. Her small flashlight and the meager spill of illumination from backstage offered little in the way of light in comparison to the generous expanse of the void in front of her.

When she walked out onto the stage—something she'd done countless times when she was young, and yet not for a long time—her heart was in her throat, her stomach in knots as she waited to see if anything would happen.

She stood there near the edge, just out from the wings: silent, still, her breath rasping a little with nerves.

She thought of Liv, of course, as she stood there. The two of them had rarely been onstage at the same time, but usually whenever one of them was, the other would be in the wings watching. Silently rooting.

Everything remained dark and silent, but the ambience she'd experienced earlier—that sense of the theater itself, the spirit of the building, the memories of the words and songs and actions that had lived here—lingered.

"It's going to be all right," she said. Not in her stage voice. More like a murmur, but still loud enough to be heard.

Nothing happened. She relaxed a little more and stepped to center stage.

She turned, shining her flashlight upstage to see the threat that had been emblazoned on or near the back wall.

But all she saw was the black hole of nothing.

No words. No warning.

Nothing.

CHAPTER FOUR

"OH MY GOD, I've missed this," Vivien said with a heartfelt groan.

She was on the floor stretching on her yoga mat in the asana known as Pigeon, with her left leg bent in a reverse-seven position flat in front of her while her right leg was extended straight out on the floor behind. Her hands reached in front of her, fingertips touching the floor, and she eased her torso down so her belly settled onto her left calf.

The position caused a beautiful sort of pleasure-discomfort that opened her hips and reminded her that sitting or even walking every day still required her to stretch her muscles to remain flexible.

Helga was next to her doing the same thing, but her forehead was actually resting on the floor, because she, unlike Vivien, hadn't skipped yoga class for the last month. "It hurts so good," she said, taking a deep yogic breath.

Vivien did the same, and when she released the long, steady breath, she was rewarded by sinking deeper and flatter into her mat. *Oh yes...almost as good as sex.*

"I know what you're thinking," Cherry Wilder murmured as she approached Vivien. Cherry, who was one of Maxine Took's cohorts and a Tuesday Lady, was the studio owner and teacher. Somewhere over sixty, she looked like a very fit Sharon Stone with slender, cut arms bared by a skintight tank in neon blue and short platinum-blond hair.

"You do?" Vivien muttered. Hell, she certainly hoped not.

Cherry placed a firm hand on the center of Vivien's back, right between her shoulder blades, and said, "Deep breath, Vivien, and now...exhale..." Her hand, flat and gentle, helped coax Vivien down into an even deeper stretch. "You're thinking, *When is she going to let me come out of this so I can do the other side?*"

Vivien huffed a laugh as Helga snorted into the floor next to her. "She likes to torture us," said Helga in a muffled voice.

"That's right," Cherry said lightly. "But all right, class, time to switch sides."

Everyone made little groaning noises of relief as they came out of the position and pulled right legs up and slid left legs straight back.

"What did you need to talk to me about?" Helga said a while later as they rolled over onto their backs for shivasana—the final position of simply resting, face-up, hands at sides, eyes closed, breathing deeply.

"Shh," murmured Vivien as she took inventory of her body while stretching long and low on her mat. She was a little achy but felt energized deep inside as well. This last hour of simple, easy movement had almost enabled her to put away what had happened yesterday morning at the theater.

Almost.

But now that class was over, it all came back.

She'd decided she had to tell someone, and Helga, being a cop, a very practical person, and Vivien's oldest and best friend in Wicks Hollow, was the obvious option.

"Tea shop?" asked Helga as they retrieved and put on their shoes in the foyer of the yoga studio. "I'm in the mood for one of auntie's cinnamon scones. She'll give us a table in the back."

"Mmm," said Vivien. The last thing she wanted or needed was Maxine Took to catch wind of what had happened. "How about we get a glass of wine on the patio at Trib's instead? You're not on call tonight. Besides, I owe you for picking up my tab yesterday."

"Wine after yoga?" Helga looked at her with raised eyebrows. "Don't you want to at least bask in the wholesomeness of listening to your body's wisdom before you contaminate it with the wickedness of alcohol?"

"Yada, yada," Vivien said, flapping a hand at her friend. "Like you don't snag a chocolate bar half the time after yoga instead of drinking a liter of water like you should."

"Chocolate after yoga?" They both turned to see Cherry standing there with a bemused look on her face. "I hope it's at least seventy-five percent cacao."

"Of course it is, Aunt Cherry," said Helga with an innocent grin. Cherry wasn't her aunt, but she'd always used the term for each of her Aunt Orbra's friends. "And fair-use-sourced and stone-ground and in limited, recycled packaging and everything else that makes it okay for consumption."

"Whatever it is, if it requires wine after yoga, make sure Trib pours you some of that Sancerre he keeps in the back.

It's by request only," Cherry told them. Then she leaned closer so none of her other students could hear. "If I didn't have a hatha class right now, I'd invite myself to join you. It's been a hell of a week."

"But it's only Wednesday," said Vivien with a laugh.

"Tell me about it!" Cherry clapped her on the back, then turned to speak to a student who'd just come in the door.

"Oh, hi, Melody," said Helga as they turned to leave.

It took Vivien a moment, but then she remembered the woman from high school. Melody Carlson had been her name back then; Vivien had no idea whether it still was. They hadn't been friends, but it was a small school, so they'd known each other.

"Oh, hi, Helga. I'm glad to see you here—I wanted to thank you again for helping me with that little fender bender the other day. I was late going to see my daddy up at the assisted living place, and I was just so out of sorts, and—Vivien Savage? Is that you?" Melody removed her sunglasses. "You've not changed a bit. Bella mentioned you were coming back to town."

"Yes, I just bought the old theater—she was my realtor," Vivien said proudly. "Maybe you can do a stint there someday. I'm trying to keep locals involved as much as possible." She didn't remember thinking Melody was all that talented back in high school when she had the lead in every play, but she was part of the community, and Vivien was definitely going to be building relationships with as many people as possible.

"Oh, how sweet of you to think of me. It's been *years* since I've been onstage," said Melody, adjusting her yoga mat.

"Well, I'd best get in so I can grab a spot in the front—it's easier for me to see up there. Ta-ta!"

"See you later," Helga said as they walked out.

"Was she a little...chilly?" Vivien muttered as they walked down the street. "Or did I imagine it?"

"Oh, she's always like that—kind of brittle. I think it really upset her when she had to put her father in the assisted living home a while back. He was only sixty. She's nice, though, once you get around her and she relaxes. I've been out with her and Bella and some of the others a few times."

"Maybe I can tag along next time," Vivien said.

"I'll let you know," said Helga.

Although they were both dressed in yoga pants and tank tops, their attire wasn't a problem for Trib's, even though it was the fanciest place in the surrounding area. Tourist towns like Wicks Hollow didn't stand on ceremony, and certainly didn't require dress codes. Why would they, when their patrons might be coming in from fun in the sun at any time of day, starving and ready to relax—and spend money?

It was barely four o'clock in the afternoon, however, and so the restaurant was in the lull between lunch and the dinner rush, as the tourists were swimming, boating, fishing, shopping, or napping.

"Darling Vivien Leigh!" Trib himself swooped down on them the moment they stepped over the threshold into the restaurant.

He was a neat and fashionably groomed fifty-ish man with hair styled in a modern version of a flat-topped buzzcut. It was salt-and-pepper around the sides and ears, blending into a stark platinum white on the brush top. He wore a closely trimmed, mostly gray goatee and mustache. Today his attire was a summery lime-green shirt with a bowtie of orange and cobalt in Harlequin-style diamonds. His crisp, pleated trousers were probably bespoke, if Vivien knew Trib (and she did), and they were charcoal gray with the faintest of blue pinstripes. He looked, as always, utterly smashing.

"I thought you'd never come in here to see me! It's been *ages*, VL," he went on as he took Vivien's arm. "Tell me how our dear Frankie is doing, will you? I miss her *so*."

"Oh, she's doing fantastic. She's working at a very chichi pastry shop in Manhattan—they're even letting her do her own macarons—and she says her summer internship here was the best thing that ever happened to her."

"Well, you've never steered me wrong with summer internships, darling. All these wannabe chefs—I just *love* gobbling up their energy during these crazy summer months! And Benjamin is working out just fine—although he's unequivocally *not* a pastry chef," he added in a conspiratorial voice. "I think the best I can expect from him is doing sous work, but that's just fine with me. He can prep to his heart's content." He smiled at them both. "Now, inside or outside today, my lovelies?"

"Outside, in the shade, and Cherry says we need to ask about your secret stash of Sancerre," Vivien replied.

"Ooh! So it's one of *those* kinds of days." He grinned. "I can't wait to hear all about it. And Officer Sugar, don't lie— you've done something brilliant to your hair. *Love* the new shade. It's like a honey-lemon, and it makes you look absolutely *delicious* with your creamy skin tone and that splash of freckles—I've always said it looks like a natural bronzer. You're simply a goddess."

Her cheeks a little pink—for she was much shyer and

more subdued than Vivien—Helga reached up to touch the high ponytail she'd worn for yoga. "Only you would notice, Trib. It's just a slight tweak in the color, but Emily did a great job."

"She always does. It's simply delicious," Trib said, taking her arm as well. "Now, let's see about a couple glasses of that crisp white for you both, and I'll check whether I have something interesting in the kitchen for you to nibble. Marty wanted to try something with grilled peaches, toasted pepitas, and Brie, and who was I to say no?"

Moments later, Vivien and Helga were seated in a prime location in the corner of the restaurant's front patio—prime because it was in the shade beneath a vine-wrapped pergola with a nice view of the street but not close enough that passersby or vehicles would interrupt their tête-à-tête. A tall pot placed strategically to give some privacy for the diners from pedestrians held an equally tall boxwood trimmed into a conical spiral. There was a small vase bursting with pink sweet peas and yellow pansies on the table.

"Damned birds," Trib said as he delivered two glasses of nearly clear white wine and a small platter of grilled peaches topped with oozing brie and a side of house-made crackers. Toasted and seasoned pumpkin seeds—pepitas—were scattered on the plate.

Trib paused to shoo away a pair of wrens that had perched among the red-flowering vines above them. "I've got nothing against them personally, but I don't want them sitting —and shitting—above my customers while they're eating!"

Vivien laughed and pretended to duck as she looked up. "Oops."

"Yes. It wasn't part of my master plan when Hector

convinced me I needed to install the pergola with trumpet vine. That's the last time I listen to that gay old fart. Should've just put in a retractable awning, but no, he said this would create a better ambiance." He pursed his lips. "I've got a guy coming to install some netting a few feet above it to keep the birds off, but until then, it's a manual project to keep them from crapping all over everything. Now, how's the wine, darlings? And what do you think about the Brie?"

They concurred it was excellent, and although Vivien was itching to tell Helga about what happened at the theater, she was also pleased when Trib pulled up a chair to join them.

"Now tell me true, VL, you really wanted *me* to play Mortimer, didn't you?" he said, preening a little.

"Of course I did," she replied. "But then you'd steal the show from Roger Hatchard and Michael Wold. We couldn't have that, you know—a small-town restauranteur showing up national celebrities."

Trib laughed uproariously. "Oh, you're good, darling. You're *very* good. All those years in advertising and PR have served you well. But admit it—you'd be more worried what Maxine would say if I stole the show from *her*."

Vivien laughed and toasted him with her wine. "You caught me."

"Anyway, I admit, I'll be in the front row on opening night. Roger Hatchard is *such* a lovely piece to look at. All that *leg* and that thick head of dark hair even at his age. I had no idea he could act."

"We are looking for someone to play the dead body in the window seat," Vivien told him with a sly look. "No lines, you can wear whatever you want, and you'd only be in Act Two."

"And then I could be backstage, couldn't I? Can I have my own dressing room? Or, better yet, share one with Hatchard?"

"Nice try. But you can share one with Doug Horner, whoever we get to play Mr. Witherspoon, and Juanita's friend Ricky."

"Oh, Ricky's going to do the show? That's good—I think his son's been trying to encourage him to get out more since Clara died. He'll like that. And you say Doug's going to be in it too? Poor guy. I wonder how long it'll be before Juanita accidentally-on-purpose stumbles into his dressing room."

Doug Horner was the Wicks Hollow veterinarian, and he was a confirmed bachelor in his late sixties. He had snowy-white hair and a bristly gray mustache that looked like a toothbrush. Juanita, who was at least ten years older than he, had had her sights set on him for years.

Trib sighed, shaking his head sadly. "If those two would stop dancing around each other and playing games and just tear off each other's clothes and *do* it all ready! She's so delicious with all those opera-singer bodacious curves—if I were straight, I'd go for her myself."

"Ew!" Helga was holding up two fingers in the shape of a cross, warding him off. "That's a picture I don't need in my head. Let's talk about exactly how Vivien got Roger Hatchard to be in the show."

"Ooooh?" Trib made the word undulate like a writhing belly dancer. "Do tell, VL!"

"Well, I've been sort of seeing his son Daniel," Vivien said. "It's nothing serious—in fact, I don't even know if we'll continue on now that I'm here and he's back in Hartford. He's a great guy, but he has no interest in moving away from the East Coast, and I'm not going anywhere now that I've bought the theater. But it was Daniel who suggested I ask his father to be in the show."

"Spectacular," said Trib. "That'll be a nice draw, and I'm not just speaking for me."

"That's it?" Helga was disappointed. "I was hoping for more scoop about the Hatchard family."

Vivien laughed and shook her head. "Really, it was pretty low-key."

"So I assume you're playing the young and lovely Elaine Harper, VL," said Trib with a smile and a quirked brow.

"No. I'm directing," she replied, squashing a little pang. "I've got Penny Stern—you know, she had that little stint on *Bull*?—to play Elaine. She grew up in Muskegon—did you know that?"

"But VL...you're the biggest local celebrity we have—next to that darling Ethan Murphy." Trib seemed genuinely surprised. "Roger Hatchard notwithstanding."

"This man. Who even says 'notwithstanding' anymore?" Vivien said to Helga. Then she looked back at Trib and smoothly changed the subject. "We've got so much to do to get things ready at the theater besides actual rehearsals. There's a Scout troop that's going to come in and help with some of the cleanup, and the high school football team, the pom squad, and the drama department are also going to volunteer some time. The students all have to do service hours over the summer, and helping with the restoration of the theater is being considered community service. That's going to save me quite a bit of money. In fact, I've got to meet them tomorrow morning at eleven."

"Eleven?" Trib said. "That's getting to be the hottest part of the morning."

"They're teens. I'm lucky to get them there before noon on summer break," Vivien said dryly.

"Good point." He was looking at her curiously, but to her relief, he didn't press on his earlier question. "Speaking of Ricky, have you met his son? I've been trying to figure out whether he's a prospect or not. I've only seen him from a distance—but that was enough."

"I've met him several times," Helga said. "And no, I don't think he plays for your team, Trib."

He sighed. "I was afraid of that. And he's a doctor, too!"

Vivien stilled. Something jangled in the back of her mind. *"Be seeing you around."*

No. Surely not...

With a feeling of impending doom, she was compelled to ask, "So, this Ricky—what is his last name, anyway?"

"DeRiccio. His name is actually Fabrizio, but everyone calls him Ricky. What's the matter?" Helga said.

Vivien took a big sip of wine and shrugged. "Nothing." But inside, she was shrieking epithets at the universe.

"Speaking of cues, that's mine to get back inside," said Trib when his assistant manager poked her head out of the restaurant and beckoned. "And I was just getting comfortable. Ah well, a genius's work is never done. I'll come by the stage soon, darling, and take a look at the dressing rooms—and the actors. You might just get me to play dead after all. I'll send Benjamin out to say hi if I can spare him for a few—though he showed up late for his shift yesterday morning, so I'm still annoyed with him." He smacked a kiss onto Vivien's cheek, then Helga's, and then was off in a swirl of lime green.

"Who's Benjamin?" Helga asked.

"Younger brother of Louise London, believe it or not. Wants to be a chef, obviously, so I helped set him up with Trib for the summer. Speaking of Louise, oh-em-gee, she is driving me a leetle crazy." Vivien held up her phone to show Helga the fifteen text notifications from the actor. "This is just in the last hour."

"Well, she is your biggest client. And her voice is so amazing," Helga said. "I just loved her in *Wicked* when I saw her in Chicago. Too bad you couldn't get her to do Elaine Harper…"

"I know. I really do like her—and she is so very talented—even though she is a little high-strung. But, ugh, she thinks just because I'm in Wicks Hollow that I've fallen off the face of the earth." Vivien shook her head. "She was really upset when I told her I was moving, but I don't need to live in her zip code to do my job. After all, I've been working with Tanya Rheim out of L.A. for years. Anyway, Louise should be happy—I've got a line on her doing some paid posts for…"

She trailed off when she saw the way Helga was looking at her—with that *don't even* try *lying to me—I'm a cop* look.

"What?"

"*You* should be playing Elaine Harper," said Helga. Then she just looked at Vivien, whose expression must have said it all. "Do we need to order another glass of wine to get through whatever this is?"

"I'm thinking a whole bottle," replied Vivien. "Ugh."

"We'd probably better get some food too, then," said her friend, and flagged down a server.

And then, being the patient, pragmatic, close-to-perfect friend she was, Helga settled back and waited for Vivien to talk.

It took a few minutes for Vivien to figure out how she was going to unload everything, then she decided to just start at the beginning and walk her friend through the upheaval of her life.

"The phone call yesterday was from the bank with the final approval on the loan," she said, then raised her almost-empty glass in response to Helga's congratulatory toast. "Yes. I am very excited."

"You should be, but you don't look it, VL. I know you're probably a little scared and nervous. Look, we really need something like the Stage here in Wicks Hollow, and who better to make it happen than Vivien Leigh Savage? You've got the name, the experience, the contacts—and you're basically a local girl. A child actor who never went off the deep end. The Olivia Dee Theater is going to be great, girlfriend."

Vivien gave her a sad smile. *The child actor who never went off the deep end—despite her tragic life.*

She hadn't known Helga when she and Liv were in their "heyday," such as it was. In fact, Vivien hadn't met Helga until she and her mother moved permanently to Wicks Hollow, five years after Liv died and right when Vivien was about to start high school.

Helga, who had already been taller than everyone in their freshman class—and most of the sophomores and juniors as well—and seriously sensitive about it, had been assigned as Vivien's mentor for the first day of school. They hit it off, and feeling like misfits, they'd clung together like Jack and Rose on the scrap of wood through the stormy years of high school. Fortunately, neither of them had been dumb enough to let go of the scrap of wood that was their friendship.

Therefore, Helga didn't know how close Vivien had actually *come* to being a child actor who went off the deep end, so to speak, because by the time she got to high school, her Gran had made certain Vivien, at least, was in therapy. Her mother was a different story.

"I appreciate your confidence," Vivien said. "Thank you. But I'm actually not so worried about that. The business plan is solid, and my goals for the year are achievable. The bank wouldn't have approved the loan if they didn't think so too. But something weird happened at the theater yesterday."

Helga leaned forward as Vivien described her experience walking into the theater, the sudden burst of light, and then the glowing words on the wall after.

"You should have called me," Helga the Cop said flatly. "Right away."

"I... Well, I thought about it, but it seemed pretty benign, all things considered, and—"

"Benign my ass. You were alone in the theater, the lights came on, and there was a threat painted on the wall? That's not benign—"

"But wait, there's more," Vivien said, then settled back in her chair as the server arrived with a full bottle of the Sancerre. There was a pause while their glasses were refilled and they agreed on a pizza to share—Trib's famous Wise Guy —and then they were left alone again.

"So I got out of there, went to my car, and then decided I wasn't going to be chased away from my own business. And I went back inside and...there was nothing there."

"Nothing there meaning no lights?"

"Nothing there meaning no words painted on the wall. And no lights either."

Helga frowned. "I'm not going to ask if you're sure because, duh, I know you are, but...wow. That is concerning. I want to see it."

"I figured you would. I've come up with several possible explanations—that's pretty much all I've been thinking about since yesterday," Vivien confessed.

"Have you been back there since?"

Pursing her lips, feeling like a coward, Vivien shook her head. "No. I had some work to do—other work; you know I'm keeping a bunch of my clients, and I didn't even check my email on Monday when I was driving here, which is why Louise has her panties in a twist—and so I haven't been back inside the theater. I had a good excuse," she added with a self-deprecating smile.

Helga nodded sagely. "All right. I'll go with you after dinner. It'll still be light till at least eight thirty."

"I'm not worried about the dark," Vivien replied. "This all happened yesterday morning. And that's not all of it." She sighed and poked at the half a cracker that was left over from the Brie appetizer.

Her friend watched her carefully but said nothing.

Vivien sighed. *Ugh.* "So there was a guy running by who happened to see me come bursting out of the theater, rush to my car, and then sit in it, and when he was coming back around from the end of the street, he saw me going back in through the side door. So he came over to see if everything was okay."

"A creeper?" Helga's mouth went flat.

Vivien had to shake her head, though she was sorely tempted not to. "No. It turns out...it was Jake."

Helga's hazel eyes were uncomprehending, then confused, then hesitant. "Jake...? As in your ex, Jake, the supreme, cheating asshole—from when you were at NYU?" She squinted and tilted her head. "Here in Wicks Hollow?"

"Yup. What're the chances?" Vivien said, then she started to get annoyed. "What are the freaking chances that not only would my college boyfriend, the one who—well, a guy I was pretty damned serious about—that he would not only be here in Wicks Hollow, *now*, but be *running past* right after I had the freakiest experience of my life?"

Helga was shaking her head. "Girl, you've got some really bad luck. Some effed-up juju."

"I know, right? *How?* How does this happen?"

"So...what happened? Did you talk to him? Was he civil? Were *you* civil?"

"He was... Well, he was Jake. But older. Just as cocky." Just as hot. "Civil, I guess, but cocky."

"What is he doing here?" Helga's question was obviously rhetorical, but unfortunately, Vivien had the answer.

"Here's the best part," she said in defeat. "I'm pretty sure Ricky—Juanita's friend who's going to be in the show—is Jake's *dad*."

"*No. Way.*"

"Yeah."

"How?"

"Jake's actual name is Elwood DeRiccio. Ricky's name is Fabrizio DeRiccio. Apparently the family has a problem giving their sons normal-sounding names."

"Well, I kind of like Fabrizio—"

Vivien nearly snarled at Helga, who lifted her glass to drink quickly—probably to hide a smirk. "That's not helping."

"Elwood? But you call him Jake? I don't— *Oh*, I do get it." Helga chuckled. "Elwood and Jake Blues—the Blues Brothers. Yeah, if I had to pick a name, it would be Jake instead of Elwood. 'We're on a mission from God!'" She giggled a little. Apparently, the wine was going to her head. It was a good thing Helga could walk home, or *she'd* be the one texting for a ride from a cop friend.

"I guess they started calling him Jake in middle school when he unequivocally told his friends and parents he wouldn't answer to Elwood. I can't blame him. Can you imagine the nicknames they would have come up with in middle school?"

"Well, at least his friends knew their pop culture," Helga said, still smirking behind her glass.

"You're still not helping."

"Right." Helga snapped her expression back into a sober one. "So your Jake—the infamous lying, cheating dickwad—is Ricky's son," Helga mused aloud. "Bummer. He's really hot. And—because I'm not sexist or overly preoccupied with looks —he also seems like a nice, solid guy. I've met him a few times, just briefly. Once there was a little car crash in town and he happened to be nearby. He was really calming, helping a pregnant woman who was involved in the accident—"

"He's a doctor. He's supposed to do that kind of stuff," Vivien growled. Then sighed. She was an adult. She could be more magnanimous. "Yes, he's really nice. And can be super sweet. And charming. And then he turns into a—"

The pizza arrived at that moment, and Vivien became wholly distracted by how hungry she was and how amazing the pie looked—and smelled. Topped with smoked mozz, caramelized onions, and sausage, along with a spicy tomato sauce, the Wise Guy was one of Trib's most popular pizzas.

But Helga wasn't quite as easily distracted from things Vivien would rather left undiscussed. Probably the cop in her. "I think it really bites that you have to deal with Jake showing up while you're trying to get the theater open. I know how much he hurt you." But instead of staying on that topic, Helga went down another path she had no idea was even worse. "So...you're really not going to be onstage for the show?"

"No." Vivien's response was short and sharp.

Helga did that bird thing she did where she tilted her head and looked at Vivien with a penetrating expression, as if her friend was a worm Helga was about to drag, kicking and screaming, stretching and undulating, from the soil.

Maybe the wine was going to Vivien's head too.

"You'd be perfect to play Elaine Harper. You're a local celebrity, it's your theater, named after your sister... It seems so obvious you should be in the inaugural production. Why not?" The humor that had been dancing in Helga's eyes was gone, and Vivien suddenly felt as if she were in an interrogation room with the steely-eyed cop.

She started to respond, but suddenly, horribly, her throat closed up and a thick lump settled there. Her eyes stung. The words wouldn't come. She shook her head soundlessly and looked away.

"All right. I'm sorry for asking." Helga pressed a

comforting hand over Vivien's. "I just want you to know I'm here if you want to talk. *When* you want to talk."

Vivien nodded quickly, then turned her attention to carefully cutting off the tip of her piece of pizza.

It was silly. She was a fool. She had to get over the memories and move on. Not just Jake—not even mostly Jake.

But not today.

Not now.

____

CHAPTER FIVE

"*POP!* What the *hell* are you doing up there?" Jake stumbled from his Lexus and bolted toward the house, heart surging into his throat. "Get the hell down from there!"

"You watch your tongue, young man," snapped his seventy-seven-year-old father, *who was crawling along the roof of his house.*

A ladder that had seen far better days was leaning drunkenly against the gutter.

"Pop!" Jake grabbed the ladder with both hands—which was at least more helpful than clutching his head and tearing his hair out; something he'd wanted to do more often than not lately when it came to his father—and looked up in trepidation as his *hardheaded, idiotic* remaining parent blithely continued his task of crawling along the edge of the roof and clearing out the gutter. The ladder shifted a little in Jake's grip, indicating how *not* stable it had been when his pop had ascended it and climbed onto the freaking *roof.*

Thank God I came by. A rush of cold sweat erupted over him as he imagined what might have happened if he hadn't...

Pine needles, leaves, and other debris tumbled to the ground as Fabrizio DeRiccio stubbornly ignored him and inched along, tossing the detritus from the gutter like he was sowing seed.

"Pop, *please*. I can do that. *Let me do that.*" Short of climbing up there and muscling his far-too-frail parent to and down the ladder, Jake was helpless to stop him, and he barely controlled the terror in his voice.

"Now look here, sonny, I've been doing this— Whoa." Pop lurched a little when his hand missed the gutter and flailed in midair for a sec. It wasn't enough that he lost his balance, but it was close enough that Jake nearly fainted.

"That's it. I'm coming up to get you right now," he said, starting up the ladder. If he had to drag his dad back down he would, dammit, because there was *no way* he was going to watch Pop fall off the goddamned roof.

"All right, all right, put a sock in it, Elwood," grumped Pop. "I was about to take a break anyway. It's almost lunchtime."

Jake didn't take a full breath until his father's feet were on the third rung from the bottom—except when he nearly fainted (again) as Pop's foot missed the second rung as he was lowering himself back down onto the ladder from the edge of the roof. The *roof!*

By the time Pop stepped onto the grass, Jake had himself under control. While he wanted to lambaste the idiot for doing such a crazy thing—why else had he moved to freaking Wicks Hollow if not to help his parent with this kind of stuff? —he knew that was not the way to handle his hotheaded Italian father.

Because he was sort of the same way.

At least Jake saw reason once in a while—unlike Fabrizio. His mother always said the two of them were as identical as two cannellini beans. But Jake was a little more grounded—at least, he liked to think he was. Medical school and residency did that to a guy.

Not that he'd felt all that grounded when he ran into *Vivien Leigh Savage* of all people yesterday.

What were the damned chances?

Damn. She'd looked *good*. Different—her whisky-blond hair was much longer than it had been back then, brushing past her shoulders now, and there was a little more definition to her features than before, and she was clearly upset about something—not just seeing him, he figured...

Vivien Leigh Savage. Here in town, presumably permanently, since she was the owner of the theater.

What was he going to do about that? Nothing...or everything?

He shook his head and followed Pop into the house, where, ostensibly, his dad was going to eat lunch. But Jake was almost certain his father's hand was trembling a little. Maybe his rock-headed pop had learned a lesson, nearly taking a header off the top of the damned house.

Maybe not.

Probably not.

"I got tuna salad," said Pop, rummaging in the fridge. "You want some?"

"Sure." Jake was about to sit down at the table to eat when his father turned around holding jars of mayo, capers, and pickles, along with a small container of chopped onion.

"Well, get the tuna out of the pantry, will you," snarled Fabrizio. "Ain't gonna make it itself, Elwood."

"Right."

No one called him Elwood anymore, thank God. In middle school, he'd loathed his parents for giving him such a horrific name (in Jake's opinion, horrific first names ran wildly in the DeRiccio family—Fabrizio being case in point, and his grandfather had been Aldobrandino). It didn't help that until he hit sixteen, he looked like a short, dark-skinned Italian frog.

Thus, Jake had heard every ugly twist on that name in fifth and sixth grades—Frogwood, Smellwood, Tinywood, Elweird, and more—and it wasn't until the older sister of one of his loyal friends called him Jake over the summer between sixth and seventh grade that he got past the name-calling.

The fact that she'd watched *The Blues Brothers* and given him the coolest nickname ever—along with the fact that she was tall, blond, and *seventeen*—made Ashley Grifton his goddess forever.

He still thought about her fondly, even though the one time he'd worked up the courage to ask her out—when he was sixteen—she'd turned him down flat.

"Don't splash the juice every-damned-where," grumbled Pop when Jake came over to drain the tuna at the sink. "Makes it stink. Rinse it down the sink, too."

"I will," Jake said calmly. Since when had his father become such a nitpicky micromanager?

He knew the answer to that, unfortunately: since Mom died.

Ten minutes later, they were sitting at the small kitchen table eating tuna on whole grain—a shocker in itself, because throughout his entire life, Jake had lived through the ongoing battle between his parents about bread. It was always Mom wanting her husband and children to eat more whole-grain breads, and Dad insisting that the crusty white Italian bread *his* mom used to make was the only bread worth eating.

Which was probably why Jake had developed a hobby, he supposed you'd call it, of making all kinds of bread. Crusty Italian bread. Sourdough. Whole-wheat, onion rye, olive bread. Ciabatta. Focaccia. He'd even tried his hand at pumpernickel.

So he couldn't help needle his pop. "Guess you've developed a taste for whole-grain bread, huh?" Jake said with a sly smile. "After all those years. Look at all the sunflower seeds in this one slice. Yum!"

His dad curled a lip at him. "Was the only thing at the grocery store."

"Yeah, right." Jake grinned and took a gulp of the iced tea he'd poured.

"Besides—you haven't brought me any of yours for a while."

"I haven't made any, but I've got some ready to bake tomorrow," Jake replied. "Been working on the main bathroom, you know? The tile's on backorder, of course."

"You shoulda let me call my guy," Pop said, jabbing his sandwich at Jake. A caper fell out and rolled onto his place.

Jake knew all about his father's "guys" back in Grand Rapids and was very glad he'd declined. He might've ended up with the tile on time, but someone could've also been stuffed in a trunk getting it here. "Anyway, Mom would be proud of you, eating seeds in your bread and all."

Pop snorted. "She'd have just found something else to nag at me about. Never stopped—even to her dying day, she nagged at me to pick up my socks and eat *healthy*. Nothing wrong with a good pasta and some white bread to sop it up with, but she'd get on me about that too! Well, my poppa and my *nonno* both lived over ninety and ate as much damned pasta as they wanted every day of their lives!"

Jake merely nodded. This was an old refrain, a familiar argument. Pop made it sound like he and Mom were at each other's throats all the time—and though they often were, they'd also loved each other well enough to stay married for over fifty years and raise four children.

"I know you miss her," he said after a few minutes of Pop grumbling about how his wife had cut back on the amount of red meat he'd eaten ("You can't have Bolognese without any damned veal! And it has to be soaked in *whole milk*—none of that two-percent crap."). "I know I do."

"It's been over a year, Elwood. I'm old, she was old, all our friends are old—and we're used to it. Gets so I don't even want to look at the newspaper from up in Grand Rapids anymore to see all the obituaries." Beneath his orneriness was a layer of grief, though, and Jake felt another little stab of his own.

"Well, don't look at the paper, then," he responded tartly to cover the moment.

"Well, how'm I supposed to know if I gotta go to a funeral if I don't know who ate it?"

"Well, if you hadn't moved away seven years ago, you could just go to church and ask Father Stan who died," Jake said with a grin.

"Your mom wanted to live away from the city and by the water," grumbled Pop. "Got half of it right—no city—and close enough to walk to the lake on a good day."

Jake smiled, even though his eyes stung a little. "You always gave her whatever she wanted."

"I did—and so why did she always want to take away my beef and bread and cheese? At least she let me keep my Chianti and olive oil."

"There are a lot of studies about how one glass of red wine a day is healthy."

"So speaks the doctor," said Pop—but the jest was said with a layer of pride.

"Right. So you should listen to me when I tell you not to climb on the damned roof. That's why I moved back here, Pop, remember? So I can help you with some of that stuff? And you stay away from that beehive I saw—all right? I'll take care of it."

"Don't need your help," he snapped. "I'm not an invalid."

"You're almost seventy-eight years old. You have no business crawling on the roof—or climbing on a ladder for any reason. All right?"

"I suppose you're going to tell me I can't mow my own lawn now, aren't you? You better not try and take away my car keys, sonny, or—"

"So tell me about this play you're doing," Jake interrupted quickly. He didn't need to hear that lecture again.

And fortunately, he didn't need to have the battle about car keys yet. His dad could keep them so long as he didn't drive at night.

"I told you already. That damned Juanita Acerita bullied me into agreeing to play some guy named Gibbs. I didn't know he was a damned *Presbyterian.*" He shook his head woefully, staring at the single caper on his plate. "She and Maxine are two giant boils on my ass."

"What? The great Ricky DeRiccio is afraid of two old ladies?"

"You haven't met them yet, have you?" retorted his pop. "Just you wait, Elwood. That Maxine Took—she'll chew you up and spit you out if you don't give her enough respect. And Juanita is just as bad. Everyone thinks she's so nice and sweet—well, compared to Maxine, I suppose she is—but she's got this little dog she likes to sic on people, and—"

"So, Pops, about this play you're going to be in— Oh, here we go." His phone alerting with the special chime from work cut him off. "I've got to get my laptop and take care of this."

"Just like always—when it's time to do the cleaning up, you've always got something to do," said Pop, pursing his lips and pretending to be annoyed.

Jake ignored the familiar teasing and went out to grab his laptop, which he'd left in the car when he'd been trying to save his dad from falling off the damned roof. Fortunately, the little one-story cottage Pop and Mom had bought ten years ago was on a small side street just off the main drag of Wicks Hollow. It had a narrow view of Lake Michigan between trees and a couple of buildings, and there was a mile-long path that led to the lakeshore. Fortunately, their quiet residential street didn't have a lot of tourists coming through, so the laptop was safe in his unlocked car. Whew.

"Don't know how you can be a doctor without ever going into the hospital," Pop was grumbling when Jake came back in. "All that money and schooling on a medical degree and you don't ever go in to the office or visit the hospital. Are you sure you're not just a quack?"

"Might I remind you that working remotely is what

enabled me to move here to be near you," Jake shot back as he flipped open the laptop. With HIPAA, he had to make certain no one could see anything on the screen—which, even though his dad would have absolutely no clue about how to read an X-ray image, and nor could Pop even read the notes without his thick bifocals—Jake still had to maintain privacy standards. So he sat in the corner with the computer screen facing the wall and logged in to the highly secure VPN for his radiology group.

"What do ya know—this one's from Sydney," he said when the patient info came up on the screen.

"You're looking at an X-ray from a guy from Sydney? As in Australia?" Pops turned from the sink—*whoa*, he was wearing pink elbow-length dishwashing gloves!—and stared at him. "Why the hell they want to send their X-rays all the way here?"

"A female," Jake said absently as he read the notes from the emergency physician before opening the image so he could read the film. "Hmm? Just a minute, Pops, I need to take care of this first..."

He carefully examined the image, made his assessment, typed up detailed notes, then sent everything back—a total of twelve minutes after the alert came in. Just as he did, another notification chimed and he had a second film to read and interpret. That one took longer because he had to hunt down previous X-rays from a different system so he could compare the baseline to the new images.

Forty minutes later, he closed the laptop and looked at his dad, who'd taken a seat at the table across from him and was eyeing Jake with an unreadable expression.

"What?" Jake asked.

"Were you really looking at X-rays from Australia?" His dad appeared both skeptical and fascinated.

"I was. It's one in the morning there, you know, and sometimes they don't have radiologists on staff at the smaller hospitals or care centers—or they're unavailable—and so my group is on call for some of the hospitals in Sydney. That way, the Australian radiologists can sleep through the night." He grinned.

Pop shook his head, scratching at the thick, wavy hair that still grew there. "You can really do all that just on your computer?"

Jake nodded. "Yes. I really can. It's pretty common for radiologists to work remotely nowadays. There's usually no reason for us to be on site."

Working from home most of the time made for an interesting lifestyle. It allowed him to be flexible and comfortable—hell, he worked in his boxers sometimes and had stopped shaving daily three years ago—but it also could be pretty lonely, not leaving the house regularly and having few human interactions. And since his relationship with Mandy had gone south, his social life had been even worse.

He'd spent a *lot* of time making bread.

Which was one of the reasons he hadn't minded moving permanently to Wicks Hollow. And why he'd bought his own place instead of living with Dad, because the two months he'd bunked here in this twelve-hundred-square-foot cottage had been enough to turn his own thick head of hair gray. And Jake wasn't about to go salt-and-pepper at thirty-four.

"That just means I have more time to help you with things around here," Jake went on. "So no more climbing on the roof, please? I don't want to be looking at *your* X-rays someday when you fall off and break your damned neck."

His dad snorted. "Fine. But I'm still mowing the lawn, and I'm going to finish painting the living room."

"Only if you don't have to stand on a ladder to do it. I'll get the ceiling, all right? And the beehive I saw out there. So, when do rehearsals start for this play of yours?"

"I don't know," Pop responded. Then he gave Jake a sharp look. "Why are you so interested in the play?"

"I... Well, I was just curious. After all, rehearsals will be cutting into your lawn-mowing time, and that might mean I'll have to come over here and do more of the yard work. I've got my own place to take care of, you know."

And he did—he'd managed to snag an unusual but promising house on a bluff overlooking Lake Michigan. It needed quite a bit of updating (something he could do while waiting for his pager to go off or his dough to rise), so he'd snagged it for a sweet deal. That was because it had been in the dead of a lake-effect January winter in the middle of a blizzard and subsequent snow-in that the house had gone on the market. It had to sell quickly—and he'd been here to snatch it up. He owed his realtor *big* time, even though he'd had to remove a freaking *tree* from the middle of the living room.

"I told you I don't need your help around here. All that much," his dad added quickly. "I won't climb on the roof again, all right?"

"No climbing anything but the stairs—you hear me? Pop, I'm not kidding," Jake said.

"Don't take that tone with me, sonny. I'm still your father."

"Yes, and I want you to stay that way."

"I don't know when those rehearsals start, but they want me to come in and help with the set." This bit of information was obviously his father's version of a peace offering—maybe an acknowledgment of Jake's concerns.

"You mean building the set?"

"Yes, and painting it and things. I hope Maxine's not there. Last thing I want is to see that woman running around with a goddamned saw. Or an electric screwdriver."

Jake shook his head. "I don't know whether to be disappointed or relieved I haven't met her yet."

"Be glad. Be very glad. Maxine Took makes your mother look like a kitten."

"Don't tell me you have a crush on this Maxine person," Jake teased.

"Hell no! What the hell is wrong with you, boy? That Maxine makes my balls wanna shrink way up inside."

Jake grimaced. "Thanks for that image, Pops."

His dad shrugged, but Jake caught a glimpse of his lips as they twitched beneath his thick mustache. "So what're you doing hanging around here, Elwood? Get on home and make your pop some more of that rosemary and olive focaccia. I don't want to eat any more bread with damned *seeds* in it. They get all up inside my stupid dentures."

THE NEXT MORNING, Vivien arrived at the soon-to-be-christened Olivia Dee Theater a little after ten o'clock.

She and Helga hadn't ended up coming here last night once they finished dinner at Trib's—after several glasses of wine, neither of them had any business driving. So they'd strolled around town before walking back to Helga's apartment and hanging out there for the rest of the night, and she'd told Helga not to bother to come by in the morning, since all of the other people would be there.

Vivien was glad to have an excuse not to go back to the theater last night—although she wouldn't have admitted it. And if pressed, she *would* have gone back. Especially with Helga (who was, as one might expect, a bit of a badass). But she'd been just fine delaying her return.

Now, Vivien couldn't help but glance around as she fitted the key into the front door's lock. The last thing she wanted was Jake DeRiccio showing up again, all sweaty and in those tight running shorts.

But the parking lot was empty, and so was the little street in front of it. She wondered where he'd come from that he'd been jogging down this road outside of town. There were a few houses nearby, but they didn't seem the type for a doctor and his possible family.

She wondered if he'd ended up with Lissa Kirkland.

The very thought of the bitch whose bed Jake had dived into about ten seconds after Vivien and he semi-broke up made her stomach churn and the fury come roaring back all over again.

Put it away.

It's over. It's done. It was a long time ago.

Distracted by the memories and emotions attached to Jake and that upsetting time of her life made it easier for Vivien to walk through the entrance into the lobby.

To her relief, nothing seemed out of place. There were no strange lights or sounds, and the air was still and quiet.

"I'm back," she called to the ghosts lingering from shows past. "And I'm not leaving," she added for whoever thought they could chase her away from her dream.

As if in answer, a soft shift in the air—very, very cold—buffeted her skin, and she thought she heard the faintest whisper of a sigh—relieved, relaxed—from deep inside the building.

"That's right," she said, the sound of her voice giving her comfort as she walked in and looked around. "I'm here, and here I'll stay."

She had a real flashlight this time, but didn't turn it on yet and instead relied on the same dismal collection of light bulbs as before. The teen volunteers would be here in less than an hour, and she wanted to have a defined list of tasks for them before the hordes (she hoped there was a horde) descended.

But before that, she needed a moment of her own to do what she'd meant to do when she came in on Tuesday.

Once more, she walked down the center aisle from the lobby through the house to the stage. And once again, she felt the presence of those who'd come before—who'd entertained and danced and sang and soliloquized—and whose spirits remained.

They were ghosts of solidarity, phantoms of familiarity, spirits of tradition and memory...nonthreatening and benign, yet insistent that they be acknowledged.

And acknowledge them she would.

This time, nothing interrupted her as she approached the front. The orchestra pit located down and in front of the stage was small but functional and required her to veer to the left in order to ascend the five steps that brought her onto the stage.

For some reason, her palms felt damp and her heart was beating hard as she walked onstage and stood, facing the house...just as she and her twin had done twenty-some years ago.

She looked out over the empty seats, the rows where faces would be, the place that she would fill with people—she *would*—and remembered: the heat of the lights, the energy pushing at her, the music surrounding her, the excitement, the exhaustion, the triumph.

Memories flitted through her mind: pieces of dialogue, measures of song, steps of a routine...and then, when they began to overwhelm her, when her eyes filled with tears and her heart squeezed and hurt, she sank to sit cross-legged on the dusty wooden floor.

Liv.

"I wish you were here with me, Liv," she said—but in a low voice. Just for her twin to hear. The other spirits didn't need to eavesdrop. "I mean, I know you're with me, but I wish you were corporeal, you know?" A skitter of sensation brushed over Vivien's left arm—Olivia always stood on her left side—lifting the hair gently.

Tears stung her eyes, and she dashed them away with the palm of her hand. "It would be so much better if we were doing this together. You know?"

Silence. But she didn't need to hear or feel an acknowledgment. She knew Liv was there, and that she heard her.

This is for you, Liv.

A rush of warmth and the glitter of energy surrounded her, gently buffeting her, filling her, comforting her. Her sister was near.

Then something caught her attention. A movement, from the corner of her eye.

She turned, heart lurching into her throat, and saw a shadow—what she thought was a shadow—*move*.

Tall, long, it spilled across stage left...dark and obvious even in the poor light. It wasn't the shape of a person—no, it was angular and smooth...except for the top, where its rectangular shape distorted into something that wasn't human.

The hair on the back of her neck shot to attention, prickling and tense, and Vivien felt goosebumps erupt all over her arms and legs. Her breath came out in short, hard pants, and it was visible, little foggy clouds of white.

The shadow slid silently across the stage—dark, slick, and amorphous—rippling over the slats in the stage, dipping off the edge until it came so close that it nearly brushed over her feet and arm...

And then it was gone.

It happened so quickly, smoothly, silently...the shadow was there and then it was gone.

And everything was still.

And Vivien was alone once more.

CHAPTER SIX

THE SCOUTS and high school volunteers brought much-needed life and energy into the theater. Vivien freely admitted it was a relief to have so much activity—*normal* activity—going on in the abandoned building, especially after what had happened just a short while ago.

She'd looked around backstage and found nothing that could have created that eerie, long shadow…and the realization made her stomach more than a little queasy.

The teens were loud and rambunctious, calling out to each other, laughing, and—since someone had brought a speaker—blasting music that was, surprisingly, from artists she recognized.

She could *feel* the place waking up.

She wanted to stand out there on the stage and sing "Climb Ev'ry Mountain" or "Defying Gravity"—something bold and anthemic.

Vivien opened the huge rolling garage door, which allowed in a lot of light and fresh air to the backstage area, and did the same with all of the other doors. Dumpsters had been set up in the parking lot, and the gloved and masked volunteers began the process of removing trash and damaged parts of the theater: broken chairs, tattered curtains, set pieces that could no longer be used, boxes of old programs, mildewed and shredded office supplies, paint, hardware, and other miscellaneous items. The basic structure of the building was sound, and most of the interior walls were as well, except for one corner in the back where a small leak in the roof had created some damage. There, rotting boards and mildewed flooring had to be taken up and disposed of. Three of the football players attacked that task with alacrity—and sledgehammers.

"Miss Savage, what about these?" called one of the students. "Do they go or stay?"

There were too many of the teens for Vivien to know their names, but she thought the girl was Stephanie—a member of the pom squad and the daughter of a blacksmith (an actual blacksmith!) who lived in town.

She came over to find Stephanie and one of her friends flipping through a stack of large framed photos of shows that had been done over the years. There were more than two dozen of them, and they were each the size of a movie poster, depicting productions from the 1920s through the early 1990s. *The Wizard of Oz, The Nutcracker, Noises Off, A Midsummer Night's Dream, Hamlet,* and more.

These were the spirits, the ghosts that lingered—and now they had faces and shapes to go with them. She felt a shimmer of awareness as she looked through the images, feeling the burst of joy and intensity that glowed from the actors in each exuberant shot.

"Definitely keep them," Vivien said, noting that they

seemed to be in good shape except for the dust and dried dirt on the protective glass. "We can hang these in the front lobby and on the walls in the house—and we'll continue the tradition and make our own."

"Miss Savage! Can you come here?" called one of the guys from the wings.

She left the pair of girls with rags and glass cleaner and answered that call—and then went on to see to countless others that took her all over the building.

It wasn't until the volunteers had been there for over an hour, with Vivien answering nonstop questions and giving direction, that she had the opportunity to step back onto the main stage. There'd been no strange breezes, no shifting in the air, no unexpected lights or shadows...and for that, she was grateful.

And yet trepidatious. It was as if she were waiting for another shoe to drop.

With that in mind, with an icy chill reminding her of the creepy shadow and the strange lights, Vivien walked upstage to the back, where the words *GO OR DIE* had seemed to burn.

As before, there was nothing there.

But this time, she went all the way up to the rear of the stage and examined the black wall carefully, using her flashlight. To her right were two cheerleaders using push brooms, sweeping up dust off into the wings. To her left were more volunteers gathering up miscellaneous pieces of garbage and fabric that been left on what were probably prop tables. Someone was testing the floods and spots, and lights were coming on and off, making her feel like she should start singing "Stayin' Alive."

The wall was blank and empty, with no sign of anything that could have been glowing letters.

She was just about to walk back downstage when something made her look up. Maybe it was the blazing crimson light that was blazing down on her as if she were in a red-light district (someone was having a lot of fun up in the light booth). Nevertheless, she looked up, and that was when she noticed a fly—a backdrop—hanging there, a little lower than the others.

It drew her attention because it wasn't ratty and tattered along the hem like the others that still swayed gently above.

It looked almost new.

Something prickled down her spine, and it wasn't Liv or any of the other spirits in the theater.

It was suspicion.

Vivien didn't hesitate. The ladder to the catwalk was metal and solid, and she tucked the flashlight under her arm as she clambered up to the sound of soft creaks and squeaks (it would have to be tightened and oiled before the show).

The narrow walkway that stretched across the top of the stage, behind the proscenium that hung like the top of a frame over the performance area, shivered a little when she stepped on it. The floor of the catwalk was made of wood, but there were metal fixtures suspending it from the ceiling every four feet, and a slender metal chain that acted as a safety barrier, which she would replace with a real railing as soon as possible.

Vivien hesitated, then took her foot off the bridge and moved back onto the ladder's landing. "Everyone off the stage! Everyone clear the stage and the wings—now!"

The half-dozen teens in the area did as instructed, but they all gawked, looking up as they backed away and off.

"Everyone stand clear—way clear—until I say otherwise," she called down, and watched to make sure they complied. They did.

Then she reached out to grab the chain railing along the catwalk. She rattled it violently using her hand, and then kicked forcefully at the narrow bridge with her foot—once, twice, a third time...and then it happened: a shudder, a creak, and then part of the walkway just *fell*, like the piece of a drawbridge collapsing down instead of lifting.

It swung down, hard, fast, and loud, with awful metallic groans and one long, piglike squeal. Gusts of dust flew up and around, and Vivien even felt the whoosh of air from up where she was. When it was all over, a section of catwalk dangled there—still attached at the other end—swaying madly like a heavy pendulum ten feet above the stage.

The volunteers gasped and a few shrieked, and then the crew broke out into nervous chatter as they stood around, unharmed but obviously freaked out by the event.

"Whoa," said one of the football players unnecessarily.

Vivien felt ill and lightheaded. *That was close.*

In more ways than one.

"All right, everyone stay clear," she called, climbing back down the ladder, which, thankfully, remained intact and stable. "I don't think it's going to come all the way down, but I want everyone off the stage and to stay out of the right wings until we get it fixed."

Her heart was still thudding wildly as she thought about all of the things that could have gone wrong, and her breathing was so shallow that she thought she might faint.

She should have waited until all of the teens were gone. Of course she'd been careful, but still…

"And that," came a familiar voice from somewhere in the house, "is why you're not climbing any ladders, Pop. Ever. Again."

Vivien spun to see Jake—*why? why?*—striding down the center aisle toward the stage. He was followed by an old man who looked a little like a squat toad with a very thick head of dark, rumply hair and a mustache to match. Her first impression was: adorable. He would be a perfect Mario, as in the video game, if he were wearing overalls.

Despite the mad shock, Vivien's brain worked fast, and she put two and two together that Jake was with his father.

"Is everything all right?" Jake asked as he vaulted easily onto the stage, taking only two of the five steps.

"Yes" was all she had the wherewithal to reply. The syllable came out tight.

His hair was loose today and fell in dark waves like those of the narcissistic Gaston to just past his jaw line. Vivien couldn't help but wonder what his patients thought about a doctor with hair that belonged on a model or movie star. The female ones probably loved it, and some of the male ones as well. Jake tilted his head, lifting one of his thick, dark brows as he looked toward the hanging piece of bridge.

"I was testing it out. That's why I know everything really is okay," she snapped. She paused to take in a deep, slow breath, then exhaled it long and easy. She was very calm. "So, what can I do for you, Jake?"

Honestly, it really wasn't fair that the cheating bastard looked so good—and she knew that she, on the other hand, was disheveled and dusty and probably had dirt streaks all over her face. But despite his longish hair, Jake was clean and pressed in dark gray board shorts with a crisp, summery button-down shirt and fine leather loafers that she was sure had cost a couple hundred dollars. He even smelled good—fresh and cool, as if he'd just showered.

"Nothing really," Jake replied. "But I might be able to do something for you." Once again, he looked pointedly at the dangling piece of metal.

"Oh, I don't think so," she said breezily. "There aren't any lying, cheating bastard roles in *Arsenic and Old Lace*."

His eyes widened at the direct hit, and she swore his cheeks—already a dusky olive—flushed a little darker.

She turned away from him and started down the steps to greet the darling man who probably stood no more than five feet, three inches. But what he lacked in height, he made up for with that dark, luxurious hair and mustache.

"You must be Mr. DeRiccio," she said, extending a hand. She couldn't bring herself to call a man forty or more years her senior by his first name, even if it was a nickname. "I'm Vivien Savage—the owner of the theater and the director of our show. Thank you so much for taking on the role of Mr. Gibbs."

"I came here under duress," replied Jake's father as he took her hand. He smelled comfortably like Old Spice and was much more casually dressed than his son, in dark chinos that bagged at the knees and a button-down plaid shirt. A white t-shirt peeped from behind the open collar of his button-down. "At least, I *did*. But now that I've met *you*, young lady—well, I've changed my mind." He had to look up at her a little, as she was five feet, six inches, but he didn't seem to mind in the least. His dark eyes danced as he lifted her hand—not to shake it, but to press a very quick, very light kiss on the back of it. His mustache, soft and glossy, brushed her skin. "It's possible I might enjoy this after all."

"That makes two of us," Vivien replied. *As long as your son doesn't stick around.*

"Jake, this here's Vivien Savage," said Mr. DeRiccio. "I guess she's gonna be telling me what to do up there."

Vivien was relieved that he seemed to have missed the brief exchange between herself and his son, considering that she'd called Jake a lying, cheating bastard. Which was pretty much the truth, but maybe not the best thing to say about his son in her actor's hearing.

"I wish her luck with that," Jake replied. But he didn't look at Vivien as he climbed down from the stage.

Nor did he correct his father's assumption that they hadn't met before.

Just then, Vivien heard a familiar sound...one that could raise the hairs on the back of her neck almost as quickly as a falling catwalk bridge.

Thump. Thumpity-thump. Thump.

She looked back out over the empty seats of the house to see Maxine and Juanita—with Maxine's cane creating the unholy rhythm on the floor—making their way down the center aisle. Behind them followed the much taller Orbra and a shorter woman with cotton-ball-white hair done in a simple grandmotherly style. Each of them were toting a shopping bag.

"Stages—nothing but health hazards, I'm telling you," Maxine said to Juanita in her carrying voice. "People always getting flattened by things falling from above. Every murder-mystery show has at least one falling sandbag or backdrop, you know. Better make sure you have good insurance, Miss Vivien Leigh," she called. "Or this star ain't setting *foot* on that stage."

Her voice carried in the empty space (at least Vivien wouldn't have to remind her to project when delivering her lines), causing everyone to turn.

Ricky DeRiccio said something to his son, and Jake turned to look at the group of older ladies. "That's Maxine Took? The woman you're afraid of?" His reply was just loud enough for Vivien to hear. "She's got a walking stick, for Pete's sake, Pop."

"Hello, Maxine," Vivien called, chuckling inside over Jake's blithe ignorance. He'd learn about Maxine soon enough. "How nice of you to drop by."

"Had to see where I'ma make my *debut*," replied the old woman, emphasizing the first syllable of the word. "And we brought summa Orbra's scones and sandwiches for the workers. It was *my* idea."

"It certainly was *not*," Orbra said testily. "I told you I was planning to bring some things, and *you* started telling me which ones you wanted to eat."

"Whatever," Maxine retorted. "Now, where is my dressing room?"

Vivien drew in another deep breath, for Jake had gone back up onstage and was examining the broken catwalk. Why didn't he just leave everything alone?

Why didn't he just *leave*?

He was messing up her mojo. Bringing bad juju.

Bringing back memories.

"The dressing rooms are backstage, but they're—"

Vivien's warning that it was no place for a woman with a

cane was cut off when the dainty lady with fluffy white hair hurried over to her. "Oh, I can just *feel* the energy here! The ghosts of musicals past! You must be Vivien Leigh Savage. I remember your record album, you know. Yours and your sister's." Her eyes showed a hint of sympathy. "And the fantastic performance at the Tonys."

"Yes, I'm Vivien," she replied, watching askance as Maxine Took made a beeline toward the steps at stage left even while she hoped the lady in front of her wouldn't start singing "Happy, Happy Me"—the biggest track from The Savage Sisters' one-hit-wonder album. It had hit number ten on the Billboard chart.

"I'm Iva Bergstrom. I'm so happy to finally meet you!" The cotton-haired woman was the epitome of the kindly grandmother type with her bright blue eyes and round, delicate cheeks. She was dressed sensibly and not quite so grandmotherly in dark blue capri pants and a light summer sweater twinset of lemon yellow. A perfect Mrs. Claus, if you were going for tiny, elegant, and not quite as chubby as the mister. Or maybe even a Mrs. Potts...

"Same here," Vivien replied, then called desperately, "Maxine, it's not really safe to be—"

"I'll be *fine*," retorted the woman, already thumping across the stage like she owned it. "It's Juanita you gotta worry about. I got three legs to balance myself, and she's got but two."

Sure enough, Juanita was following in her costar's wake, climbing up the five steps a little more carefully, but hardly less enthusiastically.

"I guess I'd better go with them," Vivien said with a sigh.

"I'll come too," said Iva. "Orbra, come on—we're going to

go see Maxine and Juanita's dressing rooms!"

Orbra set down her shopping bag (presumably filled with scones) next to the other ones that had been abandoned. "It's been more than thirty years since I've been in here," she said, following Vivien and Iva onto the stage. "I think the last performance I saw was *Little Shop of Horrors*, back in '85, I think it was. Wonderful show, but a very strange one. I had nightmares about that horrible plant for weeks after. All I could hear was 'Feed me, Seymour!' over and over in my head intertwined with the dentist song."

Vivien was more interested in catching up to Maxine and Juanita (for ladies in their eighties, they moved *fast*) than hearing about Orbra's memories. There were tripping hazards all over, as well as old nails and splintered set pieces that could injure any of them.

"Maxine, Juanita, if you could just wait..." Vivien called, already envisioning news articles (*Octogenarian Star Injured During Stage Reconstruction Honoring One of the Savage Sisters*), lawsuits, and the tripling of her liability insurance.

As she darted across the stage, she passed Jake (who was still standing on it by the dangling piece of catwalk like he had a reason to be there), and he gave her a sidewise look with brows raised, along with a smirk.

"You can get off my stage any time now," she said from between clenched teeth as she strode past.

He said something that sounded like *But I like your stage...*

Which made no sense, because *he'd* been the one who'd messed things up with them...

...and why was she even thinking about him?

Even further behind in her wake, she could hear Iva, who

seemed to have decided to take the opportunity to deliver her own soliloquy about theater phantoms and the metaphysical to whatever audience was around to listen. She'd continued on in the vein of "ghosts of performances past" and was talking to Orbra about shows she'd seen.

"Maxine, Juanita, if you want to see your dressing room..." Vivien said, desperately projecting her voice to where they were just making their way beyond the wings. "I'll show you. If you'll just wait."

To her relief, the two women finally stopped. Frazzled and annoyed (mainly because the unwanted Jake had to be witness to a group of elderly ladies running roughshod over her), she calmed herself as she caught up to them.

"I told you they have to be back here," Juanita said. "It's always in the back area—"

"Well, I remember coming around to see Melvin Millhouse when he was playing Hamlet, and they were definitely to the lef—"

"I'll show you exactly where it is," said Vivien firmly, relieved that she was now within grabbing distance of either of them. "Now, perhaps we should wait for Iva and Orbra so they can see your dressing room too?"

"Room? Only one?" Maxine said, pursing her lips. "I don't remember there being a sharing-the-dressing-room clause in the contract, Miss Vivien Leigh."

Vivien didn't bother to respond. She didn't think she could without her voice coiling up into a high, tight spiral and her eyes bulging. And she'd thought handling a rising Instagram influencer had been a challenge...but dealing with Betsy Baker's Better Self (a self-betterment guru that made Goop look like a redneck) had toughened her up.

And seriously, Maxine Took and Juanita Acerita were even worse than the Broadway diva Louise London, who was Vivien's biggest client. High-maintenance didn't begin to cover it.

"All right, now that we're all here," she said smoothly and a little loudly so as to drown out Maxine's bitter demands for her own dressing room, "I'll show you where all the magic is going to happen." She managed to infuse a rush of enthusiasm and warmth into her tone and began to carefully lead the way into the depths of the backstage area.

The wings spread out on either side of the stage, and then gave way into short corridors that led to the dressing rooms, prop room, tech room, and the huge, high-ceilinged workshop that was accessed by the massive roll-up door—all of which sprawled behind the back wall of the stage.

A team of volunteers had been assigned to come through and replace as many light bulbs as possible, so there was a decent amount of illumination in the corridor and the rooms. But in the wings it was still a dim, shadowy warren of space right now, littered with crates, scaffolding, chairs, tables, and other items that had just been left around after the last show closed quickly and unexpectedly.

"It was *The Nutcracker*," Iva said. "Now I remember! They just closed the place right down. People showed up with tickets for the Christmas Eve Eve performance—"

"Christmas Eve *Eve*?" Maxine said, thumping her cane in emphasis. "You got a stutter now, Iva?"

"I certainly do not. You know what I meant—it was the twenty-third of December, and—"

"That's right," Orbra cut in. "I remember. They were doing a one-week performance—a local woman was playing the pretty ballerina with the traveling group—and then *bam!* No one really knew why it shut down just like that. Something about a member of the cast getting sick at the last minute. I don't remember much about it. Christmas is a very busy time at the Tea House. Everyone wants to have high tea with their grandma, aunts, cousins, whatever."

"I heard the Sugarplum Fairy ran off with the Nutcracker," said Juanita, giggling a little. "And that's why they had to cancel the show."

"And the dish ran away with the spoon?" Maxine demanded as if she were cross-examining someone on a witness stand.

Vivien suddenly realized she had a raging headache.

Iva rolled her eyes. "Well, I don't know about that, Maxine, but the holidays were here and everyone was too busy to pay very close attention to what was happening. I don't even remember who was running the theater at the time...someone local, I'm sure." She frowned, as if trying to remember.

"And then it was January," Orbra said, "and no one really thought about the whole thing, since there were never any shows in the winter back then—we didn't have *any* tourists until the end of June back in the eighties and nineties, you know, when all of the Big Three Autos—back then they were the Big Three, anyway—shut down for two weeks in July. Everyone would come over here from the east side of the state."

"So the theater never opened again the following summer —I don't know why—and after that, everyone must've given up on the place," said Juanita, looking around with bright eyes. "So very sad."

"I wonder what happened," said Iva as she trotted along.

Vivien hardly listened to their chatter, as she was more interested in keeping all of them upright and unscathed as they navigated through. Whoever thought it was a good idea for Maxine and Company to show up today? Surely Helga wouldn't have suggested it... No. It was probably Maxine's idea.

"This is the costume room," Vivien said, pausing so the Tuesday Ladies could look inside.

Three long rows of clothing racks were stuffed with hangers holding all types of costumes. They'd once been bright and showy, and now most were dingy and sagging and smelled of must and mildew. Vivien had hoped to be able to save some of the more complicated, show-specific costumes like the Tin Man or Audrey II, but her hopes had begun to fade once she began to look through them. It was a shame, because Cleopatra's headdress and the ballgown from the "Shall We Dance?" scene in *The King and I* would have been stunning in their heyday.

"I see the Cowardly Lion," said Iva, pushing her way into the room. She began to paw through a row of costumes. "Ooh! And this has to be Titania!"

"Oh, and here's Eliza Doolittle's hat!" said Orbra, perching the wide-brimmed straw bonnet on her blue-white hair. She didn't seem to mind the cascade of dust wafting down from the faded red ribbon. Or the spider that dangled from the back...

"And this must be from one of the witches in *Macbeth*—" said Juanita.

"Shh!" said Iva, looking around nervously as Vivien

automatically winced and hunched her shoulders. Old habits died hard.

"What?" demanded Juanita.

"You're not supposed to say that word!" Iva told her.

"What word?" demanded Maxine, turning from where she'd been digging through a stack of hat boxes.

"The name of that play," Vivien said. "It's a sort of superstition for theater people. So we don't say it in a theater."

Maxine looked at her from beneath Elphaba's pointy (but semi-crunched) Wicked Witch hat. Her expression spoke volumes: she thought Vivien was the crazy one. "You mean *Macb—*"

"*Maxine!*" Iva lunged toward her friend and put her hands over her mouth. "Don't say it! It's bad luck!"

The hat fell to the floor as Maxine batted her hands away. "Why not? Why does saying the damned word make a difference? It's a *play*, ain't it? How can a play be bad luck in a theater? What happens when they're actually doing it? You can't do a play and not say its name—"

"Miss Savage! Miss Savage, could you come here?"

Vivien had never been so relieved to hear her name than at that moment. She fairly bolted from the wardrobe, leaving the four ladies arguing at the tops of their lungs about *Macbeth*. She figured if she didn't hear the name being spoken (and it continued to be, regularly, by the contrary Maxine), it didn't count for the bad luck.

At least, she hoped it didn't.

GO OR DIE.

She couldn't control a shiver.

Maybe the bad luck had already begun.

CHAPTER SEVEN

DESPITE VIVIEN'S SNARKY COMMENTS, Jake couldn't help but feel a twinge of sympathy for her. After all, he could hardly manage his own pushing-eighty father...and here she was trying to herd a stubborn and determined cluster of old ladies through the danger zone of an old building.

Lots of things could go wrong, and the Tuesday Ladies (as he'd learned they were known, although "ladies" might have been an exaggeration) seemed worse than a group of toddlers on the loose—which he'd experienced the one time he'd been stuck babysitting his nieces and nephew solo. Three of them, ages two, three, and five.

"Jake's a doctor—he can handle it," his older sister Mathilda had said when her husband, Jake's brother-in-law, protested. She had a malicious gleam in her eye, a sort of *He deserves every bit of it* look. She'd looked at him that way when she washed his favorite white tee shirt *and* tighty-whiteys in hot water with a red blouse, back when he was ten. Of course, that was after he'd dumped a jar of spiders into her bed...while she was in it. "He made it through his residency, didn't he?"

"They'll nap most of the time anyway," agreed his other sister Irene, who was also older than Jake, with her own smirk.

Which was a lie.

The nieces and nephew hadn't napped for more than thirty minutes. And none of them at the same time.

Still feeling sympathy he didn't want, Jake turned his attention back to the huge piece of metal that was suspended from somewhere above. Damned good thing no one—Vivien —had been standing on it when it fell.

He and Pop had just walked into the area where the audience sat when he heard the strange whooshing sound and saw the piece swing down in a wild arc. The fact that it hadn't crashed to the floor barely registered in his mind as he bolted down the aisle. Only when he saw that the metal piece was swaying madly, unencumbered and yet still fettered, did he stop and swallow his heart back into place.

He'd gone up on the stage to make certain its harmlessness wasn't temporary, and after gingerly pulling on the dangling piece, he was convinced it wasn't going to come tumbling all the way down anytime soon. Still, it should be removed or repaired sooner rather than later.

"Better go up there and take a look," said Pops, who'd climbed onto the stage with him. Apparently he wasn't interested in seeing the dressing rooms with the Tuesday Ladies. "I'll make sure everyone stands clear."

Jake barely heard him, as he was already clambering up the nearest ladder—on the opposite side of the stage from where

Vivien had been. Once he got to the top, he tested the part of the catwalk still attached on this side. It jolted sharply from the force of his foot kicking at it, and although the squeaks and creaks were wild and alarming, nothing seemed loose or even weak.

After assuring himself that he wasn't about to go tumbling to the wooden floor below, Jake cautiously stepped out onto the trembling bridge. It shivered a little, but he held on to its chain railing—which was a safety hazard Vivien was going to have to fix pronto.

On his left were clusters of stage lights, most of them in rows on long metal beams—all hidden by the top overhang of the stage. The, uh, proscenium. That was what it was called. On his right hung rows of what looked like pieces of backdrops—

"What are you doing?"

He spun so fast that the narrow platform swayed, and he tightened his hold on the wimpy guard railing—someone definitely needed to replace that death hazard *immediately*—and saw Vivien nearly to the top of the ladder he'd just stepped away from.

"Hi," he said. "I was just checking things—"

"Get off there right now," she demanded from between tight jaws.

"It's fine," he told her. "I tested it out first." Even in the dim light up here, he could see the fire blazing in her golden-brown eyes. There was a smudge of dirt high on her left cheek, and her caramel-blond hair was sagging loose from its ponytail beneath the ball cap she wore. She wore stretchy athletic shorts that ended above her knees and a kind of ratty hot-pink tee that said, *I'm not yelling, I'm projecting*. Looking at her here, standing so close, he felt an unexpected pang of sorrow...and awareness.

"Come back over here," she said, now at the top of the ladder on the small landing. "No one is going out on there until I have it—"

She'd trailed into silence and was staring into the space toward the back where all of the scenery pieces hung high above the vast stage. "So that was it," she muttered. Even in the faulty light, he could see her face had gone pale and tense.

"What? What is it?" He was already back to the landing and she hadn't responded. "Viv? What's wrong?"

"Nothing," she said, but there was a hard edge to her voice. And he didn't think that anger was directed at him this time. But as he stepped onto the small platform next to her, she seemed to regroup, and as she turned to him, the ire in her expression was definitely just for him. "Jake, I don't know what you think you're doing, but I don't need—or want—your help. All right? So just...go away."

He might have simply climbed down the ladder at that point and done as she'd ordered if he hadn't glanced toward whatever had caught her attention. He couldn't have seen it from his previous position out on the catwalk, but here, now, the view was unencumbered, and he saw what had surely caught her attention.

GO OR DIE.

Large words in glowing green emblazoned on a black backdrop, way up high at the top of the stage.

"I've never seen a background that looks like that," he said casually, although his pulse had sharply spiked. He might not have thought much of it if it hadn't been for

Vivien's reaction (considering there was a musical called *Urinetown*, he supposed anything was possible when it came to stage scenery). But the tightness of her mouth, her sudden arrested stillness, as if she'd been jerked to attention, told him there was something else definitely going on here.

"Jake," she said in a voice that trembled with warning. "I—"

He touched her then—touched her for the first time in eleven years—putting a hand on an arm bared by the short-sleeved, snug tee she wore. A strong sense of awareness, a flash of heat at the skin-to-skin contact, zipped through him before she yanked away.

"Vivvie, tell me what's going on—"

"Don't call me that," she snapped, her eyes blazing. "You don't get to call me that anymore. Ever."

"All right. All right." He put some space between them on the small platform, holding up two hands—but he also made sure he was positioned so she couldn't get past him to the ladder and escape. Not yet. "I won't touch you. Won't call you anything but Vivien or VL. Or would you prefer Miss Savage?"

And that was when it occurred to him it might not *be* Miss Savage any longer. And something hard and heavy clunked into his gut.

"Vivien is fine." Her voice was clipped. "Now, for the last time—"

"Who put that there?" He decided there would be no more beating around the bush. Direct hits only from now on, because the entirety of their interactions since he'd first seen her again had been a series of dances—circling about, tap-dancing around their past and whatever was going on in the present.

It seemed to be the right approach, for she wilted a little. "I don't know." There was still a bite in her tone, but at least she'd given him an answer.

"Tell me what's going on," he said, and when she stiffened, preparing another runaround, he added, "Look, it's obviously new—so someone put it there recently. What's the deal? I have a right to know, since my father's going to be coming here regularly." The last bit he threw in there as a Hail Mary play, but it seemed to work.

She wilted a little more, but responded firmly, "All right, you've got a point, but there's no reason to think anyone's in any sort of danger. It's just—I don't know, some sort of practical joke, I guess."

"That piece of bridge fell—"

"Catwalk."

"Catwalk, then, fine—it fell, and if someone had been walking on it, that might have been a tragedy—"

"No one would have been walking on it without testing it out first, like I did," she said flatly. "If you're suggesting that it was sabotaged—"

"I don't know whether it was—or at least I didn't even think it might have been sabotaged until I saw *that* over there." He jerked his thumb toward the GO OR DIE backdrop. "But that sort of puts things into a whole different light, doesn't it?"

"Maybe. I don't know." She shook her head and rubbed her temples with one hand—a strikingly familiar gesture of frustration and likely an encroaching headache.

"I want to examine it to see whether it was, well, sabotaged," he said.

"So, what, you're a detective now, Dr. DeRiccio? Wasn't med school enough of a career for you?"

Caught by surprise at her use of his title, he couldn't hold back a grin. "You know how much I liked to watch *Criminal Minds* and *CSI*."

She folded her arms over her middle, which happened to draw his eyes to the pair of very fine breasts that he remembered far too well. "That doesn't make you qualified to examine anything."

His heart bumped a little when he noticed the tiniest tug at the corner of her mouth, like she was almost going to smile. That was the first time she'd looked at him with anything other than contempt or dislike.

"Still. I'd like to take a gander, all right? Look, Vivien, obviously something's going on here, and it's not pleasant. Even aside from the fact that my pop's going to be here—along with a slew of other people—it worries me because... well, I mean, it's you—your thing."

That little tug at her mouth disappeared. "If only you'd cared that much about me and my *thing* eleven years ago."

"That's not fair," he said, his voice tight. "You know that's not fair. I did care about you—"

She snorted. "Yeah, until you decided you wanted to bang Lissa Kirkland. How's she doing, by the way?"

He gritted his teeth. Of course she would go there. "I have no idea."

Before he could formulate any more words, there was a shout from below. "Miss Savage? Miss Savage! Could you take a look at something?"

"That's my cue," she said, and pushed past him to the ladder. "I'll be right there. Stay off the stage, please," she called down.

As she went down the ladder, just as her eyes were about to disappear, she looked up at him. "Please go away, Jake. It'll be a lot easier for both of us if you just leave me alone."

It *would* be a lot easier if he did.

He just wasn't sure he could.

VIVIEN HADN'T MEANT to leave the Tuesday Ladies to their own devices back in the area where all the dressing rooms were, but catching Jake poking around up in the catwalk area had been distracting and delayed her from returning to them.

He simply didn't have any business poking around here. Stubborn jerk. She could handle things herself. She just wished he would stop *being* here. Didn't he have a job?

Ricky DeRiccio had taken it upon himself to pass out some of the scones, sandwiches, and bottles of water brought from Orbra's Tea House, and a small cluster of teens surrounded him in the first three rows of seats in the house. There would be crumbs galore, but that was no worse than the current situation of dust and debris, so Vivien hardly winced when she noticed.

She answered several questions from a couple of the teams of volunteers (whether she wanted to save any of the old playbills—no—and where to find more garbage bags and a broom). Vivien was just about to head backstage and search out the Tuesday Ladies when her realtor showed up, walking down the main aisle.

Bella Pohlson was wearing a huge, congratulatory smile and a smart powder-blue summer suit. Her hands flashed with a large diamond, and her wrists were decorated with a glittering diamond bracelet and several thick silver bangles, and she looked far slicker and more put together than Vivien felt at the moment. Which was to be expected.

Bella wasn't alone, for Melody Carlson and another woman who looked vaguely familiar—both of whom were also dressed professionally—were with her. *They look like ladies who lunch,* Vivien thought, and that observation made her think of "Pick-A-Little, Talk-A-Little"—neither of which were accurate or even fair, but she didn't control what she thought of as her mental "casting hat."

"Hello, Vivien!" Bella said with a wave as she came forward to give Vivien the sort of hug professional women often gave each other even if they weren't close friends. "I hope you don't mind that we stopped in. Susie mentioned all the activity—that's her nephew over there, carrying one of those boxes—going on today, and I just had to stop by and congratulate you again...and welcome you to town as another small business owner."

"That's so nice of you," Vivien replied sincerely. "Thank you. The volunteers are really making quite a dent in the cleanup work. And it's nice to see you again, Melody. I hope Cherry didn't work you too hard yesterday."

"Oh, no, of course not. She's just brilliant. It really helps with my anxiety doing those long, slow yoga poses," Melody replied.

"Vivien, you might not remember me, but I'm—I was, I

mean—Susie Parminster. Now it's Wallaby—my husband's a dentist, if you need one—and I just have to tell you how excited we are to finally have a live theater coming back to town." Susie was beaming and looking around as if it was Christmas.

"Oh, yes, of course I remember you," Vivien replied, scrambling for details. And then they came to her. "You were Marty the year they did *Grease* in high school—and of course Melody was Sandy."

And I was nothing.

"That's right!" Susie seemed to be delighted to be remembered. "Hello, Robbie!" she called, waving to her nephew. "Keep up the good work!" She turned back to Vivien. "And welcome back to Wicks Hollow. I'm sure it's going to be quite a change from the hustle and bustle of— New York? That's where you came from, right?"

"The home of Broadway," said Melody with a smile. "I'll bet it was wonderful being there and able to see any show anytime you wanted." She sounded a little wistful. "We get to Chicago a couple times a year—I'll take my father even now— but they just don't have the variety there."

"Yes, I saw a lot of shows when I lived there." *Both in the audience and from backstage.*

"Well, my dear, I'm sorry to interrupt—we just wanted to stop in and say hi. Do you mind if I just show them around backstage really quickly right now?" asked Bella. "We won't be a minute. I'm just so curious to see what you've done already."

"Well, not a lot, really, but sure, feel free. It's not as if you haven't been here before—and there are people everywhere, so nothing's off-limits." Which reminded Vivien that the

Tuesday Ladies were still AWOL somewhere backstage, and that probably meant trouble.

But before she could do that, Randy Hebden, the electrician, hailed her from one of the side aisles. "Hey, Vivien, you got a minute?"

She hadn't expected to see him today, but she was happy to look at the numbers for updated lights and sound equipment and to answer some questions, especially since, until he was done with his part, there wouldn't be any air conditioning in the building. July and August in Michigan could be steamy, and as far as Vivien was concerned, the sooner, the better.

Finally, she was free to weave her way through the backstage area in search of Maxine, Juanita, Iva, and Orbra.

She found them in the props room.

"Rosencrantz would never have used that type of sword, Maxine," Juanita said. "It's too skinny—"

"I know that," snapped Maxine, who was whipping the flexible-bladed sword through the air as if her friend was Guildenstern himself and she was driving him back in a fencing match. She was also wearing the Phantom's mask, and Vivien's headache suddenly got worse. "I was just testing it out—"

"Then why did you say it was probably from *Romeo and Juliet?*" demanded Juanita, who happened to be holding a much larger broadsword type of weapon that might have been from *King Lear*. She was wearing the ruby slippers, which were missing half of their sequins.

The freaking *Odd Couple*—right here, live and in person, Vivien thought. Female version.

Only she wasn't sure who would be Felix and who would be Oscar.

"Maybe it's from *Rosencrantz and Guildenstern Are Dead*," said Iva, who was digging through a large trunk. She was a librarian and knew all sorts of random things. "Although I believe Rosencrantz used a knife, not a sword, in that one."

Fortunately for Vivien's peace of mind, the swords Maxine and Juanita were brandishing were retractable stage props made from foam and light plastic, and therefore the biggest hazard from either was the amount of dust flying through the air.

She hoped.

"Oh, look! I've always wondered how they did the change of the pumpkin into Cinderella's coach," Iva said, her voice rising with enthusiasm. "This has to be the framework for it—and heavens to Betsy! Look at the size of this!"

She was grappling with a collection of light metal rods that were covered with shimmery white material in a sort of tentlike construction. It could very well have been Cinderella's pumpkin-coach. Unfortunately, there were holes chewed in the flimsy, gauzy material, and some of the rods were bent, while others were detached from their moorings. With Iva having somehow gotten in the center of it, her attempts to set it up gave the prop—and her—a fluttery, spectral appearance.

"Oh, look at this!" exclaimed Orbra. She was examining a flying monkey whose wings still had fishing line trailing from them. "He's almost cute up close. Maybe Vivien will let me have him."

"You can hang it in your office," Maxine said in a

surprisingly agreeable tone, still examining how the blade of her sword retracted quickly and silently. Still wearing the Phantom mask.

"You're the one who should hang it in her office, Maxine," snarked Juanita. "He'd feel right at home with the Wicked Witch of the West."

"Juanita, you cad! How dare you! *En garde!*" cried Maxine, and she whipped the epee through the air so vigorously that she wobbled and almost lost her balance. Of course, the elderly woman was still holding her cane in the other hand, so at least she didn't spin and tumble to the ground, although she knocked off the mask, and her bottle-bottom glasses went askew.

"Well, I can see I'm going to have to separate the two of you before there's any bloodshed back here," Vivien said with a grin. "The scones are going fast, Maxine, so if you want one, you'd better grab one before it's too late."

"I'd really like to help clean up this place," Iva said as Vivien herded the Tuesday Ladies out of the props room. "It's just fascinating—all of these old costumes and props—"

"I'll help too," said Maxine, who hated to be one-upped.

"When are you going to learn your lines, then?" demanded Juanita. "I'm not going to be onstage with someone who can't remember their lines all the time—"

"What makes you think I won't remember my lines? I—"

"Because you can't remember your own address half the time, and—"

"At least I can see where I'm going and don't talk baby talk to my dog every minute."

"You don't have a dog, Maxine," Juanita snapped. "And

you talk baby talk to Bruce Banner all the time when you think I'm not listening."

"You're just sour because I beat you at Scrabble this morning. Again," Maxine replied haughtily.

"I would have won if you hadn't swapped tiles when I wasn't looking," retorted Juanita. "Teach me to go to the bathroom in the middle of the game."

"And here are the scones," Vivien said loudly enough to drown them out as they came down from the side stage.

"Ricky!" Juanita flowed down the stairs, her lime-green maxi dress rippling above the ruby slippers. "Thank you for saving us some of the scones. Do you like my new shoes?"

"Miss Savage!"

Vivien absolutely did not sigh at yet another demand for her attention from off in the wings. She didn't. But she really needed to find some ibuprofen.

She was beyond grateful for the work the teens were doing for the theater—and she could already see vast improvement just in the last couple of hours.

She would also have liked a moment to use the restroom and to check her phone for emails or messages. Vivien was waiting for a trendy clothing label to get back to her about the proposal she'd made for an Instagram post by Louise London —something that would make the actor ecstatic and give Vivien a welcome surge of income while she managed the project. And Louise had been texting and messaging her constantly for updates and news and, basically, for Vivien to hold her hand.

Vivien attended to the volunteer's question, was interrupted with another problem, and then was finally about to get her own hands on a fresh scone when Stephanie

Lillard, the blacksmith's daughter, caught her attention again.

"Miss Savage, we found a big trunk down in the orchestra pit." Stephanie was standing in front of the stage where the pit would be if its top (which was part of the stage) was opened up. At the moment, it wasn't open, and Vivien wondered how the teens had found their way down into it. "Should we check inside it or leave it for now?"

"Take a quick peek inside to find out what's in there, and then we can decide," Vivien replied.

Stephanie nodded, and with an enthusiastic smile—who wouldn't be interested in opening an old trunk?—dashed off to check it out. Vivien snagged a bottle of water and gulped half of it down while she waited, and then spoke briefly to the football coach—who'd shown up to help supervise his team. He'd been a year behind her back in high school.

"Your guys have been amazing today," she told him. "We've accomplished a lot more than I ever anticipated."

"They were pretty motivated," Coach Jeffreys replied. "I told them if they filled up one of the dumpsters they could come swim at my house on Wicks Lake this afternoon."

"Good plan," Vivien said with a laugh. "And they're obviously going to be swimming at your place later."

"You a football fan? You should come by sometime once we start practice—give 'em a watch. They're going to be a really good team this year, if I do say so myself," he added with a self-deprecating grin. "First home game is the Friday of Labor Day weekend."

That was when Vivien realized Coach Andrew Jeffreys was kind of, sort of hitting on her—just like he had done back in high school. And that she kind of, sort of didn't mind—

especially since she was a sweaty, dirt-streaked kind of mess. The coach was much cuter than she remembered him back in high school, with sun-streaked light brown hair, a pair of sparkling hazel eyes, and a set of broad, muscular shoulders.

But before she could reply, the sounds of running feet over the general din of work caught her attention. "Miss Savage, we can't get it open." Stephanie and her friend rushed up, looking very disappointed. "Maybe we could try a crowbar."

"Why don't you take a break and have a scone—and there are some sandwiches, too." Vivien looked at the sweaty, pink-faced teens standing around and raised her voice. "Everyone should take a break. All of you come on and take five. Thank you so much. Let's eat in the lobby, please, not here in the house, though, all right?"

This invitation spread like wildfire as she herded them out to the lobby. What had been a small cluster of volunteers sniffing around the food quickly turned into a horde of hungry, tired, but energized teens filling the lobby. Coach Jeffreys toasted Vivien silently with a bottle of water as if to reiterate his invitation, then turned to speak to his team.

"It was so nice of you to bring all this food, Orbra," Vivien said, her eyes stinging with tears. "I wasn't expecting it—I thought I might order pizza and salad for everyone—but you were ahead of me. Thank you so much. I'm happy to pay for the food."

The older lady shrugged. "It's a donation to the volunteers. Community service deserves support from the community. And don't you worry, the Downtown Business Association contributed toward the cost of the supplies—Trib made sure of it. Wouldn't have happened when Aaron Underwood was here. He was a real tight-a—er, skinflint."

"I wouldn't worry about them," Ricky said, scratching his flat, broad nose. "I can guarantee they've heard worse walking through the halls at school."

Orbra sighed. "Probably. But I don't want to contribute to their delinquency." She braced her hands on her hips and looked over at Jake, who'd just wandered into the lobby from who knew where.

"You going to bring me some more of that bread, there, young man?" She pitched her voice toward him. "Went through two loaves in less than thirty minutes. I made it a lunch special—your asiago tomato bread with a gazpacho soup and a small salad, with a pot of tea of their choice. Sold out almost immediately and had to change the specials sign because people kept asking about it."

Vivien looked back and forth between Jake and Orbra he was making bread? wasn't he busy being a doctor?—but before she could ask or even decide if she should—after all, the less Jake in her life, the better—someone called her over to the restroom in the front of the theater.

After that, she was so busy that she didn't get back to the lobby till much later, as the last of the volunteers were leaving.

"Thank you so much, again," she said as they gathered up their things. "Coach Jeffreys, I really appreciate you getting your team out here."

"They can always use different workouts," Coach Jeffreys said. "And you gave them one hell of a workout today. Don't forget to come check out our practice someday. Starting the week of August 15. It always ends by eight, and by then I'm ready for something to eat and a cold one."

"I'll do that," she replied…pretty certain he'd just asked her out after a practice. And pretty certain she'd take him up on it.

"And by the way—it's Drew, just like when we were back in school. I save 'coach' for the team and their parents." His eyes twinkled.

And now she was *definitely* certain of his motives. "Have a good practice, then, Drew."

She looked at the time as she waved goodbye and saw that it was nearly three o'clock. Four hours of work with nearly sixty people—with only a few short breaks—had made a huge dent in the demo and cleanup work. She thought she'd been being wildly optimistic ordering two fifty-yard dumpsters, but she'd have to have both of them hauled away and replaced tomorrow. They were already full.

She closed the doors to the outside and went back into the house. Everything was quiet in there too, and it was then she noticed that the catwalk was no longer hanging from above and heaved a sigh of exasperation. Jake's doing, she was certain. So much for him listening—which was typical of him. The man was sweet, charming, said the right words— then did whatever the hell he wanted.

When she saw the large piece of broken catwalk leaning against the wall in the back, she had to at least be grateful it was somewhere safe—and that she hadn't had to deal with it herself.

Now that everyone was gone and there was no possibility that a piece of heavy wood was going to fall down on her, she was able to walk through the building and take stock.

Although little swirls of dust remained from today's activities and the gentle scents of must and cleaning supplies filled the air, the space was silent and still. Vivien was exhausted but exhilarated. So much more had been accomplished than she'd hoped.

The tattered red velvet curtains were gone—as were the others that hung in the wings—and it was a strange experience to stand on a stage that was so naked and open.

Normally, the performance area was cloaked with rows of curtains, scenery, and backdrops. Now the space—usually swollen with make-believe and illusion—seemed so spare and vulnerable. If she walked out into the house, Vivien would be able to see well back into the wings and even backstage.

Today, open and unshrouded, it was like someone's private closet had been thrown wide for all to see.

What sorts of secrets lay within?

She smiled wryly at her fanciful, eerie thought. Secrets, schmecrets—she was going home for a good, long, hot shower. And then she remembered the trunk Stephanie and her friends had found in the orchestra pit.

Vivien was mildly curious why there would be a trunk in the orchestra pit, and her curiosity compelled her to take a look before she took off for the day. Usually, the pit was crowded enough with the musicians and their chairs, music stands, and microphones, so why anyone would want to add a large trunk to the space was anyone's guess. Maybe it held old supplies. The girls hadn't been able to get it open, though, and she wondered why it would be locked.

The pit was located below and in front of the stage. It could be covered or uncovered with various-sized panels as needed, and since it was currently shielded by those inset pieces, Vivien had to go around to the backstage area where a flight of steps led down to the pit.

She couldn't help but think of *The Phantom of the Opera* as she descended into the "dungeon of black despair"—not that it was that deep or black or desperate—and hummed the song a little as she made her way below. She took the stairs because she wasn't about to test the small, square elevator—which was a necessity for bringing a harp, upright bass, or a grand piano to the pit.

Despite the work that had been done earlier, a few stubborn cobwebs still clung to the top and sides of the stairway. The steps opened into a surprisingly spacious location with a ceiling that was low, but not so low that a violinist would jab it with her bow, and the top of the harp would be comfortably far enough away. Of course, the panels would usually be removed when the orchestra was playing, but there were times when a larger stage was needed or the pit needed to be hidden for some other reason.

There was a single naked light bulb dangling near where the conductor would be positioned—his or her boxlike platform was still in place. There were music stands leaning in a neat pile in a corner—obviously Stephanie and her friend's work—and stacks of chairs joined them.

Vivien didn't see the trunk at first, because it was tucked under the lip of the stage toward the front—behind where the conductor would stand. The chest was in a sort of crawlspace beneath the floor of the audience. From the scrapes on the floor, it appeared that the two girls had wrangled the large trunk further into the open space, so it must have been tucked quite far beneath.

Now she was even more curious.

It was what was commonly called a steamer trunk—large, old-looking, and roomy enough to carry a generous amount of clothing. It looked ancient to Vivien, and the leather straps that could be used to bind it closed were dried and curled with age. They lay where, it seemed, the teens had pulled them off. The chest's corners were covered by tarnished brass bumpers, and whatever color the walls had originally been was now a dull, mildew-spotted dung-brown.

Despite removing the straps, Stephanie and her friend hadn't been able to open the trunk, and Vivien shined her flashlight closely to examine the latch. There didn't seem to be any sort of locking mechanism, and so she pushed, pried, and twisted to no avail. She was about to give up when she remembered the multitool in her pocket.

"This'll do it," she muttered to herself, flipping open the small pair of pliers and attacking the latch with their tiny metal teeth.

It snapped open easily after that—though not without a little scrape on her hand—and she tucked the tool away. Good thing she'd had a tetanus shot recently, she thought, and, having nothing else, resorted to wiping off the thin line of blood on her shirt.

Then she crouched in front of the trunk. "All right, let's see what you've been hiding down here for who knows how—"

Her words strangled as a shadow fell over her from behind. She gasped and twisted around, losing her balance and falling on her butt as she scrambled away from—

Nothing.

There was nothing there.

No one behind her.

No movement, no sound, no subtle change in the air.

Nothing that could have caused that long, angular shadow to spill over her and onto the trunk...and then slide away.

Vivien sat there, her heart thudding so hard that she could barely breathe. Her palms were damp and her knees were so weak that she didn't think she could pull to her feet even if she wanted to.

She *hadn't* imagined it. No, she hadn't. It had been a tall shadow—angular and straight, not soft and organic like a living being—just like before.

She sat there staring into the depths of the orchestra pit for quite a while. She shined her flashlight around, hoping to see something that could explain the shadow—a forgotten instrument that might have somehow tipped over (what instrument looked like a long, forbidding beam with a slanted end?)...a piece of wood...a chair?

But everything was silent, still, and nothing moved. Nothing breathed except for her.

After a long while, she rose to her feet. Her knees were still a little shaky. The trunk squatted there, unopened and tempting—yet she felt a sense of foreboding. Surely her joke about finding out what the trunk had been hiding had no relationship to the strange shadow fall. After all, the same thing had occurred when she was up on the stage, right above where she was now sitting.

Vivien frowned. She didn't like that train of thought.

Part of her wanted to get outside, into the late afternoon sunshine, and forget about long, dark shadows that came from nowhere and glided over the floor...

But the bigger part of her, the stubborn part, the

determined and furious part, the part that always picked herself back up when she was knocked for a loop—the assets that had brought her this far in life after so many ups and downs—insisted she not capitulate to weakness.

She would stay.

She would open the freaking trunk.

And she fully expected nothing to happen, nothing unusual or shocking to be inside. It was the atmosphere that put those thoughts into her head. There was simply no reason for her to be nervous about opening the trunk. It would be anticlimactic.

Thud-squeak…thud-creak…thud-squeak…

Footsteps. On the stage, directly above her.

CHAPTER EIGHT

THE THEATER WAS empty and silent, but Jake knew Vivien had to be there. Her car was in the parking lot, and he'd walked in through the unlocked side door.

"Vivien?" he called, and then he saw her purse on the edge of the stage. So she was definitely somewhere around. He just hoped everything was all right, considering. "Vivien! Where are you?"

Then he heard a muffled reply. "Jake? Is that you? I'm down here."

Sounded like she was right below his feet...? Oh, she was in the orchestra pit.

Not that he had any idea how to get there...

"I'm in the pit. Stairs are off stage right," she called up from right beneath his feet.

Moments later, he was pushing away a swath of cobwebs as he descended into the dimly lit, shadowy place. There was only one light bulb working, but it was enough. Vivien was standing near the bottom of the steps, eyeing a large antique steamer trunk.

To his surprise, she greeted him with neither "What are you doing here?" nor "What do you want?" Instead, she said, "I've been working on getting this trunk open—it was locked and I broke off the hasp. I have no idea why it was shoved way under here, beneath that crawlspace."

Her words sounded normal, but there was something in her eyes that seemed…off. It was probably him. She'd made it abundantly clear that she didn't want him around.

And that was part of the reason he'd come back to the theater once everyone was gone. They needed to talk—to clear the air or something. He knew *he* had things that needed to be said.

And aside from that, he wanted to make sure she was all right.

"All right. Well, let's open it," he suggested. He sensed a slight hesitation in her manner and wondered about it.

Just open the trunk. Right?

"All right."

No, he wasn't imagining her reluctance. There was a strange look on her face. "Want me to do it?" he asked.

"No," she said, suddenly firm. "I'm just not sure what to expect."

"What do you think is in there? A dead body?" He laughed a little, and when she scoffed and reached for the lid to raise it, he felt a sudden prickle over the back of his neck. A little rush of cool air—no, *cold* air. Frigid, even. Icy.

She stopped with her hand on the trunk and looked up at him with serious brown eyes. "Do you feel that?"

"No," he replied too quickly, resisting the urge to touch the back of his suddenly freezing neck. And he ignored, absolutely ignored, the fact that his breath suddenly looked like little puffs of fog.

She glowered at him. "No? But you didn't even ask me what I meant before you answered. How do you know what I was talking about?"

"Fine. I guess there's a little bit of a draft somewhere down—"

"A very cold, freezing draft," she said. "In the middle of July? When I can see your—"

"Fine. It's cold. So what? Will you open the trunk already, or are we going to stand here—"

She flipped it open.

They bumped shoulders as they moved to look down into the chest. Their shadows obstructed the contents, so he moved back a little to let the stingy light better illuminate it.

"Well, it's not a body," Jake said with forced jocularity. That frigid chill still burned the back of his neck, and he could still see his breath, dammit. He didn't know whether he believed in ghosts, but he knew this sort of thing supposedly portended supernatural activity.

And there was a stillness that had settled around them, there in the dim belowground pit. Like a sudden absence of sensation and movement—it was like being in a vacuum.

Just...nothing.

Or like everything was holding its breath.

Vivien spoke first. Her voice sounded artificially bright. "Looks like a bunch of costumes."

Yes, the trunk was filled with old clothing, and it all appeared fairly well preserved. Jake saw a jumble of shiny fabrics like satin—black, pink, yellow—as she began to pull items out in wads. And there was a scrap of bright purple velvet just beneath that, then something shiny and green, and then the tangle of fabric gave way to something recognizable: a military sort of coat in bright red with black cuffs and a white patch down the front. It had two rows of large brass buttons fastened with black loops across the white front.

She pulled out the coat, and what was left beneath gave him a start at first. A huge, eerie, doll-like face looked up at them with unseeing eyes. It sported an obscenely large mouth with massive white teeth, both upper and lower, in a really creepy smile. It wore a tall, cylindrical hat of dark blue with a slanted top and a short black bill in the front.

"*The Nutcracker*," she said, looking down into the trunk. "These all must be costumes from *The Nutcracker*."

"I don't ever remember the Nutcracker looking so unpleasant," he said, suppressing a shiver. The freezing air was still brushing over the back of his neck. "Isn't it a kids' show? Something like that would give my nephew nightmares. That mask looks way creepier than any clown I've ever seen."

He noticed she didn't pull out the Nutcracker mask—which wasn't a mask so much as a huge, false head that would rise several feet above one's shoulders. He didn't blame her. There was something unsettling about looking down at that face.

"It might be enjoyed by children, but it's got a lot of adult elements. This headpiece is from when the Nutcracker—which is given to Clara on Christmas Eve—first becomes animated. He starts off as a regular-sized nutcracker, and then, when she falls asleep, she dreams about him. He becomes human-size in her dreams—larger than human, which is why the piece is so big—and then eventually the head goes away and he becomes fully human as the ballet goes on."

Jake was still looking down in distaste. "If that showed up in my dreams, I think I'd wake myself up right away. Look at those chompers! Forget about cracking a walnut—they're big enough to crack a skull."

She gave a little snort and pulled out the ugly-as-hell fake head. "The back's all crushed," she said, turning the thing around in her hands. Despite its ungainly size, it seemed light. It was probably made from papier-mâché. "Maybe that's why they—"

The light went out with a decisive *pop!* She made a little gasp, and, admittedly, he did too—for suddenly they were in the dark with the blazing chill still raising goosebumps on his neck...and a big, ugly, creepy mask. She moved, bumping into him sharply, then jerking away. He could hear her rough, unsteady breathing.

"Vivien, are you all right?" He felt around for her instead of digging out his cell phone with its flashlight—and that was a simple indulgence because he just wanted an excuse to touch her.

"Yes," she said—but her voice sounded as unsteady as her breathing. "Of course."

And then he found her—his hands brushing against a warm arm, which he took gently and somehow managed to tug her up against him. He folded her in his arms like it was the most natural thing to do—and, oh man, he realized suddenly it *was*. It felt right, comfortable, natural...and then there was her scent. It was so familiar, rising over the age and mustiness surrounding them in the old theater. He felt a pang of grief ring deep inside.

"I'm fine," she said, but she wasn't pulling away. She wasn't exactly embracing him back, but she wasn't pulling away.

It was so strange, standing there in a decrepit old orchestra pit holding the woman he'd loved eleven years ago as if those eleven years—and their unpleasant breakup—had never happened.

Then she seemed to regain her presence of mind, for she pulled back, and he heard her fumbling around—

"Don't know what happened," she said, and a light beamed into the darkness from her cell phone. "I'm not usually that skittish. Geez. Frigging light bulb goes out and I go to pieces? I don't know why I reacted that way."

He didn't know. He didn't care. He just knew he was already missing her being close to him.

"What do you want to do about the, uh, headpiece?" he asked. "If it's ruined, you might as well toss it."

"Let's take it up and look at it in better light. Maybe I can display it in the lobby with some of the other mementos we've found here. Preserve some of the theater's history. Liv would like that. I think *The Nutcracker* was the last show performed here."

He didn't know why she'd choose to keep that creeper of a mask, but he picked it up and carried it as they made their way up the steps with the aid of her cell phone flashlight.

"All the lights are out," she said in surprise as they got to the top of the stairs and stepped into the back stage area. "Not just the ones in the—"

She froze and grabbed blindly for him as her light tumbled to the ground. Her fingers curled painfully around his forearm as they stared at the rippling red...*something*... that undulated on the stage.

It twisted and writhed in the darkness, a glowing, screaming red...a sort of spiral, whipping and buffeting about as if it were trapped in a gale-force wind.

Her fingers were digging holes into Jake's arm, but the discomfort was hardly noticeable as he stared at the vision before them. Then, all at once, it was gone. The light went out and they were swathed in darkness once more...

Except for angry scarlet letters burning and rippling in the air, high above the audience seats in the middle of the theater:

DEATH

CHAPTER NINE

WHEN VIVIEN DROPPED HER PHONE, it landed light-side down—effectively smothering its illumination.

By the time everything was over and she lunged to the floor to snatch it back up—guided by the faintest bit of glow around the edges of the phone—Jake was already moving toward the stage.

She followed, right on his heels, brandishing the light like a weapon.

"They didn't even try to hide it this time," she said, shining her phone up and out over the house. The sheer fabric—smoke-gray; barely distinguishable even in the light—rippled gently, causing the glow-in-the-dark red letters spelling *DEATH* to shimmy as if alive.

"No, they didn't," he said grimly. "But it was a clever performance."

"If I'd been here alone, it might have been more effective as a scare tactic," Vivien admitted. "Not much more—now that I'm onto him—her—them—*whoever*—but it might have given me more of a shock."

"The lights going out first was a dead giveaway," Jake said. "Did they know you were in the pit?"

His voice was steady, but she sensed the tension vibrating from him. And for the moment, Vivien was okay with putting aside their past and dealing with what had just happened.

Because what had just happened opened up a whole bunch of questions and problems.

"If I hadn't dropped my phone, we might have seen more," she said, disgusted with herself.

"I don't know," Jake said, looking at the center of the stage —right where the twisting, undulating, cyclonic *thing* had been. "I don't know that there would be much to see. Obviously, it was some sort of silky scarf thing, lit from inside, maybe a fan blowing down on it? You'd know more about that kind of stuff—stage theatrics—than me. Probably dropped the red cloth from above, then whisked it back up when the little show was over. And then, in the meantime, whoever it was dropped that friendly little sign into place right over here."

"Distraction and misdirection. Oldest trick in the book," Vivien said. "There must be some sort of black light shining on the scrim to make the letters glow like that."

"Scrim?"

"That's what that is—a nearly transparent piece of fabric that you can shine light on or through for scenery or to create shadows or various other effects. It's a common theatrical technique."

"So whoever is doing this has a familiarity with the theater."

Whoever is doing this.

The words shook her...but they were true.

He was right—someone was doing it. Purposely. What a horrific, terrible realization.

"I suppose you could draw that conclusion—that whoever has a background in theatrics. But it's not like these techniques can't be looked up on the internet."

"Right." His face was shadowed and stark in the bright cone of light from her phone. "Well, we should probably try to get the lights on so we can look around to see whether there's any sign of who did this."

"All right, Detective DeRiccio," she replied dryly. It was easier to cling to a bit of humor, and then to focus on things to *do*, than to dwell on the reality that someone was trying to drive her away from her theater. "The fuse box is back here. He—or she, or they—probably just flipped the main."

"They probably thought you were here alone—just like the last time," he said as she opened the door to the fuse box.

Sure enough—the main breaker was off, and when Vivien flipped it back into place, the lights came back up.

"Either they have some sort of nanny-cam here or they're watching the parking lot and saw only your car," he went on. "Or watched everyone else leave."

"What about your car?" she replied. The idea of any sort of surveillance—via camera or live eyeball—on her and the theater made her feel sick. She was going to have to call the police and make a report. Helga was going to be very upset.

"I walked. I only live up that way," he said, gesturing vaguely to the west. Then he gave her a knowing look. "So are you going to tell me what happened the last time or not?"

She pursed her lips then shrugged. "Fine. It was basically the same sort of thing as happened today. Different color lights—bluish—but in the same basic location on the stage, and last time it was just lights, not the gyrating cloth sort of thing. I don't know, maybe this time he—she—whoever—was trying to evoke a ghost or something with the fluttery fabric. And there was a different warning the first time, but you already know that. When it happened before, I, uh, left in a hurry, and when I came back in—"

"That was before or after I saw you in the parking lot?"

"I had just come out after the, uh, event. When I came back in, after we talked, the 'GO OR DIE' was gone."

"And we know how that happened. Whoever it was dragged it up like a backdrop when you went outside."

"No one was here," she told him firmly. "I didn't sense or hear any other presence."

It was his turn to shrug. "You ran out quickly—that would have given the perp enough time to roll up the sign and get out before you came back inside. He probably used one of the back doors."

"Maybe." *Oh God.* She couldn't keep from rubbing her prickling upper arms as she thought about being surveilled when she was alone in the theater. "But why didn't he take away the backdrop? They just left it, and now I've seen it, and I know it's not— Well, I know someone's doing this."

"Maybe they didn't have time—or maybe they didn't think you'd see it. It was pretty far up there, camouflaged by the others. In fact, we probably wouldn't have seen it if we hadn't been up there on the catwalk. Maybe they were trying to make certain of it by sabotaging the walkway." His face was grim and set.

Vivien shivered again and tried not to think about how sick she felt. "I'll have all the locks changed tomorrow."

"We should take a closer look up there," he said, pointing to the recesses above the stage. "See if we can tell how they did it."

"All right."

Vivien didn't mention the weird, eerie shadow.

She didn't know whether it was connected to these obviously human-related events—but if it wasn't, she didn't think she wanted to know otherwise. At least at the moment.

Jake clambered up the ladder on the side where the catwalk had fallen. "We should check out all of those other backdrops," he said when she joined him at the top. "Make sure they're secure and not going to accidentally-on-purpose fall down. And the rows of spotlights, too."

Vivien bit back a "what's this *we* business?" and nodded. At this point, disengaging Jake DeRiccio was like trying to stop a bad video clip from going viral by making an official statement—too little, too late, and just drew more attention to the situation.

But when he started to walk out onto the intact section of catwalk, she grabbed his arm. "I don't think that's a good idea," she said. "What if...whoever...sabotaged that piece too. Just now."

He muttered a curse. "Good point."

"There is some scaffolding in the back," she told him. "It's behind a bunch of old set pieces. I can dig it out and wheel it onstage tomorrow and take a close look at everything."

"You have scaffolding?"

"Sure. It's a common enough piece of equipment in a theater—not only to reach the tops of high set pieces, but for repairs to the lights, catwalk, flies, and even sometimes it acts as a moveable set piece itself. Haven't you ever seen *Newsies*?

That entire set was basically built around a huge piece of scaffolding."

"Right. Never thought about that." He looked back out over the top of the stage, where tattered backdrops hung in rows several yards from where they stood. "I see a filmy red something back there, behind the *GO OR DIE* piece. I guess we know what it is."

"I didn't notice it earlier today. Did you?" she said.

"I didn't look all that carefully. But now I wish I had," he replied grimly. "Would be nice to know whether it was installed, so to speak, in the last few hours or not."

Vivien definitely couldn't control a shiver at that unpleasant thought. It was bad enough that someone was spying on her, but to have been in here while all the teens and old ladies were as well? And setting up something so ugly?

"I need a shower," she said, suddenly *done* for the day. All this—the warnings, the eerie chill, the creepy shadow, the possibility that someone was watching her—was just a little too much. She felt sticky, hot, hungry, and utterly defeated.

Vivien was self-aware enough—meaning she'd been in therapy enough—that she knew the best way for her to combat feelings of anxiety and defeat was to remove herself from the situation and take some time to reboot. A shower, then a good cocktail while she put her feet up and checked out the social media on her clients, hopefully with some good news from Gab-Wear about the proposal from Louise London.

It was too bad Wicks Hollow was short on carry-out and delivery options. She'd probably have to settle for pizza.

"My house is really close," Jake said. "You can shower there—although I don't have much you could change into except a pair of sweats my sister left once—"

"Oh, no, that's all right," she said quickly. Not a good idea to spend *that* much time with Jake. At his place. *Showering.*

Not a good idea.

He seemed genuinely disappointed. "That's too bad, because I have a really excellent Pinot gris that's been waiting for an excuse to be opened," he said. "Seems like all this is as good a reason as any."

She gave a short laugh. "Oh, thanks, Jake. Really. It's better if I just head on back to my place. I've got some work to do. Besides, I think I'm going to need something s-stronger than a glass of w-wine." She couldn't quite keep the quaver from her voice there at the end, dammit, and she turned away before he could see her blinking rapidly.

"All right, then." His tone was studiously noncommittal.

But Jake stuck with her as she locked up, then they walked outside together, with him carrying the Nutcracker headpiece for her.

"I could give you a ride home," she offered, feeling a little churlish over having rejected his invitation.

But what had he expected, anyway? Just because they'd shared that icky theatrical display didn't mean that she'd forgiven and forgotten what happened eleven years ago.

"I can walk," he said in a cool tone. "Thanks—"

Their feet crunched and skidded to a sharp halt on the gravel-strewn concrete when they saw her car.

"*Nooo!*" Vivien cried, staring at the smashed windshield and the spread of glass shards glittering among the gravel in the afternoon sun. She stared in horrified silence at the destruction—which wasn't only the windshield, but also two broken headlights.

"Geez, Viv," said Jake, sliding a comforting, protective arm around her waist as he let the Nutcracker head slide to the ground. "I'm so sorry. Whoever the asshole is who's messing with you..."

He trailed off and simply hugged her closer as she dug the phone out of her pocket, fighting tears of fury.

DESPITE HER INITIAL RELUCTANCE, Vivien ended up at Jake's house anyway. Since she couldn't drive anywhere, she capitulated when he again offered his place.

"You might even settle for a glass of wine instead of a cocktail at this point," he said with a wry grin. "Although I might have something stronger."

Instead of getting a ride from the attending police officer (not Helga, who was out on another call), Vivien and Jake decided to wait until after the tow truck came to pick up her poor, battered Accord, then walk to his house.

"I just bought that car," she muttered as they started out of the parking lot on foot. "I never had one in New York. Didn't need it." Then she shook her head as if to clear it and hiked up the duffel bag she'd retrieved from her trunk. She'd taken to keeping a change of clothes and toiletries in there in case she made it to the gym or a yoga class after a day at the theater.

She looked down the road. "Where's your place?"

"Up there," he said, and pointed to the small bluff just behind and beyond the cul-de-sac at the end of the road. "The sort of Brady Bunch-meets-Frank Lloyd Wright-looking place."

"That's *your* house?" Vivien stumbled to a halt and looked at him in astonishment. "It's... *Wow*."

She knew the house, of course. She'd noticed it every time she drove by because though it looked pretty dated—all angles with its flat, half-pitched roof that was higher in the front than the back and the huge 1960s-style windows—she knew it had to have an amazing view of the big lake.

"Yeah," he said with a bashful smile. "I got really lucky. The owner had to sell quickly, and it was the dead of January in the middle of a blizzard."

"Is the view as amazing as it seems?"

"You'll soon be able to see for yourself." He gave her a warm smile, and she was annoyed when her heart gave a little thump.

This is not happening. You're not going to let this happen again, Vivien Leigh.

"This way," he said, pointing to a narrow walkway. "Through this little park here, then it's just a little climb up a path over the rise over there. A lot shorter than taking the road, which goes out of its way to get up there."

She didn't say much as they walked, although she couldn't wait to see the inside of the house. He carried the Nutcracker headpiece the whole way while she toted her duffel, and though it took extra effort to walk up the small path (calling it a "little" climb was a bit of an understatement), it was short enough that she wasn't out of breath. Much, anyway. Though her calves might be feeling it tomorrow.

She was used to walking on flat surfaces all over the city —not climbing small mountains.

"That's why I like to take this route when I run," he said once they got to the top. "It's a nice trail, and I have to work a little harder than on the treadmill or just running through a neighborhood."

Someone had done some work to the outside of the single-story house since its original construction in the 1960s. You couldn't do much about the roof, which not only rose to a steeper pitch in the front, bluff side, but it also canted up higher on the right, giving the front an almost triangular facade.

Instead of the brown siding and orange brick Vivien imagined had been the original, the exterior was covered in slender shale-brown bricks and fieldstone. They all had different depths, giving the wall a pleasing, uneven texture instead of a flat face. The trim was cream, and the front door —which faced the road, not the lake—was ocean blue.

"I didn't pick it," Jake said when she commented on the color of the door.

"I love it," she replied as he unlocked it and gestured her into the house. "It's unusual and gives what could be a drab-looking house a nice— Oh, *wow*..."

She dropped her duffel bag and stepped into the living room with its twenty-foot, slanted ceiling, then walked toward the large windows on one wall. They covered most of the west-facing side of the living room and the wall on the right. Lake Michigan—with all of her striations of cerulean, sapphire, cobalt, navy, and mint—was below and beyond, and the vast basin rippled and undulated as far as the eye could see. The Great Lake met the pale blue sky somewhere miles away, and nearly a hundred miles beyond that were the shores of Wisconsin. Layers of long clouds lined the sky, echoing the horizon: some puffy on top, some slender like a brush stroke, swathed above the line of the lake.

The house was situated so that the land and its surrounding throng of trees seemed to cup it protectively, holding the structure out over the water. But it was just an illusion from the inside, for there was at least a half mile of land between the base of the bluff and the shore, and the house was fully supported by the land. It was the clever design of the windows that made it seem as if the front of the house was suspended in midair over the lake.

"Go on out there." Jake pointed to the side wall, which wasn't only windows, as she'd thought, but a large sliding door. "You're going to love that."

Feeling a sort of tightness in her chest that she couldn't identify, Vivien did as he suggested and found herself on a flagstone patio with its own breathtaking view. Located on the side of the house, it was protected by a tangle of trees and bushes on two sides, which, despite the chaos, offered some shade. A third side was the sliding door and wall of the house. And the fourth direction offered its own unobstructed view of the lake.

"Wow. Mike and Carol certainly did well for themselves," she murmured, drawing in a deep breath of fresh air coming in from the lake.

"Mike and Carol— Oh, ha. The Bradys. Got it." Jake folded his arms as he stood next to her. "It needs a lot of work and some updating, but this was the no-brainer selling point."

"I'll say."

"I've got a ton to do with the landscaping," he said, gesturing to the overgrown, encroaching trees. "I don't think those vines are supposed to be there, and they look like they're choking everything out. The arborvitae is way out of control—I think that's what that is." He shrugged. "Or maybe it's boxwood. I can't remember what the realtor called it."

Vivien gave a little laugh. "City girl here. I haven't faintest idea. The closest I ever got to a garden was walking through Central Park and trying to grow a tomato plant on my teeny balcony. It died."

"I had a condo in Baltimore, so I didn't do much there. I should probably just hire someone who knows what they're doing."

"Well, don't do what Trib did and put in a pergola—I think that's what it's called—with vines growing on it," she said with a little giggle that sounded nervous to her ears. *Why am I so nervous?* "He's all freaked out because the birds perch all up in it and crap all over the tables below."

He laughed. "Ouch. Well, nothing I do could be any worse than the tree that was growing in the middle of the living room when I moved in."

She looked at him, squinting a little in the afternoon sun. "A tree? Like, in a pot? Or something that had taken root and took over the house?"

He shook his head. "Neither. The previous owners—who built the place back in the sixties—deliberately planted a tree in the middle of the living room. It was over eighteen feet tall with a branch span of about the same."

She stared at him. "A real tree? Planted?"

"Yes. They had a huge, sunken area in the center of the

room that had low walls around it like a raised garden sort of thing. It was filled with dirt—and the roots of the tree." He shook his head as if he still couldn't believe it. "They had built-in seating around it—wooden benches. It was very... ah...different."

"What kind of tree was it?" Vivien asked, still trying to picture such a thing.

"I have no idea. It wasn't a pine tree; it had leaves—small leaves—and the damned things *fell off.* They were scattered all over the dirt bed and the floor. It's bad enough that you've got to rake your *yard,* but to rake—or sweep—leaves inside your *house*? Forget that."

She was laughing by now. "Agreed. And, oh, so that's what you meant by it being Brady Bunch-meets-Frank Lloyd Wright. Didn't he put a tree in one of his houses too?"

"Yes—I think he built around a tree or something. Anyway, I had it taken out the day I got the keys."

"So you moved in here—when? Last winter?"

He nodded. "Yes—well, technically, I've been in Wicks Hollow permanently since early December. Settled on the house early February, moved in a week later.

"After my mother died, my siblings and I decided Pop should have at least one of us around. Since I was the only unmarried one and I can work from anywhere for the most part, I volunteered. Pop and Mom had moved here from Grand Rapids about seven years ago when he actually retired for good."

"I was wondering how you ended up here."

"I, uh, didn't realize this was the town you were from until the other day. I guess I thought it sounded familiar, but I didn't make the connection." The way he said it almost implied it would have made a difference to him if he had. But she wasn't sure in what way.

He went on, a little more quickly. "I tried living with Pop for about two weeks, and when I realized that was *not* going to work for either of us, I started putting out feelers for my own place. And like I said, this one came on the market suddenly and I snagged it—for a little more than I wanted to spend, but..." He spread his hands to encompass the beauty of the scene. "Despite the interior tree, it was a no-brainer."

"It's beyond amazing," she said with a heartfelt sigh. "I could stare out at the lake for hours—especially on a day like this." Then, suddenly feeling a little awkward—he was, after all, her ex, and for some reason this felt far too intimate and easy, considering the fact that she hated him—she said, "Mind if I get that shower now?"

"Not at all." He opened the slider, and she preceded him back inside. "Uh...only one of the bathrooms is in working order. The master." Now he looked a little awkward, but he went on, "I'm having the other one redone, and we're waiting on the tile for the shower. So...it's back here."

Vivien was absolutely *not* going to feel strange about walking into her former boyfriend's master bedroom. Even though she immediately noticed and could hardly pull her attention from the king-sized bed. It had a massive headboard upholstered in black leather and a tumble of decorative pillows on top of a gray and blue duvet made of linen that looked very expensive. The rest of the furnishings were just as heavy and masculine, and were done in dark, washed gray.

She'd never known a man to do the decorative pillow thing on a bed—Jake definitely hadn't done that when she knew him. Obviously, he'd changed a lot in eleven years.

"It was cleaning lady day, so the bathroom should be immaculate," he said, leading the way into the master bath.

Ah, that explained the pillows—at least, why they were arranged so prettily on the bed. It didn't explain the actual presence of the pillows, however...

"You must have redone this one first," she said, walking into a very *not* Brady Bunch-era master bath. The tile was all muted, earthy greens and blues, with a healthy bit of cappuccino and cream thrown in to keep it from being too "Under the Sea."

The towels matched and were folded neatly in place over the racks, and there was an expensive terry robe hanging on a hook. A subtle, pleasing herbal scent lingered in the air, and she suspected it was some sort of natural or organic cleaning product.

"Wow. Is that a steam shower?"

He grinned. "My biggest indulgence—so far, anyway. I hope you enjoy." His voice dipped a little low at the end, and he caught her eyes with his. For a moment, Vivien couldn't seem to pull her gaze away, dammit, and her breath snagged in her throat. Her mouth went dry and she was still trapped.

They were standing far too close in the spacious master bath, and she was extremely aware that she was in the inner sanctum of his world, the most intimate area of his home...

And that they had been so intimate, so close, so *attuned* when they were together.

"Thanks," she said, literally spinning away so as to break the connection and sever the moment of intimacy. *Damn, damn, damn.* She should never have come here.

"Uh, so there's probably everything you need in there,"

he said in an unsteady, rumbly way that indicated he was probably just as unsettled as she was.

This was *so* not a good idea.

Vivien decided she would just take a quick shower and then make some excuse to leave.

"Uh, I mean, if you don't mind guy sort of shampoo—"

"It's okay, I've got all my stuff in my bag," she said, making her voice brisk.

"Oh, good, all right." He started for the door, then paused. "Um...I think I have some bourbon. Would you rather that or the Pinot gris?"

"Oh...I don't really think... I mean, I've got to get back to my place... Well, I guess a glass of the Pinot would be nice," she said weakly when he lifted his eyebrow. She'd have the one glass and then make her escape.

Although how she was going to do that without a car, she wasn't exactly sure. Not that she thought he'd balk at taking her home if she asked, but...

Ugh. It was so incredibly awkward.

She should never have come here.

"All right, then. A glass of Pinot gris on the patio," he said with a quick smile that reminded her of the Jake she'd known. And loved.

"Thanks," she said, and turned away to busy herself digging through the duffel in hopes that he'd go away.

He did, and she was finally left alone with a bundle of emotions.

The steam shower was heavenly—as well as great cover for unpacking said emotions. She had a good cry to let out the frustration and anxiety, but she didn't wallow too long. The last thing she needed was Jake the Doctor coming in to make sure she was all right.

Then she went on to singing (but not too loudly) while she scrubbed her head with scented shampoo and, yeah, she used exfoliating body wash. But not because of Jake.

When she exited into the bedroom, this time she had the leisure to notice more than the massive, inviting bed. On the table next to it was an e-reader device on top of a stack of books, each sporting a bookmark. One was the latest TJ Mack thriller, one was a biography of Alexandre Lacassagne (whoever that was), and one was a cookbook, of all strange things. Vivien simply couldn't imagine reading about cooking for pleasure—she didn't even like to *think* about it when she had to eat.

Two large windows, one on each exterior wall, faced the woods that surrounded the house. Apparently all of the lake-view windows had been positioned in the living space area, a tactic Vivien wholly approved. But the forest view was just as interesting—or would be when and if Jake cut back on the wild trees and—were those grapevines?—growing enthusiastically around the house.

The bedroom also boasted a small gas fireplace and sleek, low furnishings that somehow still maintained a warm, inviting mood. Far, far too inviting.

At least there wasn't a freaking fur rug in front of the fireplace.

She slung up her duffel, determined to have a single glass of wine, to keep the conversation very superficial, and to leave as soon as her glass was empty.

Then she had an idea, and dug out her phone. *Hey,* she

texted Helga. *Did you hear about my car? I need a girls' night ASAP.*

Helga—who surely would have heard about Vivien's car from her colleagues in Wicks Hollow's three-person police department—would give her not only a good excuse to leave but also a ride home.

Problem solved.

CHAPTER TEN

THE LAST THING Jake wanted was for Vivien to slam her wine and bolt.

He realized this as he was pulling the cork from the bottle and scoffed a little at himself. *Dumbass.* Foolish, weak dumbass.

No, he wasn't over her, and to be honest, it hugely pissed him off that he wasn't.

More than a decade later, he wasn't freaking *over* her. Close to half his lifetime ago, and he still carried a torch for the singing-all-the-time, smart-assed, honey-blond woman who'd captured his heart, body, and mind during med school.

But it was clear as day that she was not into renewing their old spark. Even though there was definitely still a spark —he *felt* it.

Hell, it was more than a spark. More like a blowtorch whenever she laughed or even smiled a real smile.

And there'd been that moment by the shower when their gazes caught and held and he felt his whole body go hot and expectant... He was pretty sure she'd stopped breathing, too.

After all, their breakup hadn't been from growing apart or their feelings for each other winding down or devolving. No, their relationship had ended abruptly one night, like a widow-maker heart attack or a fatal head-on collision. One minute they were together, happy, connected, enmeshed... and the next, it was over.

So, he supposed, it wasn't like he should be surprised that there hadn't been any closure. They both—he in particular—had their own steamer-trunk-sized baggage they were toting around.

He wondered if that was part of the reason she was so adamant about him not hanging at the theater. Because she had baggage—and not just from him—and she just didn't want to deal with it.

Unfinished business.

But here she was—at his house, showering in *his* shower (he didn't even want to think about *that*...but then, of course he did)—and now, after the weird-as-fuck events at the theater, they had something inescapable in common besides their shared history. He wasn't going to let her leave until they at least talked about *that*: who and why someone was trying to scare her away from the theater.

But Jake wasn't so confident that he didn't hedge his bets. So he wasn't going to rely on just two wine glasses and a simple bottle of Pinot gris.

Since she was still busy in the shower, that gave him time to put some other stuff together. His sister Irene had given him a fancy wooden serving tray for a housewarming gift, and as Pop didn't care about visual aesthetics—and neither did Declan, Baxter, or Drew—Jake hadn't had any reason to break it out yet. Being new in town, he didn't get many visitors except for the guys working on his house.

He pulled out some Pointe Reyes marbled blue cheese that was soft enough to spread like butter and set it on a small plate on the tray. Then he dumped olives—briny Kalamata, buttery Castelvetrano, and some pinkie-nail-sized black ones that he didn't know the name of—along with a small scoop of almonds into four tiny dishes that were meant for soy sauce with sushi. Then he arranged them in a semicircle around the cheese.

It might not be Martha Stewart or *Queer Eye*, he thought, surveying the presentation, but at least it wasn't College Boy Beer Nuts. His tastes—and budget—had improved in the last decade.

The last addition to the tray was one he actually agonized over for a few minutes. Crackers—he had some really nice artisan ones—or bread that he'd made himself?

Crackers were fancier, and putting out his own bread might be self-serving...but it was really good bread and fresh just this morning, and the crackers would keep...but there were fewer carbs with crackers (did she care about carbs? Maybe. Probably.)...

Hell.

He could still hear the shower running, and was pretty sure she was singing in it. He wondered what song was on her mind and in her heart today.

Jake smiled to himself. Vivien always sang in the shower, and whatever ballad or tune she was belting gave a good indication of her mood. She had a stunning voice—clear, strong, and vibrant—and more often than not, hearing her sing something like "Defying Gravity" or "Blue Skies" had put him in a good mood too.

There were a few times he'd slip into the shower with her and join her in a duet—often something from *Phantom,* although another of her favorites, which she had taught him, was from *Annie Get Your Gun.* Those duets had ended up far differently in the shower than they did onstage...to their mutual satisfaction.

With such a pleasant memory fresh in his mind, he started humming "Anything You Can Do (I Can Do Better)" as he debated between crackers and bread.

When he heard the sound of a blow dryer (he didn't own a blow dryer) from the bathroom, he knew he couldn't waffle any longer.

So he took the round loaf of bread he'd made early that morning in between calls during his shift and sliced a few pieces. Then he cut them in half so they were the shape of flattish semicircles and fanned them out on one side of the tray. A small dish of olive oil followed—he was half Italian; it was a requirement—and by then he realized he needed napkins and butter and cheese knives, a spoon for the almonds, toothpicks for the olives...maybe small cocktail plates, too (which he didn't have, so he had to skip).

He'd just come back in from carrying the tray out to the patio when he heard the sound of Vivien's footsteps. Perfect timing.

He poured two glasses of wine and stuck the bottle into a wine cooler (another housewarming gift—this one from his other sister Mathilda—for apparently his siblings thought he was far more of an entertainer than he was. Maybe he should hint that he needed cocktail plates).

"Feel better?" he asked as Vivien came into the room.

Her tousled, slightly damp hair hung in whisky-colored waves around her shoulders, making her appear as if she'd just rolled out of bed…which was an image he'd never forgotten and now was sharply reminded of.

She'd changed from loose cargo pants, work boots, and snug tee into a soft yellow sundress that ended just above her knees. Her feet and pretty legs were bare and blindingly white except for bright pink nail polish on her toes.

"Much better, thank you," she said, and took the glass he offered. "And this'll help even more." She smiled, and his heart gave a little shimmy because that smile seemed genuine and relaxed.

"Let's sit on the patio," he said, opening the slider. "It's hours until sunset, but there's shade."

"You got really lucky to get this place," she said, wandering to the edge of the patio. "Wow…there's not much here between you and down there."

It wasn't a straight drop-off down the bluff, but you didn't want to take a leap off the patio either, because you'd be rolling down a bumpy incline studded with rocks, trees, and other barriers. At the bottom was a well-traveled, curvy road that hugged the lakeshore.

Jake noticed she didn't take a step back from the drop-off and smiled to himself. No, the woman he'd known hadn't changed much. He could even hear her humming something under her breath. It sounded familiar, but he couldn't quite place it.

"I'm getting some huge boulders brought in to shore up the edge there," he said, coming to stand next to her and wondering why she hadn't said anything about the tray he'd so painstakingly put together. "Before any of my nieces and nephew come over. And I'll have some low bushes—I don't know what kind—planted there along the top, and a small barrier put in behind them to make it even safer without obstructing the view."

"It's going to be absolutely lovely— Oh, wow, yum!"

Ah. She'd seen the tray.

"How did you know I love Castelvetrano olives?" she said, spearing two of them with a toothpick in one quick movement. "And I didn't realize how hungry I am. It all looks so good. You didn't have to go through all that trouble, Jake," she said, even as she speared two more olives with unbridled enthusiasm. "But thank you."

"It wasn't any trouble at all," he replied as she drew the olives off the toothpick with her mouth. His knees went a little weak at the sight of her lush pink lips puckering like that, accompanied by her low moan of appreciation—and he distracted himself by taking a sip of his wine. He gave his own hum of approval over the vintage. "It's just as good as I hoped. Do you like it?"

"It's very good. I'm a sucker for unusual whites, and this one fits the bill. It's got a little bit of pear, don't you think?"

"Sure," he said, not exactly certain he tasted pear, but enjoying the crispness of it nonetheless. He sat down in one of the two Adirondack chairs he'd arranged in front of a tile-topped metal table that had a well in the center for a fire pit (another housewarming gift, one he'd bought for himself and had only used once), hoping she'd follow suit. This sort of pacing and walking around the patio that she was doing made him feel like she was planning to bolt at any minute.

To his relief, she took a seat in the other chair, stretched her legs out in front of her, and crossed them at the ankles. She tipped her head against the back and heaved a sigh. "Thank you, Jake. I really needed this."

"Not as much as I did," he joked. "I didn't eat lunch."

Vivien gave a short laugh and rolled her head along the chair back to look at him. Her amber-brown eyes were fringed by thick lashes the same honey color of her hair, softly dark against her creamy skin, and for a moment he was a little breathless, caught by her gaze. He thought she looked so soft and lovely with all the shades of honey, bourbon, cream, and amber that were Vivien next to the fresh lemon-yellow dress. She was close enough that he could smell whatever it was she'd used in her shower, and it went right to his nose and straight on into his hormones. They were very interested.

But best of all, he was happy she was here on his patio with him...and relaxed. He knew they had things to talk about—difficult things—but he was loath to broach them and risk the tension returning.

She was spreading the soft blue cheese onto her piece of bread when she paused and looked at him suddenly. "Bread."

He grimaced. "Yeah, I know—carbs—"

"No, no...did you make this bread?"

Maybe she was just as eager as he was to keep unpleasant things stowed away—at least for a while.

"Yes," he replied.

"It's *amazing*. I love the sun-dried tomatoes in it. It goes so well with this cheese." She was practically moaning again, which did *not* help the situation in his suddenly tight board shorts. "I wouldn't have guessed if Orbra hadn't mentioned that you'd made her some sun-dried tomato sourdough. It's so good I would've assumed you got it from the bakery in town."

He was ridiculously pleased. "Thanks. I'm still perfecting the recipe. I'm glad you like it. It's one of my favorites too."

"So, uh...when do you actually *work*? You are a doctor, aren't you? Don't you have an office or go into the hospital? I don't even know what your specialty is," she added with a frown. "Weren't you going to be a surgeon?"

There it was...that subtle reminder of the past. The last time they'd known each other, he had indeed been thinking about general surgery.

And it also indicated that she hadn't been asking around about him. Which was a disappointment.

"Radiology. And I work from home most of the time. A lot of us do." He went on to explain how that worked. "So that means I have a lot of time to let dough rise in between checking my messages and doing assessments and evaluations," he added with a smirk. "And I can toss a couple loaves in the oven and still be available to review any X-rays or ultrasounds that come through."

"And," she said, pointing at him with an olive-studded toothpick, "you can work in your boxers or here on the patio —or even in bed. Can't beat that."

"Nope." He sipped the wine again, then refilled both of their glasses.

She took a taste, then suddenly whipped her attention to him. "Oh my gosh, Jake, I'm so sorry...I never told you. I'm so sorry about your mom. Really sorry." She looked stricken. "I should have said something sooner. You always seemed very close to her."

"I was." He would *not* let his throat close up. "I'm sorry you never met her. You— I think you would have liked her."

She nodded, and he wondered to himself why she'd never

met either of his parents. Why he'd never introduced her to them. He'd met her mother once—that had been interesting— and her grandmother twice, both in New York.

He guessed she'd never met his parents because they never traveled to New York. Besides working all the time, his pop was pretty old school and refused to set foot on a plane, and had no patience or desire for any traveling that was greater than fifty miles away. And Jake and Vivien had dated for a little under nine months, missing the year-end holidays that might have included family visits.

He supposed part of it was that he'd always thought they'd have time for that—family holidays and such—later, and that he wanted to just enjoy Vivien and their life at NYU without the complications of family. His sisters would have had their collective noses all up in his stuff if he'd brought a woman home to meet the parents. Even now, he shuddered a little at the thought.

"It was so nice of you to move here to be close to your father," she said. "Who, by the way, is absolutely adorable."

He lifted a brow. "Adorable? Pop? How much wine have you had, Vivien Leigh?"

She gave a dusky little laugh. "Not nearly enough to forget that someone—or something—is trying to chase me away from the theater." She sobered. "Jake." Her eyes—wide and anxious—fastened on him. "I don't know what the hell is going on. And why."

"I know—"

"But I sure as hell am going to find out. And whoever they *are*, I'm going to ruin them."

He nodded. "I have no doubt of that. But VL...I want to help you. Will you let me?"

Vivien's chest felt tight. She *wanted* to. She wanted to let go, to trust, to accept the help and support, because this was the strangest, most frightening and unsettling situation she'd ever been in.

Someone was interfering with her work, her business—targeting *her* specifically.

Someone was creeping around her property and wreaking havoc that could have injured someone today. All those innocent teens... She shivered at the thought.

And someone was giving her death threats.

This sort of thing only happened on-screen or onstage. Not in real life. Not to her.

"So what do we know?" he said, smoothly moving on after she didn't respond to his question.

Vivien felt a little bad about that—about not answering it—but, dammit, it was asking an awful lot, wasn't it?

She hadn't seen the guy for eleven years—after he'd stomped on her heart and left her battered and bruised—and suddenly he'd shown up in the midst of her trying to start a new business, produce a show, refurbish a theater...while someone *else* was trying to keep her from doing it—and he wanted to get cozy? No thanks.

"We don't know much," she said. "Someone was in the theater, probably without my knowledge—what I mean is, I don't think it was anyone I'd let in, like a contractor or appraiser. They wouldn't have time to do it unless they came back later. So whoever planted that stuff somehow got in when I wasn't there."

"And they've been there at least twice. Maybe more, since whoever it was would have had to scope the place out before setting up the little surprises," he said.

"Yeah." She took a fortifying sip of wine.

"All indications are that whoever it is doesn't want you in the theater. The question is whether it's *you*, Vivien Leigh Savage specifically, or whether it's *anyone*."

"It could just be someone trying to punk me," she said. "A couple of teens fooling around. Maybe they like to use the building as Make-out Central and want to keep it that way."

"Or Party Central," he said. "But I don't know, VL, it seems like a lot of work to go through in order to keep a place for that. I mean, the planning, the equipment, the breaking in several times...seems like a lot of effort. Can't they just, I don't know, party on the beach or make out in their cars like we used to do? Besides—there'd be evidence of said parties or orgies. Did you find any condom wrappers or beer bottles around there? And would they go so far as to trash your car?"

She sighed again. "You're so damned logical, Jake. I just wanted it to be something more benign."

"Yeah. Me too."

Vivien felt him searching her with his gaze, and she studiously kept hers focused out over the blues of lake and sky. *Don't start to get personal, Jake. I don't think I can take it. The death threats are personal enough.*

"So, who has it in for you, VL? A business rival? A friend turned enemy? One of your many broken-hearted lovers?"

Well, he'd done it. He'd gotten personal, dammit.

She gave a short, bitter laugh. "I can't think of anyone. Not even a broken-hearted lover. Or a current one."

That got his attention. "A current one?"

Now she looked at him. "You don't think I've been locked up mourning you like a nun for the last eleven years, do you?"

"Of course not. Didn't I just say 'trail of broken-hearted

lovers,' which implies a multitude? I just didn't know if there was anyone in the picture. Currently."

"Why do you care?"

Yeah, she knew she was teasing fire, dancing around, playing word games.

Maybe it was easier doing that than figuring out who wished her *death*.

Jake didn't answer. He just looked at her with those intense brown eyes. It wasn't a puppy-dog gaze—a hopeful, wishful one. It was straightforward, bold, steady—like, *you know damned well why.*

"Stop it, Jake," she snapped. "Just *stop* it. I've got enough to deal with besides you and—whatever."

He gave a short nod. "All right. Back to business. But don't you think we ought to at least clear the air a little? Since we're going to be working together—"

"I don't really have any intention of 'working' with you, Jake," she said, then sighed. "But fine. I guess with your dad being in the show, you're going to be around whether I like it or not."

He blanched a little. "Geez, is it that bad? Do you hate me that much?"

"Hate's too strong a word—though I guess I did at one time," she said bluntly. "Now it's just more that I don't want to be reminded of how much you hurt me—which happens whenever you're around."

"Wow." His mouth tightened and he set down his wine glass with a very deliberate movement. "You weren't the only one who got hurt, VL."

"Why? Did Lissa dump you—"

"Stop with the Lissa crap, all right? This is about what happened with you and me, and—"

"Oh no, don't even try that, Jake. Lissa was a *big* part of what happened with you and me, and you know it."

"She wasn't. She wasn't part of it at all."

Vivien gaped at him, fury and shock battling to see which could overcome the other. "She was *every* part of it, Jake! You jumped into bed with her mere *hours* after we...after we... after things went south," she said, faltering a little.

Then she collected herself and went on, letting it all spill out in a way she'd not been able to do eleven years ago. "And it probably would have been sooner than mere hours if you could have actually located her—which surprised me, because she was always hanging around just *waiting* for an opportunity to flirt with you."

She couldn't remain seated; she rose, wine glass still in hand, and went on, gesturing sharply. "At least you waited until you had an excuse, I'll give you that. But just barely. It wasn't outright *cheating*, but it was only just barely, you know, *legal*. Literally from your apartment to her bed, wasn't it, with maybe a detour to the bar first?" In her fury, she felt tears of anger sting her eyes. *No way. I'm not crying in front of him. That'd be the worst thing I could do.* "You'd been waiting for an excuse to screw her. And I gave it to you."

Jake sat there, listening to her rant with an impassive look on his face. Only when she finally stopped—afraid that her voice would break and she wouldn't be able to control the tears—did he speak. "You're wrong about so much of it. Most of it. All right?"

She was suddenly exhausted and sank back into her chair.

"Really? All right, so let's take it bit by bit. You and I were dating—exclusively. We were supposedly in love." She managed to keep her voice steady and hard, though it *hurt*. "Right so far?"

"I wasn't *supposedly* in love, I *was* in love," he said flatly.

"Right. Whatever. Anyway, you and I were together. Lissa Kirkland wanted you— Don't deny it, Jake, we both know she did. It was so obvious."

"Fine. She flirted. She made it clear she was interested."

"And you managed to resist—at least as far as I *know*. Maybe you didn't resist—"

"Vivien. I *never cheated* on you."

"Whatever. You never *technically* cheated on me. That line of acceptability—you were barely on the right side of it, Jake. Just barely." She jutted her chin forward in an effort to keep her emotions in check. She hadn't imagined it would be this difficult to have it out.

"When I told you I was going to do my residency in Raleigh, I didn't expect it to be the end of us," he said. "I never thought you'd dump me—"

"*Dump* you? I didn't dump you, Jake— We— You— I—"

"You ended it, Vivien. You told me you weren't going to 'fricking North Carolina'—those were your exact words; believe me, I remember them. I knew you weren't going to be thrilled, but I didn't expect you to be that final about it."

"You'd always led me to believe you were going to stay at NYU," she shot back. "It was a shock when you just dropped that brand-new, earth-shattering information in my lap. You knew I'd just signed a new lease on my apartment—and it was like a slap in the face. I was even going to ask you to move in with me," she said, looking at him through watery eyes.

"You never told me that."

"No, I never told you that. Your mind had been made up and I wasn't going to stand in your way. And don't think I didn't know Lissa Kirkland was from Raleigh," she snarled. "That just sealed it all for me. You decided to go to UNC so you could be with her."

"That's so completely and utterly wrong that I don't know what to say. I had no idea Lissa was from Raleigh—"

"Don't lie to me—"

"*I never lie, Vivien.*" Now there was real anger in his face —the temper she knew he had was rising to the surface. The corners of his mouth were white. "*I didn't know.*"

"How could you not know that if I did?" she said, a little more calmly.

"I have no idea, except that maybe because I didn't care enough about Lissa Kirkland to know or remember if she ever said where she was from."

Vivien bit back the *you obviously cared enough to jump into bed with her* comment that rose to her lips. Instead she said, "Regardless. You told me you were going to North Carolina, and you knew I was staying in New York, and that gave me all the information I needed."

"Yeah," he said bitterly. "You had all the information *you* needed, and then *you* made the decision that we were over— at least, I *thought* we were over when you *told* me it was over and stormed out of my apartment—but apparently we were only sort of broken up, so that the next day you could hold that over my head after I made the biggest mistake of my life."

"Oh, don't go all Ross and Rachel on me," she snapped. "Even if there was a question whether we were officially broken up or not—"

"You never gave me the chance to talk it out, Vivien. You made the decision and you flounced out."

"Regardless of whether were we on a break or not, your screwing Lissa finalized it all. You couldn't have cared about me that much—you couldn't have *loved* me," she said, throwing the word back in his face, "if you could go from me to three hours later being with someone else. *That* was all I needed to know."

"I wasn't *with* Lissa," he said, frustration blazing in his eyes. "It was one night, and it was a mistake. A huge mistake. I didn't want or expect it—"

"You must have wanted it enough to end up in her bed," she interrupted.

"She was very insistent," he said. "And I was pretty drunk."

"Oh, for God's sake. Really? That's your excuse? She seduced you? Give me a fucking break."

He looked away. His jaw moved; his lips pursed. He closed his eyes and took a deep breath, still looking away. Then he murmured, "Men can be sexually assaulted too."

Vivien froze. There was a sudden roaring in her ears as her body went hot.

Had he just said what she thought he'd said? No, that was...

"What did you say?"

He spewed out a long breath and looked over at her. There was something in his eyes—so stark and bleak—that made her feel weak and lightheaded. "I didn't want it. I didn't want her. She asked me to walk her home, and I did—though someone should have been walking *me* home. And then we got inside her place, and she wouldn't let me leave. I was drunk, but not too drunk to, uh, get it up, but it was all her, and I was too drunk to fight her off…" He looked away, and his Adam's apple shifted as he swallowed. "It was not a pleasant experience."

Vivien could do nothing but stare at him. Her insides curdled and the wine she'd had churned in her stomach. His expression left no doubt that he was telling the truth.

"It's difficult enough for women to talk about being assaulted," he went on in a low voice, "so imagine how hard it would be for a guy. We're all supposed to enjoy it when women are climbing all over us and sticking their hands down our pants, grabbing us, and…" He shrugged. "It's not like that."

"Jake." Her voice cracked. "I'm so sorry. I'm so…sorry."

He grimaced and looked up, brushing the hair out of his eyes. "The next day, I was not in good shape. I couldn't talk to you, Viv. I just couldn't let myself—I felt sick and dirty and… then I had to worry about whether she'd get pregnant."

"God."

"Yeah." He scrubbed his forehead with three strong fingers. "And obviously, word got around—and then you just cut me off. You wouldn't talk to me, take my calls, answer my texts… And honestly—yeah, I was done with you at that point. It was too much."

Vivien's insides had gone from tight and painful to wobbly and sickly. "I'm sorry."

He looked at her with those dark, compelling eyes. "I am too."

She buried her face in her hands, then pushed all her damp hair up and away from her cheeks and looked over at him. "I should have at least talked to you. I'm sorry, Jake. I know it doesn't mean much now, but I'm really, really sorry—not just because of what happened with you and Lissa," she said, holding up a hand when he would have spoken, "but because I didn't handle any of it well. Our breakup. I was rash and immature and...you were leaving me." She sighed, feeling ugly inside. "I was wrong about so many things."

"You were. And I didn't have the strength to fight for you—for us, I mean. It was an awful, upsetting time. I told myself it was for the best, so I could focus on my residency. A fresh start."

"Right. And you did it," she said, trying to smile. "I never congratulated you, Doctor."

"Thank you." His smile was as weak as hers.

Vivien looked away. She didn't know what to do with herself right now. More than a decade, thinking the worst of the man she'd loved, and now to learn that things hadn't been quite the way she'd remembered...or thought...and facing up to her own immaturity then...and now.

"I think I should probably leave now," she said after a moment.

"All right."

She was a little surprised that he didn't argue, didn't try to convince her to stay—but what had she expected? If she hadn't been so stubborn and rash back then...and short and rude over the last few days...

Oh, damn, she was a freaking mess.

CHAPTER ELEVEN

VIVIEN HELPED Jake carry their dishes inside. "This was really nice," she said. "Thank you for putting it all together. I didn't deserve it."

"Vivien—"

"No, really, Jake, I feel like crap right now—and rightly so. I really need to go and just try to get my head on straight. I've got a lot going on...a lot to think about."

"Right," he said. "Let me get my keys. I'll drive you home."

As he went to do so, he noticed her phone, which she'd left sitting on the side table next to the sofa. "Looks like someone's been trying to reach you," he said, handing it to her.

"Oh, crap—it's Helga. She's about ready to call in the Feds looking for me," she said with a pained laugh. "Literally. I better call her. Maybe she'll pick me up."

Jake was all right with that. He needed a little time to settle his thoughts, because something had become very clear to him during their heated discussion and the churning up of the past.

Despite his own anger and pain, he very much cared that Vivien was hurting and grieving. He ached for her and the obvious shock and shame she felt...and even though he had things of his own to work through, he realized he wanted to be there for Vivien in her difficulty as well.

Damn. He wasn't just not "over" Vivien...he was still in love with her.

And he wasn't exactly sure what he was going to do about it.

***

"I REALLY DON'T WANT to talk about Jake," Vivien told Helga. "I can't. Not right now. It's just too...painful."

"All right, then," said Helga, then muttered under her breath as she braked to avoid running into a pedestrian who seemed more interested in her huge elephant-ear pastry than looking both ways. "We can talk about other things—like who's trying to chase you out of the Olivia Dee Theater."

"Yeah, that's only a slightly more appetizing topic," Vivien muttered.

"But you never really told me about what happened with the two of you—just that Jake up and decided to move to Raleigh. And that he cheated on you."

Vivien heaved a sigh. "I guess we're going to talk about it anyway, aren't we?"

Helga gave her a sunny smile. "That's what friends are for. But seriously, VL, I'm worried about what's going on at the theater."

"I am too. I'm going to set up my own nanny-cams in the theater tomorrow," Vivien said, having literally just made the decision. "I made the police report about my car, and you can come by and take a look at everything there at the stage. Maybe there'll be some clue."

"I'll come first thing in the morning. Actually, I'll have to pick you up, since you don't have a car," Helga promised. She looked smart and official in her crisp dark blue uniform and shiny badge. "I'm on till ten tonight, and there's only two of us because Joe Cap is off on a college tour for his twins." Police Captain Joe Longbow was better known as Joe Cap to both his staff and the locals. "I guess he figured things would be semi-quiet on a Thursday?" She shook her head.

Moments later, Helga had parked her police cruiser in a no-parking zone a half block from the tiny bungalow Vivien was renting until she found a permanent place.

"Perks of the job," said the cop when her friend gave her a jaundiced look. "Makes up for being called out of bed in the middle of the night to break up a bonfire on the beach after it's closed, or not being able to have a beer while at Maxine's birthday party in case I've got to run to a call or break up a fight. Which, by the way, you missed this year."

"The fight at Maxine's birthday party, or just a fight in general?" Vivien climbed out of the car, then opened the back door to pull out the Nutcracker headpiece.

Helga rolled her eyes, looking at her from over the car roof and its siren. "The party, of course. There hasn't been a fight for a while—not since Trib found out his pastry chef had slathered whipped cream all over, and presumably licked, the new, very hot produce guy earlier that day. Watching two gay men having a catfight is something I could have done without."

"I miss Maxine's party every year," Vivien replied, walking across the road with the mask tucked under her arm. "Ever since I came to the one back in...what was it, four years ago, and she was trying to get me to hook her up with a tattoo artist? Remember that? She wanted me to bring one from New York, like I could put him or her in my suitcase or something. As if there aren't any tattoo artists here in Wicks Hollow—or anywhere in Michigan." She shook her head, happy to have a reason to laugh.

Helga chuckled. "No one in the entire county is dumb enough to try to ink Maxine Took."

"True dat," replied Vivien, digging out the key to her cottage.

"What did she want tattooed on her, anyway?"

"I think it was something like *Exceptional and Eighty* with a woman flexing her bicep...and this was three years *before* she was turning eighty," Vivien said, shoving open the door. "That was pretty damned optimistic of her."

"That sounds like Maxine. And oh, VL, I just love what you've done to the place," Helga added dryly, stepping inside the cottage. "Geez."

"I haven't had time to finish unpacking. I've been a *little* busy, you know. And I've had to actually *cook* instead of ordering takeout, which is a real pain—"

"Cooking is what most people do."

"Not people who live in the city."

"Well, you're not in the city anymore, Dorothy."

Helga walked into the tiny kitchen, which had been done with happy blue and white tile on the countertops, probably back in the eighties, Vivien guessed. There was no island and about a square yard of counter space, and the cabinets were decades-old medium brown that might eventually be called "vintage" but were just plain ugly (in her mind) right now. Someone had put blue and white china knobs on them and hung matching blue curtains over the small window that looked into the backyard.

"I can see you've been doing a lot of cooking," said Helga, eyeing the single pot in the dish drainer and the one plate next to it.

"I hate cooking," Vivien replied, putting her keys, purse, and the Nutcracker on the kitchen table. "I love eating but I hate cooking. Food, glorious food!" she sang with a grin. "You know that's my theme song— Hey, where are you going?"

"Gonna check around a little."

"Check around for what?" Then it dawned on her, and Vivien put a hand over her middle as her insides sank. Her cop friend was making sure there was no one here lying in wait for her—or that no one had *been* here, vandalizing or stealing anything.

"It's really hard to tell whether someone's come through and searched your things or whether you just dumped all this stuff on the bed yourself," Helga called from the back of the cottage—which was near enough that Vivien could hear her sigh of exasperation.

The bungalow was only five hundred square feet with two bedrooms, a single bathroom, and a compact living room/kitchen area, so it didn't take Helga long to do her "checking."

"It's not like I didn't *just move in* three days ago," Vivien retorted. "I'm still trying to figure out where to put everything."

"I'm sure you'll figure it all out. Someday. Anyway, all clear," Helga said as she walked through to the kitchen while Vivien just stood there, watching her home—and then her fridge—being invaded, for now her cop friend was poking in there too. "I can see you've been doing a lot of cooking with this entire apple and a sad-looking box of romaine. What the hell is this? A carrot? *One* carrot? Who buys *one* carrot? But at least you've got wine."

"I thought you were on duty till ten," Vivien said when Helga pulled out the bottle of Viognier. "And you didn't look in the freezer or the cupboards," she added grumpily. "There's frozen pizza and macaroni and cheese and ramen."

"The wine's for you not me." Helga handed Vivien a glass of the Viognier then plumped down on the beige and blue plaid sofa that looked like it had been on the set of *Stranger Things*. "Lord, that thing is creepy," said Helga, eyeing the Nutcracker headpiece. "Tell me again why you have it."

"I'm going to display it at the theater as a relic from shows gone by," Vivien replied.

"Having that thing in my house would give me nightmares."

"It's the Nutcracker! From a *ballet*. It's not like it's the mask from *Halloween*."

"If you say so." Helga didn't sound convinced. "All right, so I've got maybe another twenty minutes before I have to go back out on patrol—there's a live band playing at the gazebo by the beach from seven to nine, and it's ripe for drunk and disorderly—so let's get on with it. Give it to me: high-level overview. Quick, so I can give you my two cents' worth."

Vivien sighed and set the wine aside. She didn't want it right now. All she really wanted was to lie down and sob herself to sleep, or binge something light and airy on Netflix. Maybe she'd dig up *My Fair Lady* or one of the best musicals ever: *Hairspray.* She deserved it—it had been one upside-down, ugly, emotional day.

But she gave Helga the basics, sparing herself no mercy over her actions both eleven years ago and recently with Jake.

"So what I'm hearing you say is that you freaked out when Jake told you he was leaving—leaving *you*, basically. It was sudden and unexpected and it probably reminded you a little bit of Liv, didn't it?" Helga said in a soothing, knowing voice.

"When did you turn into a psychologist?" Vivien grumbled, but she couldn't deny that what her friend said had hit the right button.

"Part of cop training, babe. I did a workshop on hostage negotiating a while back, too."

"Well, I'm not holding any hostages, but you might be right about it," Vivien replied. "About me equating him leaving to Liv dying."

Had she ever thought about it that way?

No. She'd blocked it all off because it hurt too damned much. And so she'd focused on the "cheating" part of Jake's actions, not the leaving part, because the cheating part was cut and dry and easy to understand, easy to hold against him.

The leaving part was a lot more nebulous.

"Not just Liv, but your mom too." If Helga had been

wearing glasses, she would have been looking at Vivien from over the tops of them like Blanche from *Grease.*

"And Mom, too. Geez," Vivien said, tipping her head back against the chair. Her mother had been in and out of rehab for the last twenty years and was currently sober...but who knew for how long. "She didn't die, but she sort of left me too, didn't she? I mean, I knew I had issues with abandonment, but—"

"You were only ten when it happened, right? That shit leaves a deep scar at any age, but at ten? Losing your twin suddenly and without warning? Not only your twin, but your career and life as you knew it—right?"

Vivien's eyes were stinging and she blinked rapidly. "Why did it take me eleven years to figure that out?"

Helga heaved a sigh, then rose. "Because you're human. And humans protect themselves from hurt." She came over to the chair, and Vivien stood to accept her tight, heartfelt hug.

"This is cop training too, you know," Helga said, giving her one last squeeze before stepping away. "But that doesn't mean when I go all emotional and anxious you won't be able to do this for me." She grimaced. "I have to go, Viv. Are you going to be all right?"

"Yes. Thanks. I'll be fine. Really."

Helga nodded and went to the door, but she paused and gave Vivien a meaningful look. "Lock up tight. I know it's warm tonight, but at least put a wedge in the windows so they can't open too much, all right? I'll drive by or have someone drive by every half-hour until I'm off. Hey! Why don't I go get Butch? I was going to pick him up anyway—he likes to go on patrol with me at night. He can stay with you instead."

Vivien loved Helga's dog—a big, super-friendly, but

ferocious-sounding German shepherd—but she didn't want the extra hassle, nor even to have to wait up for Helga to return. "Thanks for the offer, but I'm just going to go to sleep. I'm not worried, really. There are houses on all three sides, and these lots are tiny, so they're close enough to hear anything—and I'll leave all the exterior lights on and lock the doors and wedge the windows and keep a baseball bat next to the bed," she said, forcing a smile.

"All right. I'll pick you up tomorrow morning. Nine o'clock?"

"Yes," Vivien replied, then did as directed and locked the door behind Helga. She finished securing the tiny house as promised, made sure the lights were on outside—front and back—and climbed into bed at five o'clock in the afternoon without even checking her email.

CHAPTER TWELVE

JAKE DECIDED to stake out the theater.

He didn't know what else to do, but he needed to do something.

He didn't have to work tomorrow, and he was pretty sure he wasn't going to sleep tonight, so he packed himself a cooler with a sandwich, some water, and an array of snacks, charged his tablet, and was just about to leave when his friend Baxter texted him.

The message was short and to the point: *Sup?*

Jake hadn't been in Wicks Hollow all that long, but he'd been there long enough to meet and befriend the town's brewmaster: Baxter James, the creator of Baxter's Beatnik Brews—also known as B-Cubed.

It helped that Jake had been sitting at the Roost with his pop for lunch back in March when Bax brought in a case of his latest creation, broke a bottle when he accidentally dropped the case on the counter, and ended up cutting himself on a piece of glass while trying to fish it out of the box.

Though Jake was generally most useful when looking at images of fractured bones or organs with shadows or other abnormalities, he was certainly able to butterfly up a deep cut without breaking a sweat. His payment had been half a case of the latest B-Cubed (the Straw Lager) and a two-hour mutual rant about Star Wars and how Disney had ruined the franchise (this topic came about because of the vintage poster from *Return of the Jedi*, which was hanging on the wall of the Roost along with that of about fifty other eighties movies).

Going on a stakeout. Want in? Jake texted back to Baxter.

His friend definitely wanted in.

So, fifteen minutes later, Jake and Baxter pulled into the theater parking lot in Jake's car, taking care not to drive where the glass from Vivien's vandalized Honda had been, and settled in the darkest corner behind the theater. If anyone cruised by, or even pulled into the parking lot, Jake and Baxter wouldn't be noticed unless the newcomer drove all the way behind the building.

Jake had given his friend the short version of what was going on—after all, it wasn't a secret that Vivien's windshield and headlights had been smashed, since she'd filed a police report—and explained that they suspected someone had been making their way in and out of the building. And since there'd been an incident today, he thought whoever it was might want to come back and remove evidence.

"If I can catch the bastard red-handed—or at least *see* the asshole, even if he gets away—that would shut this down pretty damned quick," he concluded. And he was more than happy to have company, just in case things got ugly.

In fact, if Jake could have gotten into the theater, they would have waited inside to surprise the culprit...but, of course, he didn't have a key. He also realized he didn't have Vivien's phone number to ask her to borrow a key. Even if it was the same cell phone number she'd had back at NYU (which was possible, as he still had the same one himself), he'd deleted it from his phone years ago.

Nor did he know where she was living or staying in Wicks Hollow. He supposed he could have asked any of those questions of Baxter, but pride won out—because how awkward would it be for Bax to find out Jake was doing all this and he didn't even know how to get in touch with the woman he was doing it for?

It was around ten o'clock, not long after the sun had set, when they rolled down the windows, turned off the car, popped open their first set of beers (of course Baxter had brought appropriate supplies), and waited to see what would happen. Jake had thought far enough ahead to bring a cool little bug zapper device that the gadget-happy Mathilda had sent him, and he set it on the console between the two front seats. The fresh air with its pleasant breeze was great, but the rabid mosquitos were not.

"So...why're we doing this again?" Baxter asked as he lifted the beer to his mouth. He was a good-looking guy of about thirty with a neatly trimmed mustache, goatee, and a tight-cropped Afro. He was almost always dressed like he was going to a dinner club in neat button-downs tucked into creased chinos or dressy jeans.

"Ah," Jake began, then figured he owed it to Baxter to spill some of the details. "Well, Vivien and I used to date about eleven years ago when we were both at NYU. So I kind of know her, since we had a thing."

"A thing."

"Yeah."

"Seems like one of you still might have a thing," Baxter said, grinning around the mouth of the brown longneck then taking another sip.

Jake scoffed, but neither confirmed nor denied it. He guessed it was pretty obvious anyway, since he was spending his Thursday night sitting in a dark parking lot watching over an empty building. All in the name of love.

"I went to high school with Vivien, you know," Baxter told him. "She was ahead of me by one year. She and Helga van Hest—you know, the blond cop who's built like an Amazonian goddess?—were tight."

"You mean the hot blond cop who's built like an Amazonian goddess? Yes—I've met Helga. And she and Vivien are still close."

"Right. Anyway, I didn't know Vivien at all back then, but I knew who she was, of course. Everyone did."

"I can imagine," Jake said.

"Biggest celebrity we ever had in Wicks Hollow—but she just kept to herself. I heard rumors—she had a twin, right?"

Jake nodded. "Yes. Liv—Olivia—was her name. They shared roles in stage plays and musicals because of child labor laws limiting the number of hours young children can work. Being identical, they could swap out whenever necessary. I think they had a song that was kind of a hit too—she didn't like to talk about it much. I barely got it out of her that they sang together live at the Tonys one year."

"Her sister died before she moved here."

"Yes. Car accident. They were supposed to go to a costume fitting, but Vivien was sick, so she stayed home, and Liv and her mother went without her."

And she never came back, Vivien had said when she told him about it. *She was my best friend, my soul mate—and then suddenly I didn't have a twin or a best friend or a costar anymore.*

"Their mother had minor injuries—which eventually helped lead to an addiction to painkillers and alcohol—but Liv died at the scene."

Baxter made a sound of sympathy and stared out into the darkness, the beer settled, forgotten, between his legs. "She was, what, fifteen? At least, that's how old Vivien was when she moved here—to get away from the memories, I gather."

"No, she was ten when Liv died. There was a period of mourning and adjustment after, of course—and lots of press over the tragedy, from what I understand—and then her mother wanted her to keep going with her stage career. Sounded like she pushed Vivien pretty hard for the next few years, and it didn't work. VL—you know, Vivien Leigh—didn't want to sing or dance or act without her counterpart. I got the impression she had serious anxiety about going onstage. So it was after that—after she was done with that career—that she and her mother moved here to be near Vivien's grandmother. I guess her father died when she was really little, so she never knew him."

"Well, that explains why Vivien never went out for any of the plays or shows here," Baxter mused aloud. "When we were in high school, I mean. Everyone thought it was weird that a big-name actress didn't want to hog the stage—but she didn't. Not even in the chorus or bit roles. Melody Carlson claimed it was because Vivien was too stuck-up— That was *her* term, dude; I don't think I've ever used that phrase before," he added when Jake snorted. "Anyway, Melody

Carlson—who was always the lead in all of the shows and had all the big choir solos—said Vivien wouldn't try out because she thought she was too important to be in a pitiful high school or community theater show."

"Well, I guess things worked out just fine for Melody Carlson, then," said Jake, imagining a sly-faced girl with a mouth pinched in jealousy and dagger eyes.

"Trust me, Melody wasn't anything spectacular onstage. I played opposite her a few times—not that I'm talented either. Small town, small school, small pool of talent...I'm guessing Melody was just relieved Vivien didn't steal her limelight. Melody still lives here in town, in fact. She's the music teacher at the elementary school. Got divorced a few years ago, I think."

Jake considered that information for a minute, then said, "I don't know anything about this Melody, but you don't think she still has a hard-on for showing up or harassing Vivien, do you?"

Baxter shook his head. "Nah. I can't see it. Over a high school rivalry from almost twenty years ago—a rivalry that never even happened? But you never know."

"That's the truth. I've seen enough X-rays to know that people do strange things for strange reasons all the time. Case in point: I once got an image—came in from the ER, of course —that showed a ballpoint pen inside someone's urinary bladder."

Baxter whipped his head to gape at Jake, a horrified look on his face. "Really?"

Jake nodded. "Yep." He shook his head. "I didn't ask... didn't even want to know."

"Yeah, no doubt." Baxter gave a little shudder. "So you

and Vivien met at NYU? And you both ended up back here? Small world," he said, then took another pull from his beer.

"Yeah, we met at NYU. I was finishing med school there, and a mutual friend introduced us because we were both from Michigan. I grew up near Grand Rapids, and when my pop retired, he and my mom moved here because they'd visited a few times and she wanted to be near the lake. Pop didn't argue—I don't know, maybe he had a feeling she was going to get sick and go sooner than he was...and so they lived here about seven years before she died. Small world for sure that Vivien and I both ended up back here, eleven years after we—after our thing. This is pretty good, by the way," Jake said, gesturing with his longneck. "What is it?"

"Oh, it's an IPA I'm testing with a hint of orange and clove," Baxter replied. "It might do well around the winter holidays. I'm thinking of calling it Firelight."

"Works for me," Jake replied. "Works for me just fine."

He was just tipping out the last bit of brew when a pair of headlights swept the dark parking lot. Jake jammed the bottle into a cup holder, and they both tensed as a car pulled into the lot and drove slowly around...then eased up right next to his Lexus.

Before he could react, a bright light blared into the car, blinding him, and he heard someone say, "Both of you step out of the vehicle. Keep your hands where I can see them."

It was a female voice, but it wasn't Vivien. Baxter swore furiously under his breath and gave an unhappy sigh as he set down his beer to comply with the order.

Jake also did as instructed, and just as he stepped outside the car, he recognized the woman standing there in her blue uniform. A very large dog sat on the ground next to her, and he didn't appear very happy. His ears were up, his eyes were sharp, and he was showing a few teeth.

"Oh, Officer van Hest," said Jake in a hearty voice, hoping it would tell the dog they were friends. "We were just talking about y—"

"Jake DeRiccio. And Baxter? What are you doing here?" The fact that her voice showed surprise and had lost its cop tone indicated she didn't consider either of them a threat. But she didn't exactly sound friendly, either. "Well, since I'm pretty sure you're not doing what the two guys were doing in the *last* car I found in a dark parking lot, let me guess...you're watching out for whoever is breaking into the theater."

"Hi, Helga," said Baxter weakly.

"It's Officer van Hest when I'm on official business," she said in a no-nonsense tone, and shifted so the badge pinned to her spectacular rack glinted in the headlights. "Like now."

Baxter exhaled a pained sigh, but didn't reply.

"I'm guessing Vivien doesn't know you're here," Helga said.

"No, she doesn't. Can I put my hands down now?" said Jake.

"Yeah, go ahead. It's okay, Butch," she added to the dog. "They're harmless. Especially him," she said dryly with a look at Bax.

The German shepherd changed immediately from ears perked up, mouth closed, eyes sharp to panting happily. He came out of his sitting position to approach Baxter, who crouched to greet him.

"I expect you had the same idea," said Jake. "Checking on the property."

"Yes." Helga looked past him, shining her light into his

car as she walked around it. "Is that an open bottle of alcohol in there? No, *two* bottles?"

Shit. Crap.

"Um...I don't know what you're looking at," he said innocently as Baxter muttered something again, standing upright once more.

"And the keys are in your ignition, Dr. DeRiccio," she went on coolly. "Looks like you were going somewhere with open alcohol in your vehicle."

Jake kept his mouth shut and hoped Helga had heard more than Vivien's side of their breakup story...otherwise, he was in deep shit.

"Mr. James, it appears there's an entire case of beer from B-Cubed in the conveniently located back seat of this vehicle —not in the hatch—and there are several bottles open in the front seat." Helga was not amused, and Jake felt Baxter squirming next to him.

Neither of them said anything as Helga continued her circuit of the vehicle, shining her light through each window. Baxter managed to give Jake a miserable look when she was at the back of the car, then he erased the expression when she came back around, looking into the driver's-side rear window.

"All right, you two—both of you know better than to—"

She stopped abruptly at the sound of a vehicle crunching over the gravel near the front of the theater. They all spun around as a car came into view from around the front. The approaching vehicle stopped suddenly and then, with a sudden roar of its engine, accelerated, turned with a spurt of gravel, and blasted out of the parking lot.

"Shit! Shit!" cried Helga as she sped toward her patrol car. "Butch! Let's go!"

But she was moving so fast, and the dog was suddenly whipped up into such excitement from the tone of her voice, that when she took off, Butch ran in front of her. She tripped over him and nearly took a header onto the hood of Jake's car.

Baxter caught her just before she connected with metal. She pulled roughly from his grip, still trying to get to her car... but by then, it was obviously too late.

The other vehicle was gone and the night was silent of any sound but the distant rumble of a car engine.

"*Shit!*" Helga exclaimed again, and ran to her car anyway. "I'll be back," she said to Butch as she yanked open the door. "Watch him," she said to the guys.

Her dog obviously thought this was a game, as he was running around in circles and barking and generally getting underfoot. Baxter grabbed the dog's collar to keep him out of the way as the patrol car roared to life and squealed out of the parking lot, sending another spray of gravel shooting toward the three of them.

"Hell," said Jake, staring after the red taillights. "That was—"

"Quick, get rid of the beer and empty bottles before she gets back," Baxter said, already diving into the Lexus.

"All of it?" Jake said, shocked and dismayed. "Don't be silly, she's not going to—"

"Oh yes she will," Baxter said, emerging with the two empty bottles. "Dude, I'm serious. Get that case out of there. We'll stash it somewhere and come back for it later. *If* she doesn't find it first."

A little shocked at his friend's tight nerves, Jake nonetheless did as he was told. After all, Baxter knew Helga better than he did.

But he wasn't about to throw the beer away, so he took the case over to one of the Dumpsters and put it on the ground behind it, safely in the shadows.

When he came back, he found Baxter giving Butch another good scratch.

"We could just take off if she hadn't left him, you know," he said, standing as Jake approached. "She planned it that way. She is *so* going to arrest us."

Jake smothered a laugh, shaking his head. "If you say so."

"Trust me, I know that woman. I—" He bit off the rest of his words as a pair of headlights turned rather sedately into the parking lot.

Butch perked up—he must have recognized the sound of his mistress's vehicle—and sat, waiting expectantly with his eyes trained on the police cruiser. By contrast, Baxter sagged a little and leaned back against Jake's car, arms folded over his middle as if waiting for the axe to fall.

"I didn't catch him," Helga said as she approached with long, easy strides. "Did either of you see a license plate? Or anything to help identify the type of vehicle?" Her blue eyes were sharp and demanding in the glow from the headlights.

"Uh," Baxter said. "It was dark and pretty big...not an SUV but larger than a compact. I didn't see anything on the license plate except that it was a dark color and the numbers were light or white."

"Yeah, it looked blue or black to me," said Jake. "Probably a sedan of some sort."

Helga slapped her hands on her hips and heaved an exasperated sigh. "That's all you got? You were facing it as it drove into the lot, guys. You didn't see anything else that might help? The shape of the driver, maybe—general height or anything?"

Jake closed his eyes, trying to call up the image in his memory. "No, I didn't really see anyone inside the car—well, just the head of one person. So they were alone. And the headlights weren't on. Obviously they were trying not to be noticed—so that's probably an indication they were up to no good."

Helga muttered something that sounded like *duh.*

"Okay, wait," said Baxter suddenly. "The brake lights—I saw them come on as the car turned around before it sped away. They were an unusual shape... Let me think about it. I might be able to draw a picture."

"That would be good," Helga said in a slightly less aggrieved tone. "That might keep you out of jail tonight, anyway."

"Jail?" For the first time, Jake thought she might be serious. "Tonight?"

She lifted an eyebrow at him. "Yes. Jail."

"What for, officer?" Baxter said innocently. "We didn't do anything wrong. We were just sitting there in the car."

She looked at him and shook her head. "I suppose you've disposed of it. I can't believe you'd destroy a whole case of B-Cubed, so where'd you put it?"

"I have no idea what you're talking about, Officer van Hest," Baxter replied. "Go ahead and look around—Jake won't mind if you search his vehicle, will you, Jake?"

"Just draw the damned lights for me," she retorted. "I'm going to take a look around."

She pulled the long, powerful flashlight from its mooring

at her belt and turned it on. Damn, it was so bright that Jake's eyes burned.

He wasn't sure whether he should go with her or not, but figured she had her dog, the flashlight, and she was a trained cop—plus they'd already run off the intruder—so she was probably just fine on her own.

Instead, he stood there exactly where he'd been when the dark vehicle pulled into the lot and tried to remember the details. There was no question that whoever had arrived and then so speedily departed had been up to no good, and the probability was very high that the driver was the perpetrator of the nasty things that had been happening to Vivien.

He was certain there'd been only one figure in the car, for there was an instant when the moonlight threw illumination into the vehicle, front to back, and he remembered seeing only one head. So whoever it was had been working alone—at least tonight they were.

He hadn't seen the strange, distinct brake lights, and he hoped whatever Baxter sketched out was helpful—and accurate.

"Didn't find anything of interest back there." Helga's smug voice caught his attention, and Jake turned to see her carrying the case of B-Cubed he'd stashed behind the Dumpster.

"Told ya," Baxter muttered.

She sauntered up with the case tucked under her arm, and without even asking, she went around the back of Jake's Lexus and opened the hatch.

"Come on, Butch," she said, inviting the dog to leap into the back of Jake's car as she perched on the tailgate. "Take a load off, big guy."

A moment later, Jake heard the distinct *thook* of a cap being popped off a longneck, followed by a feminine sigh of pleasure.

He looked at Baxter, who just shrugged and wandered around the back. "Why, officer, I'm shocked to find you drinking while on duty," Baxter said.

Helga lifted her chin and took a good, long drag from the bottle. When she put it back down, she took her time swallowing then said, "I've been off-duty for almost an hour now."

"I had a feeling," Baxter replied. But when he reached for one of the beers in the case, Helga smacked his hand back.

"Excuse me, sir—this is official contraband."

"Contraband? You didn't confiscate that—"

"No, but I found it. Last I heard, possession is nine-tenths of the law...which also says I don't have to share if I don't want to. And why," she said, tipping the sweating bottle up to her lips again, "would I want to share such an excellent brew?" She grinned around the lip of the bottle, and Jake couldn't help but chuckle at Baxter's consternation.

"So how are *you* going to get home, then, now that you've had some 'open alcohol'?" Baxter demanded.

"Why, Dr. DeRiccio is going to drive me in this very nice vehicle in an hour or two after we wait to make sure no one decides to come back and poke around here at the theater. Since the doc won't be having any more to drink, he can be the DD."

"Hey, wait a minute—" Jake began, but Baxter was already reaching around Helga to fish out a beer for himself.

"You heard the officer, Jake," Baxter said with a grin as he popped the top and took a long pull. "You're the designated driver."

"You know, Helga, all you had to do was ask for a beer," Jake said dryly. "We would have shared."

"But, you see, the way it all worked out, I've acquired an entire case of B-Cubed—and I've got some backup in case anything else happens here tonight." She smiled brightly, leaned against the car, and took another long pull from the longneck. "Now, Baxter, get me that drawing so we can figure out what kind of car that bastard is driving. And since he drove through all that glass, let's hope he's got a flat tomorrow."

IT WAS dark when Vivien awoke, and very quiet. She had to scrabble around for her phone to see what time it was, then squinted and blinked when its light blared into the darkness. Two thirty a.m.

She lay there for a moment, listening to the silence—so unusual for someone used to being in the city. No horns, no engines or planes, no shouts or music or clangs or sirens...

Did she like it? Or did she wish she were back where everything was happening all the time, where she could get takeout of any ethnic—or not ethnic—cuisine in the world whenever she wanted?

Where she was safe from whatever threatened her here.

Vivien's wry laugh was sharp in the silent darkness. "Imagine that, Liv—I was safer in New York City than I am here in little Wicks Hollow."

A light brush over her left arm, lifting the hair there, told her Liv heard her and was amused as well.

Then the flash of dry humor evaporated, because what was there to laugh about?

She threw off the bedcovers and rose, the flimsy summer nightgown light and airy around her thighs. There was no air conditioning in this little old bungalow, so fans, open windows, and cool clothing were *de rigueur* for July and August. At least it wasn't as hot as it was in the city, where the flat concrete absorbed and reflected all the heat—and baked all the smells from the perennially waiting trash cans.

She padded out from the bedroom on bare feet, heading toward the kitchen for something to eat. Light streamed in from the front door and the windows beside it, as well as by the back door leading into the fenced-in yard, so she didn't need to turn on any of the interior lights.

She came into the living room and saw a dark shape rearing by the sofa. She froze, her heart surging into her throat as she strangled back a scream.

The shadow spilled over the floor in front of her, and its shape was horribly familiar: long, straight, with a flat, slanted end.

CHAPTER THIRTEEN

VIVIEN LIVED an eternity of horror before she realized the horrible shadow was from the Nutcracker headpiece she'd set on the table.

Its grinning white teeth caught the light from outside and seemed to glow in the dim light, and the mask's wide-open eyes appeared to fixate on her as she fought to get her heart to start beating again.

"All right. I'm good. It's all good," she said, walking past the living room into the tiny kitchen.

She was hungry—the olives and bread at Jake's had been a long time ago, and not nearly enough of a meal after the way she'd been running around all day at the theater. But, as Helga had pointed out, there was very little in the cupboards and next to nothing in the fridge. And since it was two thirty in the morning, there was nowhere she could order from in Wicks Hollow.

"Guess it's gonna be frozen pizza," she said. Again. And hummed "Food, Glorious Food."

She really needed to go to the grocery...but now, she

realized with an unhappy sigh, she didn't even have a car to get her there. She would have changed her tune, but she couldn't think of a song that was called "I'm So Screwed" or "My Life Is a Hot Mess."

Ugh.

Vivien sank into a chair at the Formica kitchen table and rested her forehead in her hands.

No car. No transportation. And no Uber here in town.

Someone was trying to scare her away from the theater. Threatening her.

She'd been an asshole to Jake, who wasn't as much of a dickwad as she'd been telling herself he was for a decade and a half.

And...something very strange had happened at the theater with the eerie shadow that glided across the stage and the floor of the pit. Very strange, very creepy...very unsettling.

The oven beeped suddenly, startling her so much that she squeaked a loud gasp. Vivien swore at herself for being an idiot as she rose to put in the pizza.

Then she opened up her tablet and began to scroll through the messages she hadn't gotten to earlier today, and tried not to think about all of the other icky things.

She lost track of time dealing with her clients—but at least things were progressing. She had just closed two influencer deals for clients who'd be posting videos or pictures on social media (which Vivien would help design and produce), and that would bring in a commission of a couple thousand dollars over the next two months.

And she was still waiting to hear whether GetBack Togs was going to accept an even more lucrative proposal for Louise London. Vivien was so engrossed in her work that she didn't even realize how much time had passed until she smelled something unpleasant... Something was burning—the pizza!

Crap! She bolted from the table so fast she knocked over her chair just as the smoke detector went off, shrilling horribly in the silence.

Black smoke leaked from the decades-old oven, and when she opened it, more smoke billowed out, making the screaming alarm even more insistent.

The inexpensive, soft frozen pizza had folded, somehow sliding between the wires of the rack, cheese melting (and burning) everywhere, tomato sauce sizzling on the bottom, and pepperoni charred to black.

So much for her dinner.

A LOUD POUNDING jolted Vivien out of a low-level sleep. It took her a few bleary seconds to realize someone was knocking on the front door—Helga—and that it was very light outside. She stumbled out of bed, staggering from the bedroom as she pushed the hair from her eyes. "I'm coming. I'm *coming*."

She flung open the door, and it was Jake, not Helga, who stood there—and she was suddenly awake enough to feel the weight of his attention as it swept over her from tousled head to bare toes...then back up and down once more.

"Oh, hi," she said, resisting the desire to hide behind the door. After all, it wasn't anything he hadn't seen before—although things were a little curvier now than they'd been when she was twenty, and she no longer had a ridiculously concave belly that displayed her hipbones. "Sorry, I overslept. Uh, I was expecting Helga...why are you here?"

It took Jake a full ten seconds to respond—which didn't sound like very long, but was an eternity when you were standing in the doorway in a barely-covering-your-bare-ass nightgown of paper-thin blue fabric—and when he did, he sounded like he'd swallowed sandpaper. "Uh...Helga's feeling a little under the weather, so she asked me to pick you up."

This statement prompted a multitude of questions and more than a twinge of something that might have been jealousy—or at least a low-key niggle of something like that.

"Oh" was all she said.

"Uh, can I come in? I'm guessing you're going to want to, uh, put something else on." Still with the gravelly voice. "Before we go to the theater. She's going to meet us there, I think."

"The theater? Oh, right," Vivien said, stepping away from the door. "Sure. Come in. Um...don't mind the mess. I'm still unpacking, as you can see. I really need some coff— Oh. *Wow.*" She teared up a little when he handed her a to-go cup of something that definitely smelled like coffee. "Thank you, Jake," she said with great emotion.

"Still black and three sugars, I hope." He closed the door behind him.

"God, yes, thank you." She took a gulp of the coffee and felt more alert almost immediately, but was aware that the caffeine and sugar were going to wreak havoc on her totally empty, painfully gnawing stomach. She wondered what the chances were of getting Jake to stop somewhere for her to grab a breakfast sandwich or something.

It didn't take her more than fifteen minutes to brush her

teeth, take a super-quick shower, and anchor her hair in a loose knot at the top of her head. She dressed in a loose tank top, casual shorts, and practical shoes, since she'd be doing manual labor at the theater. When she opened the bedroom door, she thought she smelled toast and hurried to the kitchen.

"Oh, man, Jake...you have no idea how hungry I am and how good that smells."

"Well, considering the mess in the garbage and the smell of burned something lingering in the air, I was able to put two and two together that you didn't get much to eat last night. Helga warned me your cupboards were bare, and since you don't have a car..." He spread his hands as if to say *obviously*. "I brought some bread for you and thought I'd make use of it."

The toast—from the sun-dried tomato sourdough—tasted like ambrosia, and she unashamedly ate four pieces with butter, trying not to moan too loudly at the deliciousness.

"So good," she said, wiping up the crumbs and putting the plate and knife in the sink. "Thank you again."

"I guess you're ready to go now," Jake said.

"Yes. You sound disappointed. Why? Didn't I primp long enough?"

He shrugged. "I liked what you were wearing a few minutes ago a lot better." And then he gave her a sudden, devastating smile—one that made heat rush straight down her body to her toes, then back up again right to her center.

Vivien didn't know what to say, so she fumbled for her phone and bag and started for the door. "Well, a nightgown isn't very practical for digging around an old theater, is it?"

"You call that a nightgown?" he muttered, following her

out the door with the headpiece in hand. "Looked more like a piece of—what did you call it?—scrim to me."

IT TOOK till they got to the theater before Jake was able to think about anything but the sight that had greeted him when Vivien opened the door to her cottage. She'd been a vision of rumpled bourbon hair, sleepy sloe eyes, and filmy peekaboo negligee that left little to the imagination—and he had one *hell* of an imagination.

Hell, how was a guy to concentrate on blows to the back of the head and vandalized cars and theatrical threats with that sort of distraction sitting next to him in the car—and clearly unaware of its potency?

"So...when did Helga ask you to pick me up?" she asked as they pulled into the parking lot at the theater. She'd been strangely quiet during the seven-minute drive. "And don't you have to work this morning?"

"I'm off today—I have a weird schedule—and I was conscripted into being her DD last night," Jake told her. "I think she knew she wasn't going to want to get up really early today, so she asked me when I dropped her off last night."

When Vivien didn't reply, something told him it was imperative he elaborate. It was almost as if Mathilda was kicking him under the table. "Uh...so, I should tell you that I was—we were—staking out the parking lot here last night."

"You were?" She whipped her head to look at him, but there was still a funny look in her eyes. "You and Helga?"

"Baxter and I. I mean, I was, and then I asked Bax if he wanted to hang out too. And Helga caught us with a case of

B-Cubed in the car, and she confiscated it under the guise of it being official police business, but it turned out she was off-duty at the time, and so what really happened was that she got to drink several of my beers and I had to drive her—and Bax, who also got to drink some—home while getting to drink none of it myself."

Now Vivien was looking at him as if he'd sprouted another head. She narrowed her eyes and said carefully, "So... you and Baxter were hanging out here and Helga managed to swipe an entire case of your beer? *And* get a ride home?"

"That about sums it up. See, there's her cop car still parked back there. She threatened to arrest us for having open containers in the car—"

Vivien burst out laughing. "She is such a badass. I've told her a hundred times I want to be her when I grow up." Her face was all lit up and her eyes glowed with pleasure.

Jake's chest felt tight, and he hid the discomfort by climbing out of the car. *Too soon.*

He grabbed the ugly Nutcracker mask from the back seat and followed her. She was still chuckling a little as she led the way to the theater's side door.

"So while we were here last night, someone drove into the parking lot without their lights on and then sped away when they saw us and the cop car," he told her.

That got her attention, and she stopped suddenly. "Did you see who it was?"

He had to shake his head. "Helga went after them, but it was too late and they got away. But Baxter said the brake lights were unusual, so he was drawing a picture of them. And there was only one person in the car that I could see."

"You think it was them—whoever's been breaking in."

"No headlights, then taking off as soon as they saw us—yeah, I'd say so."

"They didn't come back?"

"We were here till two, two thirty. I drove Bax and Helga home—by the way, is there something going on with them?"

"Going on like how? Dating?"

"Yeah. Or something. I think I got a vibe..."

She shook her head as she fit the key into the lock. "Not a chance. Baxter is hung up on Emily Delton, and Helga's very happily single and unencumbered. I mean, she likes guys, but she's not interested in all the hassle." Then she looked directly at him. "Why? You afraid you're going to step on his toes?"

Jake was rendered speechless. Surely she wasn't that clueless... "I'd only be stepping on his toes if he was moving in on you, VL. I thought that was pretty obvious."

"Oh. No...well, maybe. Ugh. I... Jake, we have a history. I can't help it if that's the lens I look through when I—with you."

What could he say to that?

Nothing. So he followed her into the theater and put down the eerie, caved-in headpiece on a table.

"The scaffolding is back here," she said, leading the way into a spacious workshop with a thirty-foot ceiling and a massive garage door. There were walls lined with worktables and hung with tools, including an old table saw, piles of ratty paint cloths and sawhorses, trash cans, and acres of scrap wood. It was a lot cleaner than it had been yesterday, though.

"If you help me wheel it out, we can look up at the flies and see how they're attached, and maybe how they were manipulated. And at the very least, take them down for evidence."

"Flies? You mean the backdrops?"

"Right."

They muscled the scaffolding out and wheeled it onto the stage with little trouble but some godawful wheel squeaking. It was metal and had been tucked behind a bunch of old set pieces, so Jake was reasonably sure it hadn't been tampered with. Nonetheless, he insisted that they check every step and bar before putting any weight on them, even though he was certain Vivien would have done so anyway.

"So, I was thinking about timing," she said as they worked their way slowly up the steps, one on either side of the scaffolding. "When and how those events happened...either someone was watching and knew when to set the creepy effects off, or there was some other sort of trigger that launched the, uh, shows.

"When it happened the first time, I was here alone. I had just come into the building by myself, and no one knew I was going to come here; I didn't even know it myself. I'd just gotten the keys, and the news that the bank approved my loan for the improvements, and I was so excited that I came right here. So that first little *display* had to have been set up and ready well before I arrived. Heck, maybe even the second one had been set up at the same time—how would I know? I wasn't looking for scrims up in the house ceiling—probably wouldn't have realized what they were even if I saw it up there—and as you saw, there are a bunch of flies, backdrops, still hanging up there above the stage."

"So you'd literally just gotten the loan to buy the place

and the first thing happened right away?" He looked at her from between the bars of the scaffolding.

"No, I closed on the actual building a month ago. The loan was for the improvements and renovation." She pursed her lips. "So whoever it was had a month to set it up, I guess. I had to move from New York and everything. I just got the keys on Tuesday."

"All right. So you came here unexpectedly—right after you got the keys—and walked in..."

"Right. I was walking down the main aisle in the house toward the stage, thinking about all of the energy and memories contained in this space, and how I wanted to— Well, anyway, I was walking down the aisle, and all of a sudden, there was this bright blue light on the stage."

She'd been clambering up the ladder a little too fast for his comfort, then suddenly stopped. "Wait a sec. I remember something...I remember walking down the aisle and feeling something sort of give under my foot, like a soft spot in the floor, and I was thinking, oh crap, it's going to be another repair—and then the lights came on."

"So you're thinking it might have been a sort of tripwire— or trip pad—that you stepped on that set it off?"

"Or some sort of alarm that signaled the, uh, what do I call him—the vandalizer?—to set it off, maybe remotely. Because it was right after that, almost immediately, that the light came on."

Jake liked that theory, and he told her so as they reached the top of the scaffolding at the same time. "Good. So we can probably find evidence of that if you can remember where you were standing when it happened."

"Right. And then I ran—I mean, I left the building because I was freaked out—"

"Understandably so."

"And when I came back in—maybe ten minutes later—what I thought was painted words on the wall but was just a backdrop—a scrim, probably," she added with a sly look that made his stomach bottom out then bounce up, "was gone. At the time, I thought it had just disappeared."

"Which is probably what you were supposed to think. You were being fooled into thinking that the place is haunted by some horrible specter or gruesome phantom, but it was all a fake. Someone's just messing with—"

Crash!

The sound of many large items colliding or falling somewhere in the building—backstage?—was sudden, loud, and ominous, and the metallic echo reverberated through the empty space.

Vivien's mouth was open to either exclaim or scream; Jake couldn't tell—and then his brain couldn't even pursue that thought, because all at once, he felt the violent rush of cold.

It was like an actual Arctic front that enveloped him, as if he'd been plunged into a room of dry ice. The frigid air was accompanied by a dark, dank, unpleasant smell that he'd only experienced once before—when he got a whiff of something that turned out to be necrotic diabetic foot with wet gangrene during a stint in the ER. This was nearly as bad—and worse, he didn't know what was causing it.

Vivien made a noise that sounded as if she were in distress—probably gagging—and it came out in a distinct puff of white in the freezing air.

The metallic cacophony ended as abruptly as it had begun, but the scaffolding, the catwalk, the rows of light pots above suddenly began to shake wildly. The lamps themselves began to flash erratically in blinding reds, greens, blues, and golds.

Jake didn't need to shout for her to climb down from the rattling scaffolding; she was already halfway to the ground. He jumped most of the way, his own breath following in a trail of white as his fingers and the tip of his nose burned with cold. He grabbed Vivien by the hand with stiff fingers, and they half stumbled, half ran off the stage, away from the clattering, jangling mess, down the aisle past the rows of chairs.

They weren't even down the aisle when the chaos stopped just as suddenly as it had begun: the lights, the violent rattling, the stench, the cold.

They staggered to a halt and turned around to look back at the stage. Then Vivien gaped up at him, her eyes so wide that he could see white all around her irises.

"Holy shit."

CHAPTER FOURTEEN

VIVIEN'S TEETH wouldn't stop chattering, and it wasn't because of the furious cold that had suddenly surrounded them.

What the hell was *that?*

She realized she was still gripping Jake's hand, but she wasn't quite ready to let go.

"That was..." he started, then simply squeezed her fingers as they stared into the theater at the silent stage.

The scaffolding was still intact, and nothing had fallen from above. The colored pot lights were all dark now, and the only illumination was that which she'd turned on when they came in.

"I don't think it was...human," Vivien finally said. Something rippled through him—she felt it because his arm was touching hers—and he gave a short bark of laughter.

"I don't know what it was," he said. "But whoever or whatever it was, it's not happy."

She reluctantly pulled her fingers from his and started to walk down the aisle back to the stage. Everything was so still and silent and normal that she could almost believe she'd imagined it.

But now what did she do?

"I'm afraid to look in the back," she said when she felt Jake come up alongside her. "It sounded like a tornado back there..."

"First, show me where you were standing when the weird light came on the first time," he said, brushing her hand with his fingers in a fleeting gesture.

Surprised by his change of subject—didn't he want to see what had made those awful crashing, falling noises?—Vivien nonetheless paused on her path to the stage.

"Here...right about here," she said, slightly relieved to be focusing on something more easily explained than what had just happened. Her fingers were still trembling. "And look, feel it—the floor gives a little."

She'd stepped on it, felt the give, and now crouched to examine the strip of carpet that ran down the center aisle. Digging out the multitool she always carried in her pocket, she carefully began to cut into the rug several inches away from the "soft" part of the floor.

"Oh...Jake, look..."

But he was already next to her and saw what she saw when she flipped back the piece of carpet.

"You were right. It looks like some sort of trigger pad—there's even a wire coming from it." He began to follow the slender black wire that trailed into a row of seats.

"I wouldn't have noticed it because it's pretty dark in here, and they camouflaged it very well, right up against the bottom of the chairs along the floor. The bastard," she said as she pulled to her feet. "What an absolute *bastard.*"

Whatever shock had lingered after the events on the stage a moment ago disintegrated and was replaced by deep fury toward the absolute, definite *human* who'd been harassing her.

"It ends here, under this seat," Jake said, holding up the wire at the fourth chair in from the aisle. "And it's connected to a little transmitter." With an angry jerk, Jake pulled the device out from beneath the seat. He said something under his breath, then stood and held the transmitter so it dangled by the wire. "Who's got it in for you, VL? Who's gone to all this trouble?"

Before she answered, he started looking up and around, and she realized he was searching for cameras. A cold shiver trickled down her spine as she was once again reminded that someone must be watching her somehow...

And was it possible that the loud, crashing, shaking, light-flashing *thing* that had just happened could have been caused by someone—not some*thing*—that wished her ill?

Vivien wasn't certain which would be worse—a human or metaphysical entity.

She just wanted it to stop.

THEY SHOWED Helga and Joe Cap—who was back from college tours and had brought his officer to pick up her police cruiser—the trip mat and its transmitter device, as well as the GO OR DIE backdrop and the red silk swath hanging up there next to it. There were the two small nanny-cams Jake had found—one was trained onto the stage, and one aimed the center aisle—that they disconnected and turned over to the authorities.

By tacit agreement, neither Vivien nor Jake mentioned the frigidly cold air or the violent shaking of the scaffolding and stage.

Captain Joe Longbow was an easygoing, rugged man in his fifties with ink-black hair in a crew cut. His uniform shirt was a little tight around the middle, but he had solid shoulders and arms, and his eyes were sharp.

When Vivien was finished explaining everything, he scratched his chin and looked up at the scrim that still hung over the center of the house. "Death, huh?" he said in his easy drawl. "Sounds like someone's got a bee in their bonnet over you, Ms. Savage. Heard your car got bashed in, too."

"I have no idea who it might be," Vivien replied. "I've been here less than a week—"

"But you did live here before," Jake reminded her.

She shrugged. "More than a decade ago. Who's going to carry a grudge that...long." She felt her face heat up as Jake lifted a brow.

Fine. He had a point. But *she* hadn't known the whole story about what happened back at NYU anyway. (*And whose fault was that?* asked her conscience—or maybe it was Liv. Her twin had gotten pretty snarky over the years.)

"Besides, I didn't make any enemies back in high school," Vivien went on. "I just did my thing—I'd had enough of being in the spotlight, trust me."

Helga shifted on her feet. Her butter-gold hair was pulled back into a professional-looking twist, and her uniform was, as always, spotless. However, there were pale shadows under her eyes, suggesting she hadn't gotten much sleep last night.

"Well, that might be your perspective, VL, but I hate to say it...there were people who didn't like you. And some who actively *dis*liked you."

Even so many years later, that announcement was enough to make Vivien's stomach drop. "Like who? Why? And even if they did, like I said, it was so long ago—who would hold a grudge that long over nothing? It had to be nothing, because I never had any conflict with anyone. I just kept my head down and tried to be unnoticed. I didn't want people asking about Liv, or bugging me about being a star, and I definitely didn't want friends just because they thought I was something—I don't know—special?"

"I get it," said Helga. "But unfortunately, that keep-to-yourself bit put some people off because they thought *you* thought you were too good for them." She shrugged and held up her hands when Vivien started to reply. "I don't agree, never did. I'm just the messenger."

"Well, like who?" Now Vivien had to know, and her stomach felt all tight and icky again. Could that be why someone was messing with her? Because of some imagined *high school* slight?

"Well, there was Melody Carlson, of course," Helga said, causing Vivien to roll her eyes, because that one she knew about. "She was always a little difficult anyway—but her mother left them when she was in kindergarten, I think, so..." she added without looking at Vivien. "And Susie Parminster —now Susie Wallaby—who was friends with Melody, and so *she* obviously thought you were a bitch, just by osmosis. I think Bella Mihalek—now Pohlson—was also one of the, uh, Mean Girls, so to speak—"

"Bella? That's my realtor—the one who sold me the

theater!" Vivien exclaimed. "So she thought I was a bitch back then, did she? Well, she sure was happy enough to have my business when I took this freaking albatross off her hands." She looked around at the theater, suddenly annoyed. Hadn't Bella, Susie, and Melody just shown up yesterday and acted like they were old friends?

What had she ever done to cause those girls to dislike her? It wasn't her fault she'd been sort of famous—for about a minute.

Helga looked uncomfortable, and Vivien spared a moment of sympathy for her. It might be a little awkward for her friend to share this—after all, it sounded like Helga was at least sort of friends with the "Mean Girls," as she'd called them. At the very least, Helga was a cop in town and had to treat everyone equally and with respect.

"If she was your realtor, Bella would have known when you got the keys to the place," Jake said. "Could be relevant to the timing of some of these incidents. And, I hate to mention it, but she also would have access to the place."

"She seemed just fine—completely professional and really sweet and friendly during all of our interactions. She even mentioned looking up the Savage Sisters Tonys performance on YouTube so she could show her daughters," Vivien said, wondering if everyone else in town was pretending to be nice to her—all the contractors she was hiring, the volunteers, and so on—but really had it out for her instead.

She felt her shoulders hunch, and her lungs began to feel as if they weren't working right, like they did when an anxiety attack was coming on.

"Vivien," Helga said in a sharpish voice probably meant

to snap her out of the spiral into anxiety. "Don't let it get to you. It was fifteen years ago, and as you said—there was nothing to any of it. I'm sure everyone has moved on. But," she added with a meaningful look at Joe Cap, "it's worth maybe taking a look at the vehicles belonging to certain people. Just so they can be eliminated."

Vivien sighed. "You're probably right." She silently did her special breathing (in-two-three-four...) and said, "Well, were there any others? Did Baxter James hate me back then too?"

"No, he didn't," Vivien said immediately. "You know how shy he was back then, but he never said one bad thing about you, ever. Now, Drew Jeffreys had his nuts in a wad because you wouldn't go to the Homecoming Dance with him, but I'm pretty sure he got over that pretty quick, because he and Bella got all hot and heavy about a week later. And then Lucas Hebden said you were a frigid bitch—"

"That's because I wouldn't let him put his hand up my shirt after we went to the movies," Vivien replied tartly. "Jerk. Oh, but I did let Jesse Prime get to third base." She couldn't hold back a smile at the memory of steaming up his old red Fiero. That had been one hell of a tight squeeze, but worth every cramp and bruise. "He was really *prime*."

"That was after he dumped Yvonne Gesslinger to go out with you," said Helga with a grin. "And she got back at him by egging his car."

"Oh, man, he loved that car. Geez, how do you remember all this stuff?" Vivien said. "High school is pretty much a blur for me."

Helga shrugged. "I've lived here all my life, see most of these people regularly, and I was a spectator—even back then,

I was practicing to be a cop," she added with a grin. "A trained observer, you know?"

"I just can't imagine any of those people still holding a grudge," Vivien said, unable to keep the tightness from her voice. "It's just..."

"Well, now," said Joe Cap, taking his time getting the words out, as was his habit, "let's just step back a minute, Ms. Savage, and see if you can think of any other reason—besides an old grudge—someone might want to mess things up for you. Ex-husband, boyfriend, anyone like that?"

Vivien felt Jake's attention shift casually to her as she replied, "Never married, so no, and I've been casually seeing someone back on the East Coast but—"

"Roger Hatchard's son," Helga said. "He's going to be in the new show Vivien's doing—Roger, not the son." When her friend gave her an irked look, Helga went on, "Details are important, VL. You never know where there might be a connection."

"Daniel Hatchard is not going to fly here from Hartford to mess up the show his father is going to cameo in," Vivien said in frustration. "It not only wouldn't make sense—he was the one who suggested Roger should do the play—but he's just too busy to drop everything and come here. And he would have no reason to do so—we only went out a few times."

"All right, then," said Joe Cap. "But it wouldn't hurt to check in and see whether either of them have left town." He squinted at Vivien. "Roger Hatchard? The center for the Pistons?"

"Yes."

"He's going to be in a play? Like, an actor?" He sounded

confused, and Vivien admitted that was a reasonable reaction.

"Yes." She went on to explain, adding, "And Michael Wold and Penny Stern are also celebrities who'll be doing the two-weekend run. The rest of the cast is local."

"Oh, yes, I've heard all about that from Maxine and Juanita," he replied in a neutral tone. "All's I can say is, if either of them offer me elderberry wine—or any other kind of wine—I'm gonna decline."

Despite her mood, Vivien couldn't hold back a chuckle. "Good thinking—although I wouldn't worry too much. You don't fit the profile of the Brewster sisters' victims."

"Anyone else back in New York who might not want you to succeed out here?" asked the captain.

Vivien shook her head. "I simply can't think of anyone like that." She hugged herself. "This is really unsettling."

"All right, then," Joe Cap went on in a soothing voice. "We'll make sure everyone drives by here more often, and I'll do some looking in on things. Helga, you said you saw someone last night here?"

"We all did—Jake, Baxter James, and I," Helga replied. "Baxter drew me a picture of the brake lights—which wasn't very helpful, because they just look like blobs—but I'm going to show him a few pictures of car back ends in case he recognizes them. I also want to look around to see whether there are any tire tracks we might be able to use to nail down the vehicle. Especially if they drove through all the broken glass," she added with a smirk. "Looked like he might have done."

"Good thinking," said the captain. "I'll check in with the tire place in town, and a couple of the dealers, poke around a little. Helga, if you get them, I can run images of tire tracks through the system—"

"Ah, that's all right, Cap," Helga said quickly. "It's best if you just stay away from the electronics, all right? I'm happy to do it, and type up the report for this morning too. He's an excellent cop," she said to Vivien and Jake, "great investigator, wonderful boss—but this man can't walk past the copy machine without it spontaneously jamming or blowing a fuse, and every time he tries to print something, he ends up disconnecting every computer from the entire network. Then I have to reboot it, and...ugh."

"Right," said Captain Longbow, shaking his head sadly. "Not being able to use all that equipment... It's a curse...and a blessing." His eyes twinkled, and Vivien realized she was glad to have someone competent at the law enforcement helm here in her new hometown, even if he was a menace around electronics.

Once Joe Cap and Helga left, Vivien and Jake were finally able to go backstage to see what had caused the chaotic crashing sounds that had preceded the earthquake-like event on the scaffolding.

"I'm almost afraid to look," Vivien said, more grateful than she wanted to admit that Jake was on her heels as she strode to the stage-right wing. "It sounded like it was coming from back in the workshop."

"It sounded pretty ugly," he replied.

It *was* pretty ugly.

The scene looked as if a cyclone had come through and tossed everything around in a jumble. Set pieces once leaning against the wall had collapsed into a pile, metal rods and tools were flung to the floor, and paint cans (fortunately, none had come open) were strewn all over. The posters of old show casts Stephanie Lillard had found were in a tumble in the middle of the floor.

Vivien stood there trying not to think about who, or what, had done this. At least it all happened after the big cleanup day, or the mess would have been much worse with so many more things to throw around.

"It won't take that long to put things back," Jake said, already picking up paint cans to restack them against the wall. "It's really not that big of a mess."

"No, it's not as bad as it sounded from out there. But how did it happen? *How?*" She picked up *The Nutcracker* show photo, which was in the middle of the floor on top of the pile, and sighed.

Of course, Jake didn't have an answer for that—or if he did, he didn't want to share it. Neither of them did. The answer wasn't pretty.

In an effort to distract herself, Vivien began to sing an old song from *The Little Mermaid* about all the neat stuff, and by the time most of the mess had been picked up, she was belting out how she wanted to be where the people were.

In the middle of the chorus, she turned to find Jake standing there watching her. When their eyes met, her heart jumped a little. Then he gave a funny grimace and returned to tipping the last of the large set pieces against the wall with the rest of them.

"Cute song," he said. "I think your voice has gotten even better over the years. It's more mature."

Feeling supremely self-conscious, Vivien brushed off his compliment. "Only because the acoustics in here are better than my apartment—or yours—was back then."

"I thought the acoustics in the shower back then were pretty damned good," he said, holding her eyes with his.

Her throat went dry and something sizzled in her belly. She gave a nervous laugh and looked away, turning her attention to straightening a row of nail cans on the worktable. "Well, that's why people like to sing in the shower—"

"I loved hearing you sing in the shower," he went on mercilessly. "I'd still be in bed, and you'd be up and at 'em, and then I'd hear you. It was a wonderful way to wake up in the morning. I could hear you right through the wall. You could be singing anything from a sad tearjerker to a big, happy dance number to a sassy, silly thing like—like 'If You Were Gay.' That one always made me smile, but I liked them all. I liked hearing you." He was looking at her so affectionately. "I could always tell what your mood was by what you sang in the shower."

She wanted to swallow, but there was something clogging her throat. And the dust was getting to her eyes, because all at once they stung. "Jake..."

"So I'm just curious what you were singing in my shower yesterday," he went on, giving her a crooked little smile and spreading his hands.

That surprised a laugh out of her. She hadn't realized he could hear her. "Are you sure you want to know?"

He nodded, but before she could tell him (should she?), a jaunty little tune broke the silence. "My phone," he told her, digging it out of his pocket. He glanced at the display, frowned, then answered, "DeRiccio."

Then every bit of levity evaporated from his demeanor as he became alert, tight, and intense. "When? Where? ...Is he on his way now? ...Who's taking hi— All right. I'll be there stat."

He was still holding the phone when he looked at Vivien. "It's Pop. I have to get to the hospital. They're taking him now."

"Let me get my bag," Vivien said. "I'll drive you— No, Jake, let me. Then you can be on the phone on the way if you need to, all right? You can concentrate on that while I get you there safely."

He was already halfway to the lobby by this time, and she was right on his tail. She was afraid Stubborn Jake was going to insist on driving, but to her surprise, he handed over the keys to his Lexus without her asking again. He climbed into the passenger side, already keying something into his phone.

"Which hospital—"

"Butterworth," he said, then spoke into his phone. "Pop's on his way to the hospital—chest pains, low BP. I don't know —they said he was out working in the yard and he hurt himself or got bit or stung—probably doing something he shouldn't—and then he started having chest pains. Can you let Irene and Mathilda know? I'll start a text thread as soon as I know more. I'm on my way there now... Probably at least thirty minutes, maybe more. Thanks, Dom."

Vivien knew better than to speak as Jake next called the hospital, identified himself, and told them he was on his way, then took two phone calls from his sisters, who clearly had gotten the news from their brother Dominic and didn't want to wait for the text thread.

"I don't know anything yet," he said to one of them. "He was working in the yard, I guess, and he might've gotten stung or done something—anyway, he started having chest pains— I don't know. The person who called was a little scattered, so I don't have... No, I wasn't with him. Look, Mattie, I don't know anything yet. It could be a lot of things... maybe he had too much tomato sauce on his pasta, maybe he strained his pectoral lifting a log— I *know* he shouldn't be lifting logs! I don't really know what he was doing. I'm on my way now, and I'll update you and— Look, Irene's calling me now, and I'm going to take it. I'll let you know— Yes, I know this is just like Mom...I *know*. I know, Mattie, I know, I'll... All right." He pulled the phone away, stabbed at it, then brought it back to his ear. "Hi, Irene... Yes, I'm on my way— Yes—no, I don't know anything yet..."

Vivien focused on the road and was grateful it was just past noon and not rush hour so they could fly on the expressway. She couldn't help but notice and admire Jake's calm, clear responses to his obviously freaked-out siblings while he must also be fighting his own level of freaked-outness.

At last, she pulled up to the emergency room entrance and he jumped out. "Thanks, Viv, I'll find you in a few," he said, and then rushed into the building.

She followed him in a few minutes later, but Jake was nowhere to be seen in the emergency room. She hoped that meant he'd been able to get back into a room with his father.

Instead of taking a seat, she tracked down the café inside the hospital and grabbed a few granola bars and a couple of waters and coffees. Who knew how long they'd be waiting, and she figured Jake wouldn't want to leave to eat.

When she came back to the emergency room waiting area, the woman behind the counter waved her over. "Are you here with a patient? Someone is waiting for you in the back, but I can't give out the name."

"DeRiccio," she said, and the administrator nodded.

"Yes, the son is back there with him and said you could come back too."

Vivien felt a shudder of relief. If Jake was inviting her to come to the examination room, then it must not be desperate.

Unless it was horribly desperate, and he wanted someone to wait with him...

The nurse who led her back past rows of curtained rooms didn't give any indication of Mr. DeRiccio's status, and Vivien didn't want to ask. She'd find out soon enough. The place smelled like antiseptic and medicine and other scents she figured were things she'd rather not identify, all things considered.

"Okay for her to come in, sir?" asked the nurse, stopping at one of the curtains and poking her head around the edge.

"Yes, please," came a grumpy, gravelly voice. "I want a witness in case he tries to kill me."

"You almost did that yourself, Pop," said Jake as Vivien slipped in through a gap in the curtains. His eyes lit on her, and the relief and warmth in them made her feel a little wobbly inside.

"Thank God you came with him," said Ricky DeRiccio, who was lying on the hospital bed. "Otherwise, who knows what he'd do."

Vivien had to stifle a gasp at the sight of the old man. He looked frail and ashen, and his face was a mess of swollen red wheals over the weak pallor of his skin. What she could see of his arms—he had an IV needle stuck into the back of his hand, and the other arm had a blood-pressure cuff around the bicep—were also covered with the same angry red bumps. His thick black hair was an unruly mess, and his mustache bristled every which way as if it needed a comb.

"Pop tangled with a bee's nest," said Jake before she could ask. "After I told him not to—"

"You did nothing of the sort, sonny. You told me you'd take care of it, but you didn't, and it was a week ago, and I wanted to trim the bushes under that window," replied his father stoutly. "So I took care of it myself."

Vivien swore she heard Jake counting under his breath before he replied very calmly, "When I told you I would take care of it, that *meant for you not to do it, Pop.* And it meant that I would as soon as I could. And it was only *two days ago* that I told you I would take care of it."

Jake looked at her with something like pleading in his eyes. She wasn't certain if he was asking for her to side with him against his father (as *if*), give him a break from his dad somehow, or simply empathize with his frustration and worry. Having a difficult parent of her own, Vivien could relate to the latter, at least.

"Well, it looks like the bees got the best of you, Mr. DeRiccio," she said, coming closer to the bed. "I'm sorry to see that. I hope you're not in too much pain."

"Not anymore. They fixed me up just fine." He pouted a little and looked even more Mario-like with those big eyes and the forward-thrust lower lip below his mustache. "I was being very careful, even though Genius here doesn't think I know what I'm doing. I used a rake to knock it down, but when I was running away, I tripped over a damned stone and fell on my a—fell, and the blasted bees attacked."

"Ouch," Vivien said. "I'm very glad you aren't allergic."

"That makes two of us," Jake muttered. "Pop, I have no idea what possessed you—"

"Now don't you lecture me, Elwood," growled his father. "I've had enough pain in my ass for one day. I don't need you on there too, like a damned boil." He turned his attention to Vivien and managed to look adorably pathetic. "Got stung so many times, I got to feeling all weak and lightheaded. Started getting a pain in my chest, too. Genius here don't care about that, he just wants to lecture me about—"

"Pop, that's not true," Jake said, his eyes bulging and his jaws clamped tight. "You almost went into cardiac arrest. Your blood pressure was dropping—Christ, Vivien can tell you I was terrified all the way here that something was going to happen to you before I could get here, like—like Mom."

That last bit plopped right down there among all of them, landing like a meteor, and Vivien winced a little inside. There was a flash of grief in Ricky DeRiccio's eyes, but it was gone in an instant. The silence was broken when the blood-pressure cuff on his arm turned on with a little hum and began to tighten for a reading.

"Well, I'm glad you're all right. I'd hate to have to recast Mr. Gibbs," she said, interrupting the two men as they eyed each other with mingled fury and sadness.

"Yeah, that reminds me," said the patient a little grumpily. "Mr. Gibbs is a *Presbyterian*, isn't he? I don't think I can play a Presbyterian—and I don't look like one of them either," he said, as if they were easily identifiable or contagious. "Can't you make him a Catholic? With a good Italian name?"

Jake muttered something that sounded suspiciously as if he were taking the Lord's name in vain, but Vivien ignored him. "I don't see why not. It's a small role and it's only in one scene. Let me know what name you'd like to use, and—"

"Excuse me," said a nurse, peeking in from around the curtain. "Mr. DeRiccio, your room is ready, and so we're going to move you there in a few minutes."

"Room? I thought I was going home! I don't want to stay here," Ricky said, suddenly looking upset and even frightened. "He's a doctor—my son—so he can stay with me. At home. I'm going to go home."

"Pop, they just want to keep you overnight for observation," said Jake, exchanging meaningful glances with the nurse. "Your blood pressure was pretty low, and you did have chest pain."

"I don't want to stay here," Ricky said again, his brow furrowing. "I don't like hospitals. And their food is inedible— no offense, miss," he added to the nurse.

"None taken. And I happen to concur with your assessment," she said with a smile. "About the quality of the food, anyway, but not about you going home. And neither does Dr. Frantner."

"And neither does your son," added Jake, "who, as you've so kindly mentioned, is a doctor. It's just overnight, Pop. Oh, I know—how about if Vivien and I go and get you something from Luciano's? It's one of his favorite old haunts from when he lived in Grand Rapids," he told Vivien. "Not far from here."

"They closed down two years ago," replied his father in disgust—probably for his son not knowing this vital information, not because the eatery was closed. "Luciano dropped dead of a heart attack while he was rolling out pasta

—ended up with imprints from the metal thing all over his face—and his wife retired and moved to Florida.

"But now that you mention it, you could go get me something from Federico's—they're down on Ionia. Their osso bucco is almost as good as my *nonna's* was." His eyes had lit up, and Vivien swore he was salivating. "I can *have* it—I didn't have a heart attack! They said my heart's just fine, sonny, so just shut your mouth and don't argue for once."

Jake sighed. "Fine. I suppose you deserve something after all of this. Oh, man, Vivien, I'm sorry. Would you mind terribly?" he asked, as if suddenly remembering she was stranded at the hospital with him for as long as he was here.

"Not at all. Italian sounds amazing to me—I haven't had a real meal in two days." She was completely fine with ignoring the fact that she had two granola bars and a couple bottles of water in her bag. Authentic Italian won the day over granola bars, Thai, and—if she were being honest—even Mexican, every day.

Plus it would give her an excellent excuse not to be back at the theater for a little while.

Just so she could think about things.

Not Jake.

Definitely other things besides Jake.

CHAPTER FIFTEEN

JAKE WOULD NEVER HAVE IMAGINED his first "new" date with Vivien would be at an Italian restaurant getting carry-out for his father in the hospital.

"You get going, sonny," ordered his pop. "It'll take 'em an hour to get me settled in my room—no, you don't need to wait with me. Where the hell am I going to go anyway? They've got me all wired up and stuff—look at this crap in the back of my hand and in my arm. It's like I'm on my deathbed or something. And I'm sure as hell not going to get lost—this pretty lady isn't going to let me go anywhere but to the john or to my room is she?" he added, giving the nurse a wink.

"Not a chance, there, sir," she replied with a laugh. "We'll strap you down if we have to, and jam a catheter up your urethra if need be." She was about fifty years old with a very capable air, and Jake figured she'd seen it all when it came to feisty old men in the ER. He concluded his dad was in excellent hands.

"The sooner you get going, Elwood," continued his *annoyingly* bossy parent, "the sooner you'll be back with my osso bucco...which I haven't had made *properly* for at least twenty years. Don't mention anything to Mattie, though, because she made it for me last year on your mother's recipe —which never turned out right in forty years, but I never told your mother—and Mattie's was so tough that I had to chew it for five minutes—how can anyone make osso bucco *tough?*— but I didn't tell her that, of course."

Jake hadn't seen his father so animated since...hell, he didn't know when. He could hardly believe that less than three hours ago, Pop had been on the verge of cardiac arrest, his blood pressure in the toilet, and he'd been almost catatonic from the numerous bee stings.

Amazing what the thought of a good meal could do for a guy. Oh, and drugs.

"Elwood," Pop said, plucking at Jake's sleeve just as he was ready to leave the little curtained room.

"What is it, Pop?" Jake asked, suddenly nervous, and searching his father's face for the truth. "Are you feeling all right? I can stay, you know—I'm sure Vivien would go and get—"

"Yes, yes, I'm fine, for Pete's sake—Jesus, Mary, and Joseph, I'm not made out of glass, Elwood."

"What is it, then?" Jake asked.

Pop glanced at Vivien, who was prudently waiting just out of earshot at the edge of the curtain, then he said in a low voice, "You take your time, sonny, all right? It'll be hours before they get me settled and get all the testing done and let me eat—I know how these prisons work—and so you just take your time at the restaurant. I picked a really nice one—God knows you can afford it. Wine and dine her a little—I'll still be here when you get back. No need to rush."

Jake straightened up and looked at his father askance. "Pop, what the—"

"She's the one, isn't she? The girl in New York? From way back? I didn't put it together right away—and you didn't *bother* to tell me, you blithering idiot—but then I remembered her."

Pop shook his head like he didn't know *what* to think of his son—like he'd just been arrested for murder—and continued, "You can thank me later for setting this up, and *don't* mess things up this time, Genius, all right? And you bring me the best damned osso bucco in Grand Rapids as a thank you—and make sure they put polenta with it, not potatoes, not tonight—and some cannoli, yes three cannoli— one pistachio, two chocolate, you got that? You do that, or I'll run off with her myself. And you *know* we DeRiccios are irresistible to women."

Jake barely managed to control a smile. "Well, Vivien did tell me she thought you were adorable. So I guess I'd—"

"She did?" Pop actually shot up from his half-reclined position in the hospital bed. "She said that?" His cheeks pinked a little beneath the bee stings.

"Yep. And since I'm a good guy, I promise not to smother you—my rival—in your hospital bed, and instead I'll go off and wine and dine her while you get poked and prodded and show your bare ass to the nurses— Oh, don't deny it, Pop. I'm a doctor. I know how things work in a hospital," Jake said with a broad smile as he made his escape.

Thank God. Thank God Pop's all right.

That sentiment—and the silly fact that his pop was playing matchmaker from his hospital bed—made Jake feel almost giddy as he came out of the curtained carrel in the ER.

"Well, you heard the man," Jake said to Vivien. "We'd better go get him some dinner. And he said to take our time so he can get settled in his room."

"What about your sisters?" Vivien asked as he started for the driver's-side door of his car. "I'm sure they're waiting to hear from you. I'll drive so you can text them."

Jake sighed and pivoted to go to the passenger door. "I might just as well call them—even if I text, they'll just call me anyway. Look." He held up his phone and she saw six missed calls from Mattie and five from Irene, along with twenty text notifications.

Fifteen minutes later, they were seated at Federico's. Even though it was Friday, because it was midafternoon, they were able to get a cozy booth tucked in the back. It was terribly, horribly, wonderfully romantic, with lush navy velvet upholstery and a cluster of three real candles on the table, along with a small bud vase of fragrant peonies. Traditional Italian music played at the perfect volume in the background, and the light sconces on the walls cast golden glows on idyllic paintings of Tuscany landscapes. Vivien felt like she was in *The Godfather*.

Vivien ordered a negroni, and between phone calls, Jake decided on a glass of Primitivo. He was still talking to one of his sisters—maybe Irene, whom Vivien was pretty sure was the second one; Mathilda, a.k.a. Mattie, was the eldest—but Vivien could tell the conversation was wrapping up. He'd had to give each of his siblings all of the same information despite the fact that he'd probably texted the info as well, and she could see that he was quite ready to be done with it.

Just as their drinks—and a bread basket—arrived, he disconnected the last call.

"I really need this," he said, lifting the wine to smell it. "Mm. Nice. My sisters make me crazy sometimes. Most of the time."

Vivien submerged a quiet pang of sorrow that she didn't have a sister to drive her crazy (although sometimes Liv did anyway, at least in her mind). She helped herself to a hunk of crusty bread and dragged it through the greenish-yellow olive oil sprinkled with salt and pepper. She was starving.

There was silence for a moment as they looked through the menus. Vivien felt both awkward and utterly comfortable —how was that possible?—sitting here at a restaurant across from the man with whom she'd once shared everything.

Finally, he put the menu down and looked at her with those dark, dark eyes as candlelight smoldered between them. "Vivien...thank you." That was all he said, but there were volumes in the tone and in his gaze.

The lump in her throat made it impossible for her to respond right away, so she nodded, then lifted her glass. "To Ricky," she said when she found her voice. "May he live another three decades or more, thus ensuring all of your thick, gorgeous hair goes completely gray."

Jake laughed, his eyes warm over the rim of his wine glass. "To Pop's health."

They placed their orders, including the to-go, and then there was nothing left to do but talk.

"What happened with your mom?" Vivien spoke first purposely in order to divert the conversation from the uncomfortable topic she knew was coming.

"She was being treated for colorectal adenocarcinoma—

uh, colon cancer—and she seemed to be doing well, responding to chemo as expected. We'd all visited her here—it'll be two years ago in September. Then one day in November I got a call from Pop—not much different from today's call—that they were on their way to the hospital because she was feeling really sick. We were all in shock when she died later that night—it was sepsis from the chemo, and it took her really fast—before any of us could even think about getting on a plane."

"So none of you really got to say goodbye to her." Vivien reached across the table and touched his hand. "That's awful. I'm sorry."

"No, we didn't—although at least we'd all seen her a short while earlier. That's why everyone was so—tense, I guess, today. My sisters and Dom were already making reservations to fly in." He turned his hand upside down so that her fingers slipped into his palm.

His hand, his skin, the texture, the shape...it all felt good. Right. Familiar.

Vivien pulled her hand away under the guise of adjusting her seat.

Too much. Too much.

"How's your mom? And your grandmother?" he asked.

"Gran died last year," Vivien replied. "She left me a little bit of money, and that's how I bought the theater with cash."

"I'm sorry. I know you were close. I only met her the one time, but she was a nice, really fun woman. I loved the way she just broke out into song and dance right in the middle of Bryant Park—remember, you were talking about some hot new show on Broadway? She collected quite the audience. I think it had something to do with the content of the song, but I can't remember."

Vivien's eyes stung a little, and she laughed through the glimmer of tears. "I remember that. It was 'Ohmigod You Guys' from *Legally Blonde*, and she inadvertently made about fifteen bucks in tips that night after singing and dancing her butt off for five minutes—which she donated to the animal shelter in Wicks Hollow. Oh, I do miss her a *lot*. But it's because of her that I was able to move back here. So I'm okay with it. She had a good, long life.

"And as for my mom—well, she's living in Boise with her husband. She's been clean and sober for six years and counting now. He's really good with her—they met at a dog park near where she lived at the time. She got an emotional support dog to help with her anxiety and addictive behaviors, and it's really helped keep her healthy."

"I've been thinking about getting Pop a dog," Jake said. "He could use someone else around the house, you know?"

"Having seen how it's helped Mom, I'd say that's a great idea." She was about to say something else when Jake lifted a hand to stop her.

"I know what you're doing, trying to keep the conversation going in every other direction. But we have to talk about it, Vivien."

She sighed and slumped a little against the back of the booth as their salads arrived. "I know. It's just so difficult to acknowledge there's a real ghost haunting my theater. But I don't have any other explanation—"

He was chuckling, shaking his head with a weird expression. "I meant we needed to talk about the fact that someone is trying to sabotage you. Not...the other." He looked a little pained.

"Oh, I see. *You* don't want to admit there's supernatural activity involved," she said, conveniently putting aside her own reluctance to talk about it. Because, obviously, it was time. "But what else can it be? We literally rolled the scaffolding out from the back room—it was unattached, freestanding—there were no wires on it, nothing that could have caused it to shake and shimmy like that—"

"The whole stage floor was shaking, Viv—that's why it felt like the scaffolding was moving."

"And how on *earth* did someone make that happen? That would have taken some serious machinery. And what about the rattling light cans and shaking flies—and the sudden, intense cold? And the smell?" She shook her head. "No way that was manufactured—at least by anyone human. It was too instantaneous, too intense, and too...whatever. Creepy."

He looked down into the bowl of his wine glass as he swirled its dark red contents.

"Are you saying you don't believe in ghosts? In the afterlife? In spirits?" she asked.

Great. He must've thought she was nuts when they were together and she talked about feeling Liv's presence nearby, or even talking to her. *Ugh.* No wonder things hadn't worked out.

"I'm not saying that at all." He looked up, his eyes hooded. "Look, I've been around death enough to have experiences...that, uh, indicate that... Well, there's a lot going on we might not understand." He gave a short laugh. "I've never experienced anything before like what happened at the theater, but when people die, there's often...things that happen."

"Like what?"

"Well, once there was a patient—when I was on a hospice rotation—who was telling me about how she was going to stay with her sister Anne, and how excited she was about going on the 'journey'—she used that word. She said Anne had just stopped by and told her to get ready for the trip, and that she'd be back for her soon...and it turned out her sister Anne had been dead for five years. But this patient had carried on an entire conversation with her that was overhead by one of the nurses. Obviously, Anne was there to, uh, guide my patient to the afterlife or whatever." He shrugged. "I'm not going to dismiss the idea of ghosts. I just have never experienced them before. Myself."

Vivien tilted her head a little and looked at him intently. "Your mom never visited you after she died? You never, you know, felt her or anything?"

He shook his head. "No. I guess...I guess some people are maybe just more susceptible or open to supernatural happenings."

"Well, susceptible or not, you and I experienced supernatural happenings today, and, let's be honest, the other night when we opened that trunk in the pit and it got all cold and frosty all of a sudden."

"I can't deny it. Doesn't mean I have to like it," he said.

"Right. But do you remember what you were saying when all that frenzy whipped up?" she said, giving him a crafty smile.

"Not really," he said, but she could tell he was hedging.

"You were saying that someone was messing around with

me, trying to make me think there was a spirit or phantom haunting the place, but that it was all a fake—and then suddenly, all hell broke loose. Pretty sure that wasn't just coincidence. It was the ghost's way of saying, 'Not so fast, buddy.'" She sipped her drink and eyed Jake as he struggled with that tidbit of information.

It was cute watching the methodical, logical man who dealt in life and death all the time try to come to grips with the fact that there were, in fact, spirits and ghosts and metaphysical layers to their world.

"Hmm" was all he said, and then was rescued, so to speak, when their dinner arrived.

"Oh...*wow*," Vivien said as she sampled her lasagne Bolognese a moment later. "This is *heavenly*. I haven't had a meal this good since I left New York. How's yours?"

He'd ordered grilled branzino with sides of pasta aglio olio and green beans. "Pretty good. Not that I expected anything less. Pop knows where to get his Italian food."

"I hope the osso bucco is up to snuff," she said.

"If this is any indication, I'd say it will be. Vivien, I'm worried about you."

She paused with a bite of lasagne halfway to her mouth. "Because of the break-ins at the theater? Or because of the ghost?"

"Because someone wants to hurt you—if not physically, then at least financially. I know Captain Longbow and Helga are working their angles, following up on their leads, but that doesn't make me worry less."

"I appreciate that. I've been thinking about this logically —pretty much nonstop. The bottom line is, someone doesn't want the theater to open, either because it's *me* or because they just don't want the theater to open. I can't think of any reason why either would be true—wouldn't anyone who lives in Wicks Hollow want another successful business to keep the economy of the place going? And have what was sort of an eyesore become a viable business? And I really can't think of any reason someone from high school would hate me so much that they'd do all these things."

He twirled the wine glass stem between his fingers. "Is there any chance Roger Hatchard or his son are involved? Or Michael Wold or—who's the actress? Oh, Penny someone."

"Penny Stern, and absolutely none. None of them are even in Wicks Hollow—and aren't scheduled to be here until the last week in August. Roger is doing this as a favor to me—"

"As a favor to his son's girlfriend, you mean."

Ah. So that was where this was going. "Daniel and I weren't serious at all. I haven't talked to him for over a week. It's not him or Roger, Jake—it's just *not*."

He shrugged. "All right." He relaxed a little. "But the fact remains, someone's out to get you. First it was just scary things, then it was your car. I'm worried *you* might be next, VL."

Her insides squiggled a little. She'd been trying not to think about that obvious escalation. "I'm best friends with a cop—everyone in town knows that. Plus, you saw my place— it's practically on top of the neighbors on all sides. Everything that's happened so far has been at the theater, so I'm inclined to think it's going to stay focused there. But," she added, "Helga offered Butch to me, and maybe I'll take her up on having him stay the night."

"That's a good idea," he said reluctantly. "But—and I'm

just going to put this out there—you don't have to stay alone. If you're nervous about being alone at night."

"I'm not, but it might be a good idea to bunk somewhere else for a night or two," she said, feeling a mischievous grin twitch her lips. "Does your dad have an extra bed at his house?"

"What?" His eyes went wide, then he laughed. "Oh, he'd *love* that."

She laughed too. "I was only joking—unless you think it would be good for him to have someone there when he gets home from the hospital. Anyway, I'm not worried about staying alone—especially if I can have Butch."

"Well, at least put my cell number in your phone. Just in case," he said.

"I already have your number—I mean, I still have it from NYU...unless you changed it."

Vivien had nearly deleted it a hundred times over the years, but something had always kept her from doing so. She'd told herself it was because she wanted to know if the lying, cheating dickwad ever tried to contact her again—just so she could have the pleasure of ignoring him.

He looked surprised, but he made no comment. "It's the same. I, uh, Helga gave me yours—for when I was picking you up this morning," he added lamely.

The server brought their bill just then, along with the to-go order, and Jake swiped up the tab before Vivien even had a chance to take a look at it. "My treat," he said.

"Jake—"

"Pop insisted. Argue with him, all right?"

When they walked out to his car, Jake paused as he opened the passenger door for her. He had a contemplative look on his face. "You never did tell me what song you were singing in my shower yesterday."

He was standing very close to her, and Vivien's heart gave a traitorous thump. God, he was so dark and sexy with all that thick hair blowing in the light breeze and his intense eyes and that amazing mouth she'd been trying not to notice all night... but it was definitely the negroni that was making her head feel light and the rest of her all warm and sizzling and not him. It couldn't be him.

She gave him a saucy look. "I was singing 'I'm Gonna Wash That Man Right Outa My Hair.' *Obviously*."

"Obviously," he murmured, and she recognized the look in his eyes a heartbeat before he moved in.

His hands, warm and callused, cupped her face, his thumbs brushing her cheeks. His hips bumped against hers, pinning her lightly against the car as he eased closer, holding her gaze. "But did it work?" he whispered, his breath warm against her mouth. He gently nibbled the top of her parted lips, sliding his tongue lightly along the sensitive underside. "Let's find out."

Vivien shivered as she stepped into the kiss and met his mouth—an event that was both wildly, terribly familiar and at the same time new and different.

And *hot*.

So hot.

He still tasted like Jake, with an underscore of wine and coffee—and he felt the same against her, felt *right* and comfortable, and yet there were so many things that weren't the same, because it had been so long and they were so different...and there was so much that had happened since then.

"I think I need stronger shampoo," she murmured against his mouth when he eased away to catch his breath. "Industrial strength."

His smile brushed her lips, then he kissed her gently at the corner of her mouth. "Won't work," he said, then, sliding his hands down along her arms, he stepped back. His gaze was shadowed as he looked down at her, but his words were firm and clear: "I've never stopped loving you, VL. No shampoo is going to change that."

And, having dropped that megaton bomb, he walked around to the other side of the car and got in.

CHAPTER SIXTEEN

VIVIEN WAS quiet on the ride back to Wicks Hollow. She was still tingling from that volcanic kiss, and still reeling from his gigantic pronouncement.

How could that be?

And what was she supposed to do about it?

In an effort to *not* think about yet another upset in her life, she spent some of the drive scrolling through the emails and messages on her tablet, responding to clients. The trendy fashion company GetBack Togs had green-lit the proposal for Louise London's social media posts, and so that project would soon be in full swing, and that meant a nice little payday for Vivien (and a much bigger one for Louise) in a few months.

She tried not to think about the man sitting next to her, whose strong, capable hands managed the drive while he spoke to his sisters again via speaker in the car. The siblings apparently needed one last assurance that their father was going to be all right overnight (although Mathilda seemed put out that Jake wasn't going to stay at the hospital with him).

Instead of stewing over the way Jake had felt and tasted,

plastered up against her—and what he'd said—she found it easier to mull over the few minutes when she and Ricky DeRiccio had been alone in the hospital room. Jake had stepped out, ostensibly to take a call on his cell, but she suspected he wanted a few private words with the attending physician and the nurse on the floor.

"Bring that chair closer," Mr. DeRiccio had ordered Vivien. "I got something I wanna ask you, and I don't need the whole floor to hear it."

The chair legs scraped over the floor as she drew closer to him. The welts from his bee stings had subsided significantly and now just looked like a splattering of zits. Having eaten his fill of osso bucco, polenta, and cannoli, he looked—as Gran would say—fat and happy, despite the IV needle and blood-pressure cuff that were still attached.

"You were going with Elwood back in New York, right?" he said, taking her completely by surprise.

"Yes. We knew each other about ten, eleven years ago." She kept it vague, not certain what Jake had told his father— and what Jake *wanted* him to know.

He nodded wisely. "That's what I thought. Took me too long to put it together—getting a little foggy in my brain. You messed up my boy but good, you know. Back then."

The lingering pleasure from her dinner and the time spent with Jake—and the kiss—disintegrated. "I didn't—"

"*I* didn't notice it, but my Margaret did. She always had a better sense of the kids than I do. Now, Elwood, he wouldn't talk about it much, but she was worried about him for a while there, with him moving all the way to Raleigh and all."

"I'm—"

"Now, if you keep trying to interrupt me, he's gonna

come back before I get to my point here. Don't know how long it takes to lecture up a doctor, but I guess my boy will take his time, do it right." He grinned under his mustache. "Still, we ain't got all night."

Vivien nodded, trying to ignore the block of stone that had settled in her middle.

"All right, then." He seemed pleased with her silence. "You had the sister, the twin, didn't you? The one who died?"

Again, he surprised her. She nodded, uncertain whether answering his question was permitted at this time or whether she was still required to remain silent a little longer so he could get to his point.

He started to speak, then hesitated, looking nervously toward the door. Mystified, she nevertheless remained quiet and waited for him to go on. He shifted awkwardly in the bed, fumbling with the controller that raised and lowered the mattress, and finally got himself positioned a little more upright—a little closer to her.

Vivien leaned nearer as well and didn't expect it when he gripped her hand with callused, gnarled fingers. "I gotta question for you." His voice was very low, hardly audible over the sounds of the machines beeping and humming in the room. "Do you ever... Does she ever...well...visit you? Your sister?"

Vivien heaved a mental sigh of relief. "Yes." She looked at him and saw hope and anxiety in his eyes, and she understood what he was really asking. "We talk, you know? I know she's there. Sometimes I feel her—her name was Liv—touching me on my arm. It's always my left arm, because she always stood on that side of me. It was a habit from when we were little because it was easier to tell us apart if we were always on the same side of each other." The hair prickled a little on her left arm just then, and she rubbed it gently. *Thanks, Liv.*

His fingers loosened a little on her hand. "Good." He was about to say something else, but the door to the room opened and Jake came in.

He gave Vivien a curious look then said, "Well, Pop, I've given them all the instructions. They're going to wait to give you the shots till after we leave—much as I love you, I don't need to see your hairy white ass—and they promise to be gentle when they jam the catheter in. Sound all right?"

His father rolled his eyes and chased them out of the room as well as he could, being in bed and wired up, as he put it.

"I'll be back tomorrow in the morning. First thing," Jake promised. "Don't bug the nurses too much, all right? I told them they could knock you out if you were too demanding. All right? I love you, Pop."

Vivien was still chuckling when they climbed into the car for the ride back, and when they got to the outskirts of Wicks Hollow, it was after eight o'clock.

The sky glowed in a showy blaze of magenta, crimson, and gold just above the horizon line, and its reflection shimmered with every movement of the lake below. Beyond the splashes of breathtaking color, the sky was still pale blue. But Vivien knew that as soon as the sun began to dip below the edge of the world, darkness would come quickly and everything would phase into dark blues and dusky purples, and end with the inky black of night.

"I'm really sorry to keep you from your work all day," Jake said, obviously noticing she was looking at messages on her tablet. "I so appreciate you going with me. And I think Pop liked having you there too."

"He's pretty sweet," she said.

"I told him you thought he was adorable. Pretty sure he's got a serious crush on you." Jake smiled in the dim light—a flash of teeth and the shadow of a dimple.

"The feeling's mutual. I think he misses your mom a lot. Getting him a dog is a really good idea."

He shot her a quick look. "You talked to him about her?"

"Sort of. Anyway, I can tell he really appreciates having you nearby, but I think a dog would give him something else to do besides poke at bees' nests."

"He and Doug Horner are supposed to go golfing next week—that's who called the ambulance today. Dr. Horner was dropping off some golf clubs and found Pop in not-so-good shape. I can ask him if he knows of an older dog in need of adoption that would be good for my dad."

"Good idea. Oh, wow, I just got a text from Helga. It says, 'Volt or Elantra.' I guess that means Baxter has narrowed down the brake lights of the car you saw last night."

Jake nodded. "That's good. Sounds like she and Joe Cap are on it."

"That reminds me—do you mind if we swing by the theater so I can just check and make sure everything's all right, all things considered? We left in kind of a hurry."

"Sure."

Jake wasn't about to admit it to anyone, but he wasn't all that excited about going into the theater at night. He wasn't afraid, exactly...he just didn't really want to be faced with whatever crazy supernatural thing was going on in there.

But all the way back on the drive, he'd been calculating

ways to convince Vivien she should go over to his house for a while—after all, it was still earlyish—instead of dropping her off at her house. Now this detour would give him more time to consider his options, but that also meant they had to face the unpleasant reminder of whatever was happening at the theater.

Once they arrived, he parked in front and they went in the main door.

"We're ba-aack," Vivien called, leaving Jake bemused as she pushed through the swinging doors that led to the house.

Was she really talking to the ghost—or whatever it was?

All right. It *was* a ghost or some sort of haunting. He guessed he had to admit that at least.

"We're here," she said, jogging up the stairs onto the stage. He followed at a more leisurely pace, looking around to see if anything else had changed since they left to meet Pop at the hospital.

"No need to be upset, all right?" she went on, speaking to the house at large as if she were delivering lines from a show. "We've come to the conclusion that you exist, that you're here —no question.

"I don't know why you're angry. I hope it's not because I want to open the theater again, because that's going to really put us at odds, and I was hoping we could just get along. I mean, every theater should have a phantom, right? I don't really want to bring in a priest or, I dunno, a medium, or whoever exorcises ghosts—unless you're trying to tell me something—"

Her voice trailed off as a great blast of light exploded from the stage, highlighting her as if it were an extraterrestrial's spaceship hovering above and beyond. A great roaring noise accompanied the burst of light, filling the space, vibrating through Jake's body.

The blue-white light poured from the stage, surrounding Vivien like a blazing, illuminated shower. She stood there, unmoving, and for a minute he thought she was somehow trapped or paralyzed—or being absorbed into the great, raging light.

He ran down the aisle to the stage, shouting her name over the tumultuous roaring that filled the theater. Wind whipped up from nowhere, and he fought against it, trying to get to the stage...but it held him back, pushed at him like a hurricane throwing tiny, sharp, icy knives at him as he fought to get closer.

"Stop!" she cried, her voice cutting through the storm. "Enough! That's enough! We're here to help—now *stop this!*"

To Jake's utter shock, it listened. The roaring fury ceased with hardly a whimper. The light fizzled into a small white circle, then popped dark like a burned-out bulb. The wind died. The air warmed.

"Vivien!" Jake cried, stumbling toward the stage after his sudden release from the rush that had forced him back.

She was cold to the touch. Her fingers were icy, her breath coming in frosty gasps even though the temperature in the theater had returned to normal. Her eyes were glassy, and for one terrifying moment, Jake feared she'd been possessed or somehow taken over by whatever haunted this place. But then she shivered and her eyes focused, and she smiled up at him, clear and lucid.

"It listened," she exclaimed. "Did you see that? It stopped! It listened when I told it to stop!"

Jake, who'd been shocked and terrified out of his mind,

could hardly fathom this gleeful reaction to what—from his perspective—had looked like she was about to be absorbed into a metaphysical fog, or possessed by, or taken away...or something. He couldn't speak. All he could do was pull her close and feel the warmth of her body against his while he tried to keep from trembling. And puking.

She hugged him back, then shrugged loose, still with that excitement in her demeanor. And that caused him to fear that she *had* been possessed or her mind had been overtaken somehow—for how could she be so lighthearted and giddy after what had just happened?

"Jake, I think we're making progress. If it knows we're here as friends, it doesn't have to be so violent. That's got to be why it's so angry—because it needs something from us, from me. *Right?*" The last word she shouted up and out into the theater as if delivering some important line.

A flicker of light from above beamed down, then was gone again immediately.

Jesus. Jake could hardly believe he was standing there while his...while Vivien communicated with a freaking *ghost.* As if it was no big deal.

CHAPTER SEVENTEEN

"WELL, THAT WAS INTERESTING." Vivien's voice was weak and thready as they walked out into the theater's parking lot. She sounded exhausted.

Jake was feeling much the same way. It had been a long and emotional day, not even including the two—count 'em, *two*—ghostly appearances. Nevertheless, he looked around to make certain no one was lurking. Hopefully, being seen by a cop last night had scared away whoever was messing with things. He only hoped they wouldn't transfer their attentions to Vivien's home instead of her business.

"I thought ghosts were only supposed to haunt in the dead of night," he said as they climbed into his car. "It's all over the place with its haunting schedule."

"I don't know the rules. Maybe Liv can talk to them and clear things up," she added with a bark of wry laughter.

He chuckled too, and realized with a start that he actually believed that was possible.

At this point, did he have a choice?

"I wish my hot tub was ready," he said with a sigh. "It would be a great night to soak under the stars."

"You're getting a hot tub? Out on the patio, so you can simmer and soak while watching the sun set, with a glass of wine in your hand?" Her eyes were big and dreamy.

"I wasn't really getting a hot tub, but I am now," he replied with a grin. "That sounds perfect." Then he looked at her. "My house or yours?"

She hesitated for a split second, then said, "I have work to catch up on. It's home for me, and a nice glass of bourbon for company."

Jake got the message, and, although he was disappointed, he understood. "I won't argue if you promise me Helga's bringing Butch over to chaperone you tonight."

"I'll text her right now."

To Jake's slight disappointment, Helga met them at Vivien's house right away, as she'd had Butch with her on patrol. That meant he didn't get to say goodbye to Vivien alone, and that he had to field questions about his pop. Apparently, Doug Horner had been filling in the Tuesday Ladies all about the events of the day, and the gossip trail went on from there.

Seeing that the two females were about to settle into a detailed discussion about Butch's overnight requirements, he decided to throw in the towel for the evening. He had to get up early tomorrow anyway to get to the hospital and get Pop home. He'd already found someone to cover his shift in the morning, fortunately, but he had sourdough that was ready to be made into bread.

Mixing and kneading bread dough would be a very

relaxing way to end a rollercoaster of a day—since he couldn't have a hot tub or Vivien.

And it would also give him time to think.

"SOUNDS like you had lots of excitement yesterday," said Orbra as Vivien ventured into the Tea House via the back entrance. She'd brought Butch to hang out with his great-aunt while she waited for Helga to come and pick her up.

"How's Ricky doing?" Orbra continued after having given Butch an appropriate greeting. "Have a seat up there with Maxine and Juanita—if you don't, they'll just shout across the place at you until you do," she added, shaking her head as they walked into the main seating area. "Not a good look for the customers."

"Mr. DeRiccio should be coming home today. He was doing much better once they pumped some steroids into him," Vivien replied.

"That's what we heard. We've got a bunch of meals put together for him—Maxine and Juanita are going to take things over this afternoon after he gets home and settled."

"That's very nice of you," Vivien replied, suddenly feeling guilty that one, she hadn't thought to do the same, and two, that she didn't cook, so she couldn't even if the thought *had* occurred to her. She supposed she could bring him a pizza—the guy was Italian; he'd probably go for that.

Vivien had no choice but to sit with Maxine and Juanita, even if she would prefer not to have to talk about everything that had been going on over the last week. But she wanted tea and food, and she'd walked here so Helga could come by when she had a spare moment and drop Vivien off at the theater. So she headed to the table that hosted the Tuesday Ladies.

Maxine and Juanita, along with Iva, were sitting at their regular table at the front window of the tea shop. A Scrabble board took over a portion of the round top, but there was plenty of space for teapots (each a different style and shape), cups and saucers, and the plate-sized three-tier servers of scones, muffins, and paper-thin sandwiches. Vivien's stomach growled in anticipation. Dinner at Federico's had been a long time ago.

"Well, look at that," exclaimed Maxine in a voice that probably carried all the way to Lake Michigan. She was definitely not going to need a mic for the show. "Our esteemed director is *deigning* to mingle with us lowlifes, Nita! Now you come on over here and sit right down, missy," she demanded. "I'm about to beat Juanita here in Scrabble for the three thousandth time, but there's room for you at the table."

Maxine thwacked her cane onto an empty seat right next to her, and Vivien understood that she was to sit there. As she did, she noticed a large leather tote on the deep windowsill next to Juanita's chair. A pair of soft, furry ears, each as large as a plum and with wispy, long hair, peeked out from the bag. They were attached to the sweetest dog face she'd ever seen, with a small button nose and two very large black eyes. They blinked, watching Vivien as she took a seat.

"That's Bruce Banner," said Juanita, noticing Vivien's interest. "He can be a little testy, so go slow if you want to pet him. But he's really just a sweet little angel, aren't you, *bebecito*-Brucie?"

Deciding it wasn't worth commenting about the dog being in a café—after all, he was in a bag and not causing any problems at all—Vivien sat down. She gave Orbra her order.

"So...Scrabble, huh?" she said in an effort to *not* have to talk about what had happened over the last couple of days at the theater. "And you're winning, Maxine?"

"She is *not* winning," said Juanita as she set down seven tiles in a row: *click, click, click, click, click, click,* click. "Because I've just played a bingo on a triple word score square with a V *and* a Z."

Maxine's eyes bugged out of their sockets as she spun away from Vivien and whipped her attention to the lazy-Susan-style game board. "There's no bingo word with V *and* Z," she snarled. "You made it up like you always do—"

"Not true," said Juanita, looking pleased as punch—and fresh as a lemon drop—in a frosty-yellow maxi dress. For once, her fingernails didn't match her clothing but picked up the same rosy pink as her lipstick. She appeared extremely satisfied with herself. "'Vizards' is a perfectly acceptable Scrabble word and you know it, Maxine. Unlike 'slidiest,' which you tried to use on me last week."

Juanita's eyes danced as she went on to calculate her score. "That'll be...let me see...ah yes...twenty points for the word, tripled is sixty points, plus fifty for it being a bingo, plus the extra word I created by adding Z to 'ax'...that's another ten plus one plus eight...that's a total of one hundred twenty-nine points. On a *single word*," she said, sneering at Maxine. "I think your highest-scoring word ever was only one hundred fifteen, wasn't it Maxie?"

"I don't remember," replied Maxine, still glowering at the game board as if hoping her evil eye would somehow move the tiles around to her advantage. "Now that Vivien Leigh is here, it would be rude to continue to play the game, Juanita. Let's just put it aw—"

"Oh no you don't, you conniving woman," snapped Juanita. "We are going to finish this game, and you are going to accept your loss like the badass witch you are, Maxine, or *Dios mio*, I'll never play with you again."

Maxine huffed and grumbled, but she put aside the game box she'd picked up and turned her attention to Vivien. "She's a sore winner," she said, pursing her lips. "Because she don't win very often."

Juanita rolled her eyes and reached for a finger-sized muffin. "It's your turn, *sore loser*. See if you can play that Q you've been hoarding for three turns."

"So tell us about all those horrible things going on at the theater," Iva said. Her eyes were bright and birdlike, and she held a delicate teacup with pink roses hand-painted on it. "Break-ins and your car getting smashed... Why, I would never have thought such a thing would happen here in Wicks Hollow."

"You wouldn't?" Maxine chortled. "After three murders last year, you wouldn't think that? This place is practically Detroit now, you know, murders happening every time you turn around—and I know Detroit because I was around during those damned riots in the sixties. And proud of it! I was out there with my baton—not that I smashed any windows or anything," she added quickly.

"Maxine, I'd be shocked if you *didn't* smash any windows," Iva said in her well-modulated, ladylike tone.

That shocked Maxine into silence as she seemed to

contemplate whether Iva's comment had been an insult or a compliment.

"Oh crap," Vivien said involuntarily when she saw the text from Helga.

"What is it, dear?" asked Iva.

Vivien sighed. "Helga was going to drop me off at the theater this morning, as my rental car won't be available till *Monday*—don't get me started—but now she's been called in to help with a big accident on the highway north of town."

"Yep. Tractor-trailer did a jackknife, tipped over, and spilled a whole slew of dried corn all over the highway," Maxine said. "They gotta detour everyone down the state route and over to the county road. Everyone's backed up for miles and there's construction over on the state route too. It's a disaster. Corn everywhere. Gonna be deer feasting for months on that, then they'll be coming after my damned hostas.

"I listen to the police scanner, you know. Can't be too careful. Gotta keep apprised o' what's going on. I'll drive you, Vivien Leigh." Without further ado, she launched to her feet with the help of her cane. "Come on, Neety. We can finish the game later. Our director's gotta get to work."

"But—"

"No, no, no," said Maxine, gripping Vivien's arm with very strong fingers as she cut off her protest. "We'll take you, won't we, Neety?"

"I'll come too," said Iva, bolting to her feet and gathering up her handbag. "I've been dying to get back in there to see whether I can sense any more of the spirits haunting the place. I have a sensitivity to these things, you know."

Vivien hardly knew what to say to this. She could only

imagine what would happen if the ghost at her theater acted up while the Tuesday Ladies were there. That would *not* be good. "Oh, no, really, I can—"

"*Ay-yi-yi!*" said Juanita. "Don't argue! Maxine'll drive you. Besides, I want to see those ruby slippers again."

Iva was still talking about her sensitivity to spirits as the ladies bustled Vivien out the door. As she passed by Orbra, the proprietress pushed a bag into her hand. "Good luck!" she said with a grin, and that was when Vivien realized Orbra was *delighted* that her front table was going to be free for customers on this Saturday morning.

"Last summer when our dear friend Jean was murdered, she was haunting her own house up over on Wicks Lake," Iva said as the three ladies directed Vivien down the street. "I knew something was wrong about how she died, but I never went to the house, so I didn't realize she was trying to send a message—and sweet Diana, bless her; Jean's great-niece, you know—didn't have an open mind at all about spirits and ghosts and hauntings...

"And then there was Cherry's adorable, *very* smart niece Leslie, who opened up Shenstone House into a B&B up on the hill outside of town. We've *all* known that place was haunted for years, and the moment I walked in, I could sense it. The hair jerked right up on the back of my neck and all down my arms...but it was really when that *darling* Fiona— who I hope is going to marry my dear Hollis's dashing Gideon someday soon—opened up that little antiques shop on Violet Way that I really began to understand how to communicate with those who've gone to the afterlife. That was after she found the skeleton there, you know. I think I'm going to have to take mediumship lessons if this sort of thing continues to happen here in Wicks Hollow—"

"And what about up to the lighthouse? Just two weeks ago," said Maxine. "*You* didn't know it was haunted, no one did, but that writer, TMJ Mack—she's still there, ain't she?—she met the ghost. It saved her life by the lighthouse—or that's how she tells it."

Vivien could hardly follow the conversation, let alone all the names and events...and she didn't think she wanted to. What she did extract from the nonstop rambling from Iva, interspersed with arguments and details from the others, was that ghosts, hauntings, and strange occurrences were rather commonplace here in Wicks Hollow. At least, according to the Tuesday Ladies...who she suspected might be unreliable narrators more often than not.

Vivien had to close her eyes once Maxine hit the accelerator on her powder-blue Cadillac SUV. She simply didn't want to see everything whiz by far too quickly and closely, corners being cut short, and how near the bumpers of other cars came to the vicinity of the large vehicle. Though she clutched the bag Orbra had given her, Vivien suddenly wasn't hungry anymore.

"And here we are," chirped Iva after what felt like an eternity to Vivien. The car swung around a sharp corner then jolted to a halt, tires grinding on gravel, and she finally opened her eyes.

"Oh, dear, is all that broken glass on the ground over there from your car, Vivien? I heard someone took a bat or something to it," Iva said. "And there've been some horrible threats against you too? I simply can't imagine who would do such a thing. Whoever would do such a thing must be a very unhappy person."

"Or totally whacked in the head," said Maxine. "I vote for whacked in the head."

Vivien didn't bother to reply as she unlocked the door to the theater. She knew better than to suggest that the ladies get back to their Scrabble game; they were sticking to her like burrs and were going inside whether she wanted them there or not.

"And how was your romantic dinner with that *delicious* Elwood DeRiccio?" asked Juanita, beaming as she slipped past Vivien into the lobby.

Apparently there was no such thing as privacy in Wicks Hollow.

"We just went to get takeout for his dad," Vivien said nonchalantly.

"That's not what Ricky told Doug Horner," said Juanita. "You were gone for over two hours, he said. You don't mind if Brucie looks around, do you?" She patted the little dog's head as he poked his nose over the edge of his carrier.

"Uh...not as long as he knows where to do his business," Vivien replied, suddenly feeling terribly guilty about leaving Ricky DeRiccio in the hospital by himself while she and Jake had a definitely non-romantic, purely businesslike dinner while waiting for the carry-out.

Until Jake kissed her at the car.

"My goodness, Vivien, your cheeks are awfully pink. Are you feeling all right?" Iva said as she walked in past her. The short, curvy woman sailed through the lobby and into the house, her blue and white silk scarf fluttering at her throat. Her arms were spread wide as if she were opening herself to whatever ghostly entities might abound, and Vivien hurried after her...just in case.

After all, the last time she'd been here, she'd given the ghost a bit of a lecture. For all she knew, the phantom of *her* opera might have taken umbrage with the set-down.

But the stage was silent and dark, the house empty and still. It was lit only by the lights Vivien had turned on—more than the other day now that many of the bulbs had been replaced, but still fewer than it would be when everything was up and running.

"Oh, it's so much *easier* to feel the energy now that the place is quiet and empty—nearly empty," Iva said from the stage. She turned in a slow circle in front of the scaffolding that remained in place, her arms still wide and open.

"I *feel* your presence, all of you," she announced to the room at large. "Speak to me if you will... I'm open, prepared to be your vessel of communication..."

Vivien's heart was in her throat as she hurried to the stage, knowing that at any moment, all hell could break loose.

Liv, if you're here, make sure it—they—whoever—doesn't do anything, please.

"I feel you," said Iva, still spinning in a slow circle. She ignored the sudden high-pitched yapping of Bruce Banner, who'd been turned loose among the audience seats and had found either a rodent or a scrap of paper that clearly needed to be put in its place.

Juanita and Maxine were arguing as they clomped down the aisle on the far left of the house, and Vivien was grateful she was far enough away she couldn't hear what this particular topic was, although she caught a phrase that sounded like "...from a trapeze..." that made her blood run cold.

Thank goodness *Arsenic and Old Lace* didn't have any elements that needed special effects.

Vivien stepped onto the stage just as Iva finished her slow circle and opened her eyes.

"Nothing yet," she said soothingly to Vivien. "Don't worry; just give them time. They must be a little shy."

Right.

"I'll just—"

A sudden chilly breeze ruffled Vivien's hair, and Iva's cornflower-blue eyes went wide.

"I feel something," she said in a stage whisper.

Vivien looked around, waiting for craziness, ready to leap into action to protect her unanticipated charges...but it was only a breeze. A definitely cold, definitely sharp, definitely *not normal* movement of the air, but that was it. No rattling, shaking, horrible-smelling, light-flashing events.

"I feel it," whispered Iva, holding her hands in front of her. "*Her*. It's a *female*... All right...I'm coming..."

She began to walk off stage right, her arms held out in front of her, almost as if she were in a trance. Vivien would have been terrified if Iva hadn't tossed a look over her shoulder at her and mouthed, "*Come on!*"

Vivien took two steps when she realized that it was dead quiet—Bruce Banner had stopped barking and Maxine and Juanita had stopped arguing. She looked over and saw the little dog on one of the steps of the stage. He was vibrating with tension, highly alert with his ears perked up, eyes wide, and a bit of a silent, snaggle-toothed snarl showing.

Juanita and Maxine—shockingly silent—stood there, looking around as if they, too, felt the change in the air.

Vivien waffled for a moment, then went after Iva.

She followed the older woman, who was still walking as if in a trance, backstage. But when Iva reached the stairs leading to the pit, Vivien rushed forward to take her by the arm.

"No, let's not go by the stairs," she said, her heart pounding. Iva could have tumbled down them without even realizing it.

"She wants me to go down there," Iva said, a little too dreamily for Vivien's comfort.

"No," Vivien said. "I think it's better if you stay up here." *And leave. Get out of here before something horrible happens.* "Uh, it's very dark and there are a lot of things down there you could trip on or cut yourself on..."

Iva blinked and jolted as the breeze became a virtual gust, cold and rough and sharp, bringing stinging air and the not-so-subtle putridness of death.

"It's time to leave," Vivien said firmly, her skin prickling and her hair standing on end. She needed to get them out of here.

"But—" Iva began.

"I've got a meeting I've got to be back for. I forgot," Vivien said. Keeping hold of Iva's arm, she pulled the elderly lady none-too-gently away from the danger of stairs down into darkness, even as the wind tossed and buffeted at them from behind.

"Maxine, Juanita," she called as she rushed Iva out onto the stage. "We've got to go— I forgot I..."

Bruce Banner was standing there onstage, legs far apart,

ears back, tail tucked. His ruff was straight up and his eyes were wide, practically bugging out of his little skull as he looked behind Vivien and Iva.

Vivien turned just in time to see the scaffolding move, barreling toward them as if some ghostly hand had shoved it with all its might. The lights and catwalk above began to shake and rattle violently as bulbs flashed on and off like in a disco.

"Run!" she cried.

CHAPTER EIGHTEEN

"IT WAS THE MOST AMAZING, frightening, exciting thing I've ever seen!" exclaimed the short, grandmotherly woman with pink cheeks and bright blue eyes. "Hollis, you would have been gobsmacked!"

Jake was pretty sure the older lady's name was Iva Bergstrom, but he wouldn't put money on it. He was still gobsmacked himself by the sudden, overwhelming arrival of three loud and excited women, each carrying various bundles of food, and one small, yippy dog at his father's house—which had already been invaded by Doug Horner and Hollis Nath, the veterinarian's golfing buddy and apparently Iva Bergstrom's significant other.

"The whole place was shaking and lights were flashing, and the *wind*—it was like being in the middle of a tornado *inside a building!*" Iva went on as she took a seat next to Nath in one of the chairs on Pop's back deck.

From what Jake could gather, she was telling his father and their friends about something that had happened earlier today, but he hadn't caught the details. Jake was too busy waiting on all of the unexpected guests who must have learned his pop's ETA at home after being released from the hospital.

He'd never believe his dad again when he claimed he didn't use his phone to text, because Pop sure as hell hadn't called anyone.

It wasn't until Jake heard "Vivien" and "theater" that he realized the context of the events, and he bobbled the stack of glasses and almost dropped them along with the pitcher of iced tea he was carrying to the shaded deck. The glasses and pitcher were all plastic (a prudent choice when dealing with excitable retirees and outdoor venues), but he still didn't want to have to wash everything again.

"Uh...what were you saying, Mrs....Bergstrom, is it?"

"Oh, honey, just call me Iva. I might be nearly seventy, but I feel like I'm barely your age," she said with a twinkle in her eyes. "And yes, I'd just love some iced tea. How nice of you! Ricky, your boy is simply the *sweetest* young man. I don't understand why some young woman hasn't snatched him up yet."

Pop grunted in begrudging assent—probably because he'd wanted a beer and Jake had nixed that because of the medication he was still taking.

"I'll take iced tea," Maxine Took informed Jake before he could press Iva for more details. "And some of your homemade bread—I know you got some inside; your daddy told us. Don't you be opening up the things we brought— those're for your daddy, you know. Bread with butter would be just about right. Been a long damned time and lots of excitement since breakfast at the tea shop. Makes a girl hangry, you know. And don't you be playing shy around us,

Elwood. We're just normal folk like the rest of you—even though we just saw a ghost throw a tantrum."

"A ghost?" Jake managed to say. "Where was this?" *Please not the theater. Please not the—*

"Why, it was at the theater with Vivien," said Iva. "Weren't you listening, Elwood, honey? It was quite a show she—it was definitely a she—put on. If only you could have been there!"

If only.

Jake gritted his teeth and nodded. "So, really? A ghost?"

"And it was most definitely a female entity—wouldn't you agree, Juanita?" said Iva.

"Oh, *sí*," replied Juanita, sitting like a queen in her chair in a flowing yellow dress. She'd inched her seat closer to Doug Horner, who was drinking a beer (which was probably why Pop was still giving Jake dagger eyes). "It was certainly a feminine spirit. Bruce Banner always puts his ears forward when he doesn't like a man, but when it's a female he's not sure about, he puts his ears back. His ears were definitely back, weren't they, *bebecito mio*?" she said into the face of the small black, white, and brown dog she held on her generous lap.

"Bruce Banner?" Jake found it easy to allow himself to get sidetracked by something more mundane than ghosts and their gender.

"He's named after the Hunk," Maxine told him as she snatched the cup of iced tea he'd just poured. "That green monster with the raggedy pants—his alter ego. Bruce Banner. 'You wouldn't like me when I'm hangry' from that old TV show—that's what he says, you know, and it's true about that rat-dog Bruce there. You're going about minding your own business and you reach over to pet him like this and—"

Snarl! The little dog nearly launched himself from Juanita's lap as Maxine's hand swept toward his head. His tiny body quivered as if he were about to attack, his beady black eyes bright and wary. He looked like a long-haired chihuahua except for the huge, butterflylike ears whose position could apparently indicate whether a spiritual presence was male or female.

Jake wondered what would happen if the ghost was nonbinary, and then decided *he* might need a beer—or something far stronger—if he was really worried about that sort of detail.

"See what I mean?" Maxine said, reaching out to pet Bruce again, and once again had to snatch back her hand before the tiny little teeth grabbed her.

"All right, Maxine, you've had your fun," Juanita said, batting her friend's hand away. "Elwood, love, if it's not too much trouble, I'll have some bread and butter too."

"Bring out the ham and cheese, Elwood," his pop said. "And the good spicy mustard—this stuff's great," he added to Doug Horner. "It's gotta be half horseradish, I swear. I can feel it burn right through my gut, and the damned mustard seeds get all up in my dentures, but damn, it's good going down."

Jake escaped inside to the kitchen and began to put together a tray of snacks. Fortunately, he'd stopped at the store after dropping Vivien at her house last night and had picked up a bunch of food for his dad to have on hand. He hadn't expected the Tuesday Ladies to bring food as well— enough to feed an army for a month. They'd paraded in carrying huge bags of casseroles, sandwiches, containers of soup, a roasted chicken, scones, muffins, and *two whole pies.* All for just his dad?

But apparently those items weren't allowed to be served right now…

He shook his head. He'd never quite understood the rules of hospitality.

He scrabbled around for the ham and cheese he'd been ordered to bring out, then found the pot of spicy mustard and the pumpernickel bread he'd baked last week and brought with him (it had been frozen, but no need to tell that to Maxine and her crew). He filled a bowl with cherries he'd grabbed at the store last night and put a few Cherry Newtons (his pop's favorite) on the tray as well. That might tide over the hordes.

And then he picked up his phone…and hesitated.

For the first time in over ten years, he was going to text Vivien. She'd know who it was, since she'd never deleted his number from her phone.

That had to mean something, didn't it? She'd never deleted his number.

He hesitated more, then chewed himself out for being an idiot, and typed the message: *The Tuesday Ladies met your ghost?!*

Her response was almost immediate: *Kill me now.* <eyes-bugging-out emoji>

Where are you? He hoped she wasn't still at the theater. By herself.

Home. Made an escape and came back to work. Louise London is making me glad she's six hundred miles away rn…

He breathed a sigh of relief. *Have been invaded by Tuesday*

Ladies and others at Pop's. Dinner later? His palms were a little sweaty and his belly fluttery, for Pete's sake, as he pressed send...and then waited for her reply.

Depends who's involved. <sly winky emoji>

The flutter went to a low burn and he started to respond, but a second text came in from Vivien before he finished: *I mean, if Ricky's going to be there...* <heart-eyes emoji>

Jake gave a short laugh and tried to decide how to respond, but before he could, he heard the unmistakable thumping of Maxine's cane approaching.

"You get lost in there, Elwood?" she demanded through the screen door. "We're all about to expire from lack of sustenance."

"Oh, sorry," he said, turning sharply. The phone squirted out of his hand into the sink, which, thankfully, wasn't filled with water. He snatched it back out and began to towel off the few droplets that clung to it. "I'll be right ou—"

The screen door slammed. "Gotta use the john," said Maxine, thumping in with her cane. "Old bladder ain't what it used to be."

"Sure, right down that hall..."

But she was already heading that way. "Just glad I didn't pee my pants when that ghost business started happening." She paused in the hallway, the whites of her eyes gleaming in her dark face. "I've seen some *scary* shit in my life, but that was just about enough to turn my hair dead white."

Jake could relate. He glanced down the hall and saw that Maxine was out of sight, giving him a moment of peace to respond to Vivien.

Sadly, Pop will be out of commission tonight. I'll make sure of it. Dinner at my place, watch the sun set?

He was carrying the tray out to the deck when he heard the text alert ding through the kitchen window, and he hurried to lay everything out so he could see whether she'd go for it. He was more nervous than when he'd asked out the goddess Amanda Grifton all those years ago.

Damn—he'd forgotten napkins, and hurried back inside to get them, still refusing to let himself look at his phone until the guests and their refreshments were settled.

Maxine was just stepping out of the bathroom as he came back in. "Now you come on and sit with us, Elwood, so we can tell you all about that ghost and you can tell us just what's going on with you and our Vivien Leigh. Iva and Juanita get all nosy about stuff like that, and I won't hear the end of it until we get all the juicy details."

She curled her gnarled, arthritic fingers around his arm and, like it or not, the next thing Jake knew, he was being maneuvered onto the deck...

...with his phone still sitting on the kitchen counter, leaving him in suspense about what Vivien's answer was.

It was over an hour later that he finally had the chance to look.

Haven't bought new shampoo yet...what time?

VIVIEN WAS ready when Jake picked her up at seven thirty.

"Sorry about the choppy comms this afternoon," he said.

"You said you'd been invaded by the Tuesday Ladies. I understood the delay," she said with a grin. "That's how they ended up at the theater today. Maxine and Co. give new meaning to the term 'railroaded.'" She picked up the tote bag that conspicuously held a bottle of wine, her tablet, and her wallet, as well as—far less conspicuously—some overnight things.

Juuuust in case.

"Ah…is it all right if we stop by Pop's house? He asked me to pick up something at the store, but I think it's just an excuse for him to see you."

Vivien was delighted. "Yes, of course. I'd love to see him. Did you already get the thing he wanted from the store?"

"Yes, why?"

"I'd like to bring him some flowers— Wait a sec. I'll cut some from the backyard."

"Pop'll be over the moon if you bring him flowers," Jake told her with a grin.

A few minutes later, she was back with a cluster of blooms. She wasn't sure what type of flowers they were, but the colors were bright and cheerful.

"Oh, no," Jake muttered as they drove down a quiet residential street a few minutes later. "They're still here. Or they came back."

Vivien had seen Maxine's car a moment before he spoke. "I almost died in that vehicle earlier today," she said when they parked next to it. "No joke."

The two of them were greeted like long-lost friends by the Tuesday Ladies, Doug Horner, Hollis Nath, and Ricky DeRiccio. From the looks of the deck, they'd been sitting there eating and drinking and talking for hours.

"There she is!" said Maxine. "Vivien, we need to tell you what we've figured out. Sit right here."

"About what?" she said, taking the chair Maxine

indicated while innocently ignoring the wild and silent plea in Jake's eyes: *No, no, don't do it!*

And damn, he looked good in the white linen button-down that fit his broad shoulders just right. Waaay too good. His hair was damp as if he'd just showered, and he'd pulled it back in a short tail so he looked far too much like Antonio Banderas as Zorro. Not to mention how delicious he'd smelled when she sat next to him in the car. *Whew.*

Vivien figured a stop-off at the parents' house (so to speak) might settle her hormones a little, because right now they were all up in her business and very interested in submitting to a medical exam by the handsome doctor.

And she just wasn't sure if that was a good idea.

"So if there's a ghost haunting the theater," Iva was saying as Vivien dragged her attention up from Jake's muscular legs, "that means it's upset about something. It needs to be put to rest, you know."

"Iva thinks she knows *everything* about hauntings," Maxine said. "My granny used to tell me all about what they did down south, you know, back when she was little and they had all them haints down there. Painted the porch ceiling blue, they did—you ought to paint the ceiling at the theater blue, there, Vivien Leigh. Mebbe that'll keep them ghosts away."

"That's an interesting idea," Vivien replied, and felt Liv brush against her left arm. She had a feeling her twin was laughing.

"*Anyway,*" said Iva, raising her voice in an effort to be heard over Maxine, "as I was saying, a ghost means a soul is not at rest—usually because some wrong has been done to them and they need to set it right before they go off to the afterlife.

So we need to find out if someone died on the grounds of the theater, and then we can determine how to make things right."

Vivien was more than a little concerned about all of the "wes" in that speech, so she demurred. "I'll definitely check into that. But I haven't heard anything about anyone dying at the theater, so I don't know."

"Maybe it's built on a Native American burial ground," said Juanita. "And that's why it's never been a successful business. You ever hear about any ghosts before this, Maxie?"

"Not a one. But who knows? Wicks Hollow's kinda like that Hell Mountain thingy from—what's her name? That skinny blond girl with the stick?"

"You mean Buffy?" said Ricky, surprising all of them. "What?" he demanded when everyone stared at him. He was just *not* the target audience for *Buffy the Vampire Slayer*. "I liked that show. She kicked some serious butt."

"And it's the Hell*mouth*," said Juanita. "I swear, Maxine, you say the wrong things on purpose just for attention, don't you?"

"Memory ain't what it used to be," grumbled Maxine. "Don't need to be mean about it. At least I can *see* and *hear* all right...unlike some other people around here. *Juanita*," she added in a stage whisper.

"All right, then," said Jake, standing purposefully. "We've got to get going now."

"Oh, but wait—I wanted to tell you one more thing," said Iva.

"What's the hurry, Elwood? Sit back down," said his father. "Always running off and leaving me. Did I tell you he took over *two hours* to get me dinner last night?" He cast a sly wink at Vivien, who giggled at the consternation and mortification on Jake's face.

"Come on, take a load off, son," said Hollis Nath, who was sitting very cozily next to Iva. He was a little overdressed for hanging around outside on a summer afternoon, in creased slacks and a suit coat, but he didn't seem uncomfortable at all. "What's the rush? Where's the fire? Have a seat, Elwood."

"I've got steaks sitting on the counter defrosting," Jake said weakly, but he sat.

"Anyway, I wanted to tell you that when the ghost—it was a female, did I tell you that?" Iva began.

"Yes, I believe you did," replied Vivien, deliberately avoiding Jake's attempt to catch her eyes. Inside, she was still giggling.

"All right, so when the ghost was talking to me—well, she wasn't really talking, she was just sort of...leading me, I guess you'd say—"

"Leading you to the stairs where you might have fallen down into the pit," Vivien said darkly, and had the pleasure of seeing Hollis straighten up.

"What's this? You didn't tell me about that, Iva! Now that puts a whole different spin on things. Maybe you shouldn't be messing around with this supernatural business if you're going to be in danger—"

"Now, darling, please don't get your boxers in a twist," said Iva in her prim voice as she patted his knee. "I was in no danger whatsoever. I knew exactly where I was all the time, and if Vivien wouldn't have stopped me, I was going to go down the stairs—they led to the orchestra pit? Very interesting—and see what she—the ghost, was trying to tell me."

"*I* heard music," said Maxine, wresting the group's attention from Iva.

"So did I," Iva snapped. "That's what I'm trying to tell her—"

"I didn't recognize it until we figured out that—"

"—it was from *The Nutcracker*." Iva was fairly shouting to be heard over her friend. She stopped and glared at Maxine, who glared back and adjusted her thick glasses.

"Took you long enough to spit it out," Maxine muttered.

"We've been sitting here all afternoon trying to figure out what it was," Juanita said in a modulated voice. "Everyone was humming it—some of us better than others"—she looked Maxine—"and that's what we wanted to tell you."

"Did you hear music too, Vivien?" asked Iva.

"Maybe." Vivien thought she might have, but she'd been so anxious and freaked out that she hadn't paid it much attention. "I was a little distracted trying to stop the three of you from being possessed by a spirit, you know."

"Oh, pish," said Iva. "The spirit— I really wish I could give her a name; hopefully we'll figure out who she is soon enough. Anyway, the spirit was quite benign, all things considered. She just wants her story to be heard and understood, that's all. It was very clear to me, Hollis, that she had no intention of harming me."

"While she was leading you down the stairs into the darkness," Vivien reminded her.

"Now, Iva," Hollis began, his voice stern and his eyes wide.

"Vivien, it's time to go," Jake said, desperation in his voice as he bolted to his feet. "Really. The steaks will be ruined. It's been great seeing you all—and thank you *so* much for all the information about the ghost—"

"*You* know about the ghost, Elwood?" Ricky said, standing up. "Have you seen it? *You?*"

Jake froze, and Vivien would have convulsed with laugher if he hadn't looked so incredibly pathetic, all frustrated and trapped and trying to be polite—and if she hadn't felt her heart smoosh and flutter for him.

Damn. She was beginning to think even industrial-strength shampoo wasn't going to help her wash him away.

"I'm really hungry, *Elwood,*" she said, rescuing him. "I think we'd better get those steaks in the oven before they're ruined. Mr. DeRiccio, I hope you're feeling better," she added, and, with the pièce de résistance that she knew would be their escape hatch, she leaned over and kissed Jake's pop right on the cheek, just above his soft mustache. "Enjoy your flowers, Mr. D. I'll be checking on them to make sure they aren't drooping tomorrow, all right? So get them in a vase right away."

"We'll see you tomorrow afternoon at the book signing, right, Vivien?" said Iva, in an obvious last-ditch effort to keep them there.

"Oh, right—yes, thanks for the reminder. I'm looking forward to meeting TJ Mack," Vivien said cheerfully. "I'm a huge fan." And without giving any of the older folks a chance to waylay them again, she took Jake by the arm and towed him off the deck.

"Make sure you go into Hot Toddy beforehand," Iva called after them. "It's right up your alley."

"Will do," Vivien hollered back. "Quick, let's go," she said, diving into the passenger seat of Jake's car.

To her surprise, he didn't say a word during the eight-minute drive to his house. She wondered if she'd somehow offended him or upset him—even though she knew he wasn't that touchy sort of person. At least, he hadn't been eleven years ago...

He was still silent when they got to his house, and Vivien was beginning to think she'd really effed things up somehow when he got out of the car wordlessly and strode over to open the front door without even looking at her.

She went inside, feeling more and more awkward and unsettled by the moment, and watched as he moved swiftly to the kitchen counter. He picked up the meat package there and tossed it into the fridge, then turned to her.

"Jake—" She barely got the syllable of his name out when he had her plastered up against the door—the nearest upright surface—gripping her hips, his mouth on hers, drowning out whatever she'd been about to say.

"Oh my God, thank you, Vivien," he said after an eternity of slick, deep, lustful kissing while she melted under his touch.

He began to nuzzle his way down the side of her throat, making her brain turn even mushier. Her knees buckled embarrassingly, but fortunately, he was holding her against the wall with his solid, warm body. She gripped his arms, reveling in the solidness of his biceps and the texture of his lips and tongue along her neck and shoulder as heat and pleasure sizzled through her.

"I thought we would never get out of there..." he murmured, sliding his tongue lazily around the rim of her ear as she shivered against him. "And have I mentioned how sexy you look in that little blue dress you're wearing?"

His lips were doing amazing things to her, and she could hardly hear the words coming out of his mouth between nibbles, nuzzles, and nips as he slid his hands up beneath her skinny-strapped sundress, sliding them over her quivering belly.

"Jake," she murmured, barely able to form thoughts, but needing to taste him, too, to touch him… It wasn't fair that he had his hands all over her and she couldn't pull herself out of the hot pleasure haze to do more than cling to him so she didn't collapse onto the floor. What he was doing to her was… well, it was insanity.

It was as if no days or years had passed between the last time they'd had their hands on each other more than a decade ago—he smelled, tasted, *felt* the same—and yet it was new and fresh and different—and *hot* as hell. Dear God, she was so hot and wet and swollen, and he was only kissing her.

"Jake," she said again, twisting her face away so she could *think*.

"Vivien?" He stilled, looking down at her with an arrested expression.

"Bed" was all she could manage. "Please. Now."

He growled agreement deep in the back of his throat and swept her into his arms. Moments later, she was tumbling onto the massive bed, Jake following.

His weight atop her was a pleasure she welcomed, a feeling she remembered: the way his leg slid just so between her thighs, pressing up against her at the warm, throbbing juncture there…the way he propped himself up on the left side, just enough to keep from crushing her, but close enough that he could capture her mouth as his right hand slid up to cover her breast, to find her nipple through the lacy bra she'd chosen, and to rub his thumb over it. He knew—remembered—just how to tease her, how she liked it, how even the gentle pinching and flicking of that tight, sensitive tip made her hot and ready and desperate for more.

She fumbled the buttons of his shirt free, suddenly *needing* to move her hands over his warm, taut chest, and to cover the corners of those square, muscular shoulders with her palms. She sighed because it was so familiar and yet different, and her eyes stung a little when she realized they'd lost so much time.

So much time.

He seemed to feel the same way, for all at once, impatience took over for both of them. In a few frenzied moments, they dragged away all the clothing—shirt, shorts, dress, bra, panties, briefs—and at last...at *last*...Jake slid his warm, smooth, hard body along hers, covering her, skin to skin, curve to muscle...and Vivien suddenly felt *home*.

"Oh, God, Jake." *I've missed you.* She was sobbing a little against his warm, salty throat as he slipped his hand between them to find the hot, swollen, oh-so-slick-and-ready part of her. She cried out and arched a little, pressing up into his palm as he found the place, his fingers as deft and sure as they'd always been.

He groaned into her ear, low and husky and needy, sending more delicious shivers down to her center. She felt the thunder of his heart against her palm as he played with her, teasing and coaxing as she whimpered a little, reaching... reaching...and then she came, fast and hard, with a little rush of tears.

"Vivien?" He must've seen or felt the tears on her face, for he hesitated. "You okay?"

"I'll be better once you suit up and start riding, cowboy," she managed in a rough voice.

"As you wi—" His reply ended in a groan as she closed tight fingers around him. Delighted by the heat and heaviness in her grip, she took her time reacquainting herself with that part of him, stroking and thumbing over the hard but velvety softness until he firmly removed her hand so he could replace it with a condom.

He cradled her face with his palms, and she brushed his jaw with her fingers, and they were kissing—deep, tonguing, delving kisses—as he found his way. They exhaled matching groans of pleasure and relief as their bodies fit together...and then began to move.

The rhythm was slow and easy at first, as if they were remembering each other, memorizing the way it felt—so right, so perfect, so exquisite—until Vivien began to need more, faster and harder, and she urged him on with her body, and soon they were panting and groaning and crying out with release...and relief.

Relief.

It was the only word that sat with her as she lay there in a haze of ebbing heat and still-rippling passion, damp and warm against Jake, whose heart thudded strong beneath her cheek.

Relief, because now she was truly home.

CHAPTER NINETEEN

"VIVIEN, SWEETHEART..." Jake said a long while later. They were curled up together in bed and he was playing with her hair, wrapping it around his finger. It was soft and silky and it smelled good—just like the rest of her—and he could hardly believe they were here, just like this again, after so long.

"Mmm?" Her eyelashes fluttered against his shoulder.

"I need to straighten you out on something you said earlier. It's pretty important." He was smiling as he said it, humor coloring his voice.

"What's that?" she murmured, stretching long and languidly against him so that a breast just *happened* to slip into his palm. And he couldn't ignore *that*, so he began to gently roll his thumb over the tip of her tightening nipple, smiling more as she shivered delicately against him. "I hope you're not going to tell me Ricky's lost interest. I brought him flowers and everything."

He huffed a laugh and tweaked her so she squeaked in outrage, then kissed the abused nipple with a long, sensual swirl of tongue. He loved the way she sighed when he was touching her, all low and sexy.

"No, and I don't know why you'd bring my pop into this moment," he said as he pulled away, and felt her lips curve into a smile when he cuddled her close again. "It's a little disconcerting."

"Oh, you'll get over it," she said, scratching his chest lightly with her fingernails. It made him want to purr, and for a moment, he just reveled. Then she stopped and said, "Well?"

"Oh, right. So...you don't put steaks in the oven," he said.

"What?" She propped up onto an elbow to give him a confused look. Her bourbon-colored hair tumbled over her breasts as she blinked matching eyes in confusion.

"What, meaning—what do you mean you don't put steaks in the oven; I thought that's how you cook them? Or what, meaning—what did I say, because you were so overcome with lust that you didn't hear me?"

She chuckled, then sobered. "Steaks don't go in the oven? Really? And why did you bring that up, anyway?"

"No, sweetheart, they don't go in the oven. They go on the grill, or on a broiler—"

"But isn't a broiler in the oven?"

"Technically it is—"

"Ah-ha!" She poked him in the belly. "So technically I was right."

"Technically, yes—but when you say 'in the oven,' that implies something else—like baking or roasting. Like, you put bread in the oven, or a cake, or a roasting chicken, or meatloaf, but not steak. *Never* a steak. You'll ruin it." He couldn't control a little shudder, thinking of the two-inch-thick filets he had waiting for them if they ever dragged themselves out of bed.

The sunset he'd promised her was long over with, and he'd been ignoring hunger pangs for quite a while in favor of other, more interesting pangs.

"And when did I say anything about putting a steak in the oven, anyway? I'd never say something like that. You know I'm allergic to cooking."

"Earlier today, when you were engineering our escape from Maxine and my pop. You said something about putting the steaks in the oven, and I thought I'd do a little PSA just in case you got motivated to get up and start dinner in order to refuel me so I have the energy to jump your bones again. You wore me out, VL," he said as she shook with silent laughter against him. "I'm going to need sustenance before I—"

He closed his mouth when she curled her fingers around his cock, which had been relaxed and basking until the idea of jumping bones had come up.

"What were you saying?" she said, her voice muffled as she slipped down beneath the sheets.

"I have no idea," he said as she closed those luscious lips around him. "And...I don't...care."

IT WAS the blackest part of night when the steaks finally made their way onto the grill. A swath of glittering stars danced above them and out over the dark blue Great Lake. The moon was high and sliced in half, but it cast a fair amount of blue-silver glow. The world was so quiet in the earliest hours of Sunday morning that Vivien could even hear the waves washing up on shore in the distance.

An owl hooted, and frogs and cicadas croaked and buzz-zapped in competing rhythm as a few bats swooped gracefully below the stars. The smell of summer and lake and the faintest tinge of a distant bonfire lingered in the air, and a gentle breeze made Vivien almost need a sweater.

"This is the best meal I've ever had in my life," she said, sighing with delight as she tasted the filet for the first time. "Red wine, steak, baked potatoes slathered with sour cream and chives, and fresh Michigan corn on the cob... And that cool little bug zapper that's keeping us from being eaten alive while we dine al fresco without smelling eau de trash. Manhattan can suck it."

She hummed her anthem, "Food, Glorious Food," as she scooped up a bite of loaded potato.

"Yeah, I'd better thank Mathilda for sending that zapper to me. I never thought I'd have a use for it—I just don't sit out here all that much." *Alone* was the unsaid but obvious word she suspected Jake meant to say.

"Jake, I need to tell you something."

The tone of her voice was meant to grab his attention and maybe even make him worry a little. She grinned inside but kept her expression blank. She owed him for the whole steak-in-the-oven thing.

"What is it?" His voice was carefully neutral, but she saw the corner of his mouth tighten just a little.

"I don't want you just for your patio overlooking the lake," she said, spearing another piece of the butter-soft steak. "Or the view from your living room. It's your dad I'm really after."

He chuckled. "I'm beginning to believe that."

She grinned at him, loving the way the moonlight limned over his features and made him look like a dark, sensual angel. His hair was loose and fell a ways past his jaw, and he hadn't bothered to put on a shirt—which she appreciated greatly. He'd filled out and bulked up just a little—just the right amount—in the last eleven years. And he certainly still had the stamina of a twenty-four-year-old.

"So, Vivvie—" He stopped suddenly, looking awkward. "Sorry—"

Her heart hurt. "It's all right, Jake. You can call me that. I was being bitchy. It's just...it reminded me of better times, and it hurt too much."

He nodded, holding her eyes. "Me too." When he lifted his glass, moonlight shot through the Tempranillo, making it appear more ruby than garnet. "To even better times."

"To even better times." She sipped—the wine was excellent, and perfect with the steak—then steeled herself and said, "Jake...I need you to know how sorry I am about how things ended with us before."

"You've already apologized, Viv, and—"

"I know, but when I think about how self-absorbed I was and what you went through, I feel— I just wanted to say it again."

He nodded. "Thank you. I appreciate it. It wasn't a fun time for me. It messed me up a little."

"I know. Your dad told me your mom was worried about you." Her eyes welled up again as she thought about the fact that she'd never meet his mother.

"I know. I could tell she was...but it was something I had to work through, and I didn't want to talk about it. Any of it.

And, honestly, what happened with Lissa was ugly and uncomfortable, and it still makes me ill to think about it, but when I think about how much worse it can be—especially for women...

"When I was in my residency, I did a rotation in the ER, of course, and there was a woman who came in who'd been sexually assaulted. My God, Vivien, what she went through was so much worse than what happened to me. I mean, it was awful, but it didn't, you know, leave me with the deep, lasting scars—physical and emotional—that she'll have—"

"But it was still awful, still a violation, Jake, and...and if I hadn't been such a bitch, maybe I could have been there for you." And beaten the crap out of Lissa Kirkland.

"You'd been left by so many other people you'd loved. I was just another one doing the same. I didn't realize it at the time either, why you were so upset, why you just cut me off. I was just focused on me, and my future—which I assumed you'd be part of. I could have handled it better."

"We both could have." She raised her glass so it caught the moonlight too. "To even better times."

"To even better times."

They ate in silence for a while, basking in each other's company. Then Vivien remembered Jake had started to speak earlier.

"What were you going to say, Jake? A few minutes ago?"

"I... Well, when the Tuesday Ladies and everyone had me trapped at Pop's, it came up that you're not going to be in the show. Onstage. They were all pretty confused and, actually, a little worried about you. Sounded like Trib—I guess you know him too?—was really sounding off about it. Are you doing okay with all of this?"

Vivien's throat closed up a little and her eyes stung at this unexpected topic. She gave a quick shake of her head and told herself to stop being an idiot. If there was anyone she could talk to about this, it was Jake.

"I just can't," she said after a minute.

He nodded. "I only wondered if things had gotten better since...since I knew you."

"No. I simply don't have any *desire* to be onstage ever again. My stage career—short-lived as it was—was tied so tightly to Liv that I get anxious whenever I think about stepping out there in front of people, knowing that she'll never be able to do it again, that I have to do it alone. I mean, we shared a womb, we shared a crib, beds...acting roles..." She shook her head and collected herself. "We even played each other sometimes, just to mess with people.

"I know it sounds weak, but I get cold and clammy, I break out in a heavy sweat...it's bad. I tried once after—after you left New York to audition for a small role in an off-off-off Broadway show, and I had an anxiety attack and couldn't even walk onto the stage for the audition. I puked in the bathroom instead. So." She spread her hands and shook her head sadly. "My acting days are over."

He tilted his head, looking at her intently, still gilded gently by the moonlight. "Things might change—there's no reason to force them to, but someday they might. After all, Liv is still with you all the time. Isn't she? She'd be with you if you ever went onstage again, wouldn't she? It's not like you're leaving her behind or moving on. She's *with* you. You're connected. You always will be."

Vivien's eyes really stung now, and there was no way she could get any words out of her mouth; her throat was closed up tight. She'd never really thought about it that way, had she? *Liv is always with me. We'd still be sharing a role, kinda.* Looking at him through a watery gaze, she nodded...and just then, she felt a very definite nudge against her left arm.

Jake was sitting four feet away from her.

But even more moving than his sensitive, honest words was the realization that he understood her relationship with Liv, that he didn't think she was crazy or delusional. Always before, she'd wondered a little.

And maybe it had taken Jake meeting a ghost himself to fully grasp how a loved one never quite leaves behind those who remember them. Especially ones who'd shared a womb, who could read each other's thoughts...who were soul mates in a way.

"Thanks," she managed to say, still blinking rapidly. "That actually makes a lot of sense...and Liv seems to agree." She gave an awkward laugh and sipped her wine. "So, speaking of ghosts..."

He scratched the stubble that had just started to show on his jaw. "I can't imagine how crazy it must have been with the three ladies there at the theater and all hell breaking loose with the ghost."

"I was terrified one of them was going to get hurt—or worse. But Jake, I've been thinking..."

"When have you had time to think? I thought I'd kept you pretty busy." He gave her a leer that lingered on her breasts, which happened to be bra-less.

"Maybe you'd better work at it a little harder," she said with a sly smile that grew slyer when she saw him shift a little in his seat. *Shorts getting a little tight there, big guy? Emphasis on the* big.

"You're such a slave driver," he said. Then he looked around and winced a little. "Great. Now I'm always going to be thinking about Liv lurking about, judging my... uh...technique."

Vivien laughed heartily at that. "I promise not to tell you what she says." When he looked nauseated, she laughed again. "Joking!"

She forked up her last bite of steak. "Anyway, I was thinking about the ghost thing. The ladies said they heard the Nutcracker music—which I honestly don't remember if I heard anything or not, I was so freaked out—and Iva said the ghost wanted her to go down to the orchestra pit. Which is where we found that trunk with the Nutcracker stuff in it.

"*And,*" she said, stabbing a piece of potato, "it wasn't until after we opened the trunk and found the Nutcracker stuff that things started to get really crazy. Up until then, it was just a chilly breeze and that weird shadow. I just wonder if somehow, when we opened the trunk, we fully released the ghost's strength."

"Like Pandora's box. And what weird shadow?"

"Oh, I guess I didn't tell you about that. It wasn't anything— Well, yes, I guess it was," she said, gathering her thoughts. "Twice this weird shadow came out of nowhere and sort of glided over the floor at the theater. And then it was gone—although both times it was accompanied by a cool brush of air. The second time I saw it was down in the pit, right before you got there."

"And it was definitely not caused by anything around you?"

"No. It was the same shadow, and there was nothing else both times—I was alone in the theater. And here's the thing—

one of the things—I just realized when I was *thinking*," she said with another sly smile, "I got up in the middle of the night at home that same night we found the Nutcracker stuff, and when I came out to the kitchen, I saw that same shadow —not gonna lie, I freaked out for a minute—but then I realized *that* time, it was the Nutcracker headpiece that was giving off the shadow. It was the shape of its hat—a tall military hat with a slanted top."

"So what you're saying is, the ghost has something to do with the Nutcracker."

"Which happened to have been the *last* show that was ever done at the theater. And they shut it down suddenly and for no reason, and no one ever really found out why. *And—* oh, I just realized this—when the ghost threw everything around in the workshop, the cast photo-poster from *The Nutcracker* was right there in the middle of the floor. I didn't think anything of it until now."

"But the ghost—according to Iva and Bruce Banner—was female. The Nutcracker is definitely male."

"Oh, yes, I know. But somehow it's connected. I just don't know how."

He nodded. "All right. That's really interesting, and it makes sense—as much as a ghost makes sense." He laughed a little uncomfortably, and Vivien found it adorable that he was still awkward talking about ghosts...especially since he'd acknowledged Liv.

She didn't say anything because he'd mentioned he had an early shift tomorrow—in only a few hours, she realized— but she fully intended to visit the theater in the morning to check out the orchestra pit and the trunk once more.

VIVIEN WALKED to the theater down the hill from Jake's (she preferred going down rather than up the hill) the next morning.

It was after nine o'clock, and she'd felt more than a little guilty about sleeping in when Jake had to get up for his shift at five a.m.—and on a *Sunday*.

But the look of pleasure in his eyes when she walked into the kitchen erased any lingering remorse.

"I heard you singing in the shower," he said, handing her a cup of ambrosia—a.k.a. coffee—as he looked up from his computer.

"Unfortunately, it was a solo, not a duet," she replied, bending over to give him a sultry kiss with lots of tongue.

Which he returned, turning up the heat and adding a boob cup while he was at it. "And what were you singing this morning?" he asked, arching a brow.

She smirked and bumped her hip against his. "It was a song from *Oklahoma!* Didn't you hear me?"

"No, I've been working for the last four hours while you were snoring away."

"I don't snore," she said.

"Mmmph," he said with studied innocence. A pair of dark-framed glasses—a new development—sat next to his laptop on the counter, and she immediately wanted to see him wearing them. Cute guys in glasses were one of her favorite things.

But before she could ask, Jake cast her a curious glance. "So what were you singing?"

She grinned down at him. "'I Cain't Say No,'" she said,

then twirled away before he could grab her and prove the point.

His eyes were laughing as he looked at her from where he was stranded at his computer screen. "I sang a duet by myself yesterday morning in the shower," he confessed as his phone beeped with an alert.

She stopped and looked at him. "Really?"

"Yes," he said, looking at the display on his phone. "Oh, good, that's not for me. What were we saying?"

"You said you were singing in the shower yesterday."

He smiled and lifted his mug of coffee to sip, watching her over it with dark, smoky eyes. "Oh, right. A duet, but, alas, I was singing it as a solo. Nevertheless, I struggled through."

"What was it?" she asked. He had a nice enough voice, true—a decent baritone—but he wasn't quite as regularly vocal as she was. And certainly not as powerful when it came to belting.

"'Agony,' from *Into the Woods*. What else?"

She burst into laughter as he grinned and checked his phone as another alert came in.

"Well done, grasshopper," she said.

"Hey, I've got to take care of this—can you feed Carmella?" he said, distracted again.

"Feed who...what?" She looked around. She didn't see an aquarium or even a goldfish bowl, and she knew he didn't have a cat or a dog.

"Carmella—over there on the counter. The Mason jar," he said as he turned his attention to the computer with a whole bunch of complicated-looking programs on it. "One and a half cups water, one and a half cups of flour, stir it all together, pour it in. Oh, but pour off the icky gray stuff first."

Huh?

She looked around and, sure enough, saw a Mason jar on the counter. Was that Carmella...or was that what she was supposed to feed Carmella—whoever or whatever Carmella was—with?

"Uh, Jake, some help here. Who's Carmella?"

"In the Mason jar. My sourdough mother." He flapped his hand in her general direction. He must have seen the bewildered look on her face. "It's the mother of my sourdough starter—fermenting there in the Mason jar on the counter. Feed her, but pour the yucky gray liquid off the top first."

That seemed straightforward enough, and she picked up the Mason jar. Yep, there was some cloudy grayish liquid floating at the top. Humming the obvious song from *Little Shop of Horrors*, she took off the top of the jar and carefully poured the ick down the sink.

What remained was something that looked like waffle batter—sort of—and the only reason she knew exactly what waffle batter looked like was because she'd had to pour her own at a Hampton Inn once when she stayed overnight and ate their free breakfast in the morning and had to make her own waffles in the idiot-proof waffle maker thing.

"Where's the flour?" she stage-whispered to him while he was tapping away on his laptop, and he gestured vaguely again toward what turned out to be a pantry.

She managed to find the flour and follow the rest of his directions, and therefore successfully fed Carmella.

Then she popped over and gave him a quick kiss on the

cheek—he was still distracted by looking at some complicated images on the screen, his glasses forgotten—and slipped outside.

Perfect—she didn't have to tell him she was going to the theater and worry the poor guy.

It was going to be a hot day—perfect for the tourism industry in Wicks Hollow, but a little less exciting for someone who had labor-intensive work in a building that had non-functioning air conditioning. Still, Vivien had work to do if she was going to open the show on time, and she couldn't allow herself to be waylaid or distracted by ghosts or vandals.

She arrived at the theater and, with some trepidation, let herself in.

"All right, everyone just keep calm," she called out, feeling a little foolish but determined nonetheless. "I'm here, I know you want me to figure out what's going on, and I'm going to go down into the pit in a few minutes and try to do so, all right? So just...don't get all worked up."

To her relief, nothing happened except that she felt the air all around her move, sort of shudder, as if the building was taking in a deep breath and then exhaling it.

The scaffolding was still on the stage, but it was at the very edge where it had obviously somehow stopped before going over to the floor after the ghost shoved it at her and Iva yesterday. The only illumination was the lights she was turning on—some in the house, many more in the backstage area. The dented Nutcracker headpiece sat, ugly as usual, where Jake had put it yesterday, casting an eerie shadow. But at least she knew what caused it this time.

Nothing seemed out of place, and there was no indication that someone had broken in and set up any other surprises for her. Maybe whoever it was had decided it wasn't worth the trouble, since Vivien was clearly not about to be chased away from her business.

Or maybe...

She smiled to herself as she pushed the scaffolding back upstage. Maybe the Nutcracker-loving ghost had scared the bejeezus out of whoever it was and chased them off.

"I'll bet that's what happened," she said, walking across toward the right wings.

She stopped in the wide-open center of the stage and looked out over the empty seats. Tried to imagine what it would be like to face rows and rows of people again, eyes trained on her, expectant...

Liv brushed her arm in a supportive caress, and Vivien felt a glimmer of *maybe*.

Maybe someday.

"But not today," she said, and then, surprising even herself, she did a little soft shoe from a barely remembered routine. She didn't even know what show it was from, but it felt...good.

Ending with a flourish, Vivien bowed to the invisible audience of her theater's phantoms and stood there, panting a little, as she looked around.

Maybe.

Maybe someday.

In his perceptive, thoughtful way, Jake had given her something to think about last night.

She shivered with pleasure. What a guy. What an amazing man. Even after more than ten years apart, he understood her in a way that even Helga couldn't.

A song dropped into her head just then, along with its

snappy, happy rhythm. And because, dammit, she *was* happy right now—and because she'd had an amazing night and Jake was back in her life *despite* her trying to keep him away—she couldn't hold it back.

She sang about a boy who'd made her helpless, improvising her own dance routine because she couldn't ever try to emulate the brilliance of the *Hamilton* cast.

And when she was done, her voice echoing to the far corners of the theater, out of breath and exuberant, she bowed once more to the ghosts who watched her and thought...

Maybe.

VIVIEN FINALLY GOT down to the orchestra pit. Jake had texted wondering where she'd gone, and she told him she'd be back by noon and would make lunch.

His response was a single horrified-eyed emoji that had her laughing as she descended into the pit.

She'd brought a flashlight to help illuminate the way and shined it around even though two bulbs were now working down here.

The trunk was just where they'd left it—closed and silent —but something else had changed.

There on the floor, in a puddle of spangled silk and glittery tulle, was a sequined white ballerina costume that could only belong to *The Nutcracker's* Sugarplum Fairy.

It was lying next to the military coat that had belonged to the Nutcracker himself.

Her palms suddenly slick, the hair on the back of her

neck standing on end, Vivien walked slowly over to the pair of costumes as something Iva or Juanita had said rang in her memory:

I heard the Sugarplum Fairy ran off with the Nutcracker...

It couldn't be a coincidence that those two costumes had been left here and arranged like this. As she bent to pick up the ballerina costume, a cool breeze buffeted the back of her bare neck and shoulders, raising goosebumps.

"All right," she said calmly, holding up the costume to look at it. "What do you want me to know about— Oh my God..."

The skimpy little leotard had rents in the back of it, and there were huge, ugly brown stains all over.

Like rust...or blood.

CHAPTER TWENTY

VIVIEN WAS HUFFING and puffing by the time she made it back to Jake's house—which wasn't a shock, considering that she'd practically run up the hill from the road where the theater was while she was carrying the Nutcracker's coat and headpiece, as well as the Sugarplum Fairy's tutu and the cast show photo.

She could have texted him to come and get her, but she didn't know what time he got done with his shift, and besides, she was a liberated woman and could handle a big-little hill just fine.

Because she didn't know whether he was still working, she let herself in as quietly as possible, then dumped her burdens on the living room sofa.

He glanced over, raised his brows at the costumes, and said, "I should be done in about fifteen minutes—I just have to finish this patient and write up my notes."

"That's okay, I want to look at this," she said, picking up the headpiece.

She'd waited to examine it closely until she got back to

Jake's house—better light, and no touchy ghosts, she reasoned, who could have a tantrum at the drop of a hat. Humming "Masquerade" (which, in her opinion, was a perfectly creepy song to accompany this task) and with her skin prickling with excitement and nerves, she took the headpiece over to the kitchen counter, where the light was the brightest.

Just as she'd noted before, the back was caved in, but it didn't look as if something heavy had crushed it in the trunk. The damage looked more like someone had whacked the headpiece with one blow or punch, for the deep indentation was a single, circular area.

Vivien examined the sharp break in the back of the papier-mâché, then tilted the mask to look up inside its white interior.

It was easy to see the dark stain inside. Right where the piece had been crunched inward in a violent indent...and below it. As if something had smeared or trickled down.

Vivien's breath caught, and she flipped the mask the other way so she could look down into it with the kitchen light shining inside, but what she saw only supported her theory: that it was a bloodstain inside the headpiece, and that the blood was from whoever had been wearing it when they were hit on the head from behind.

So the actor had been hit on the head.

Maybe he'd been killed too, because she was pretty certain the Sugarplum Fairy had been stabbed to death. The bloodstains were pretty big.

And maybe that was why the headpiece had been hidden in the bottom of a trunk, pushed away under the stage in the orchestra pit and locked up tight where no one would find it.

She was so intent that she didn't hear Jake close his laptop and come up behind her.

"What's all this?" he said, eyeing the headpiece.

"Take a good look at this," she said, gesturing to the mask. "Tell me what you think."

While he did that, she retrieved the Sugarplum Fairy's costume and the military coat from where she'd left them on the sofa.

"So?" she said when Jake put the mask aside. "Thoughts?"

He tilted his head. "Oh, I have thoughts, all right."

"Well, don't leave me in suspense."

"It looks like someone was hit on the head while wearing the headpiece. The position and type of indentation, the stains—which look like old blood to me—and their position would bear out this theory. Is that what you wanted me to say?"

She nodded. "Yes. Is that really what you believe?"

"It's plausible. More than plausible—"

"And the fact that it was locked in the bottom of a trunk that was basically hidden in a crawlspace way beneath the stage...doesn't that follow too?"

"It certainly doesn't do anything to debunk the theory." He picked up the mask again, turning it around carefully in his hands. "But the question is, was it an accident, was it fatal, and was it purposeful?"

"That's three questions, but I concur that they're all vital. Now, look at these."

She laid out the other two costumes. Jake picked them up, one at a time, and gave a low whistle. "These rents in the back of both of them—and the stains—"

"From stab wounds, don't you think?" she said. "The stains are harder to see on the red military coat, but it's really obvious on the Sugarplum Fairy's costume."

"So you think someone killed both of the people who were playing these characters—and that's who's haunting the theater," he said. "Makes sense to me."

She hugged him exuberantly. "Oh, good, oh thank goodness you agree. I thought I might be going a little crazy."

He shook his head. "This whole thing is crazy, but this actually makes a lot of sense—as far as ghosts are concerned."

"Exactly. I mean, they are logical in their own twisted way."

"So then it *also* follows that whoever is sabotaging you is trying to keep the theater from opening because they don't want the mask to be found—because they attacked and possibly murdered the Nutcracker," Jake said. "The two things have to be related...otherwise it's just too much of a coincidence."

Vivien felt spikes of relief and excitement that he agreed with her. "It just makes sense—the mask was hidden away— and Iva, I think it was, said no one really knew what happened when the theater suddenly closed down and never opened again."

"Maybe. But if someone killed the *actor* who played the Nutcracker," he said with a quirk of a smile, "and the actress playing the ballerina—wouldn't the owner of the theater or the producer or someone notice they went missing? It would have been all over the news, I'd think."

"Unless that's who killed him. The person in charge—the producer or troupe leader or owner of the place. And Iva, I think it was, said they heard the Sugarplum Fairy—that's whose costume that is; it's just as iconic as the Nutcracker's—ran off with the Nutcracker. What if that's not what happened, but that they were both killed, and the story was just put out that they ran off together or were sick or whatever happened—and that was why the show was canceled."

She brought over the poster-sized blowup of the cast photo for *The Nutcracker*. The date was December 1994, so she knew it had to be the right one.

Scrutinizing the photo, she looked for anyone who might be familiar. The core cast was in the photo, each in their costumes and in an active pose. She paid special attention to the Sugarplum Fairy and the Nutcracker, who wasn't wearing his headpiece in the picture, and felt a little pang of grief when she looked at their smiling, happy, electric faces. She could only assume the worst had happened to them.

"I wonder who that is," Jake said, pointing to a distinguished-looking man standing with his hand on the ballerina's shoulder. "He's the only one not in costume."

"Probably the director or the producer," Vivien said. "But he's standing with the Sugarplum Fairy—maybe he was her husband or something. I think Iva did mention someone from town played the ballerina. Maybe that's who she meant."

"Well, we need to get this stuff to Joe Cap right away," said Jake.

"Agreed," Vivien said. "He can take it from there. See if that's really blood on it, and let him follow through on the investigation. Oh, and I can make sure Maxine and Juanita and the rest of the Tuesday Ladies know about the headpiece and our theories when I go into town for the book signing this afternoon. It'll be all over the county by the end of the day.

Then the vandal would have no reason to try to keep a secret, because the secret's already out."

Jake was nodding. "That would definitely help. But more important, we've got to figure out if there's anyone who's been in and around the theater recently that might be connected to the 1994 *Nutcracker* production."

"Everyone I've had out there at the building—contractors, visitors, volunteers—are locals, and they wouldn't be the right age to have acted in a professional show nearly thirty years ago."

"What about those little children?" Jake asked, looking at the poster again. He pointed to three young children in the very front dressed in period clothing. "Guessing they'd be about your age now, wouldn't they?

"Well, I'm pretty sure a five-year-old girl didn't murder two adults," Vivien replied. "But I think everyone in the picture should be identified."

"Hopefully it won't take the police too long to do so." He frowned, then his expression relaxed. "Now, what do you say we have some lunch—which *I'll* make—and then we take a nap? Sundays are perfect napping days—especially when you didn't get much sleep the night before."

"I'VE GOT to stop in here," said Vivien, pausing on the sidewalk in front of Hot Toddy. They'd just come from meeting with Joe Cap at the police station, and now they were walking to the bookstore. "Looks like a cute coffee shop. And I could use an iced latte. I'm awfully thirsty after that workout this afternoon," she added, giving him a sly look. "We didn't nap much."

Jake grinned complacently and followed her into the pink cottage with lime-green shutters.

Inside, she was delighted to discover a huge framed movie poster from *Victor/Victoria*. The walls were also decorated with several photos from the same film—most of Robert Preston, but some with him and Julie Andrews, Blake Edwards, and James Garner as well. They all seemed to be signed by Preston.

"Hot Toddy—I love it," she said, then hummed the super-catchy "Le Jazz Hot!" as she approached the counter.

"I don't get it," said Jake, looking around.

"Robert Preston played an 'old queen'—as the character puts it—named Toddy in *Victor/Victoria*, which is a movie and musical about a woman, played by Julie Andrews, pretending to be a gay man who is pretending to be a woman, who performs in the clubs in 1930s Paris. It's comedic and romantic and the music is wonderful. So the coffee shop is named after Toddy, who's Victoria's best friend and mentor. Blake Edwards directed the movie and Lesley Ann Warren plays a hilarious floozy. It's perfect," she said to the proprietor as he came from the back room.

"Thank you, miss," said the barista with a broad smile on his dark face. He was well over fifty, with an Indian accent and a gold hoop in one ear. "It's my favorite movie, obviously. I met Robert Preston three times before he died, and he signed each of those for me in person. What can I get you?"

They were just getting their orders when Bella Pohlson came in, looking unusually rushed. "Oh, Jim, thank goodness you're still open. I'm just *dying* for an iced oat milk latte with stevia, and I also need an iced macchiato... Oh, hi, Vivien. And...Dr. DeRiccio, is it? Sorry to be in such a rush—my husband's waiting in line for the author signing and he wanted me to run over and get us something." She was paying for her drinks and Vivien and Jake were nearly out the door when she said, "Oh, by the way, Vivien, that little grand opening thing I got you came in finally—I can drop it off at the theater for you sometime this week."

"That's so nice of you—thanks," Vivien said. "Enjoy the signing—we'll probably see you there."

As they walked out, Jake took her arm and muttered, "She was your realtor, right? She could have had access to the building before you got to town."

Vivien stopped on the sidewalk and looked at him. "I've thought of that, but I simply can't think of a reason she'd want to ruin things for me. After all, she made money on the sale of a building that's been sitting there empty for over twenty years. And if the vandalism is related to hiding the murders, I don't see how Bella Pohlson could be involved. She would have been maybe five or six when the Nutcracker murders happened."

"Nutcracker murders?" came a familiar voice. "What are those? Is that a new TV show on that Netflax thing everyone's talking about?"

"Hello, Mrs. Took," said Jake politely. "Hi, Mrs. Acerita. And hello there, Bruce Banner." He prudently didn't reach to pet the little dog, who was peeking out of Juanita's bag as usual.

"Don't you Mrs. Took me, Elwood DeRiccio. Makes me feel old—and like you're talking to my granny. It's Maxine—or Dr. Maxine if you wanna get fancy—and nothing else, you hear? Now you tell me and Juanita what's all this about some Nutcracker murders."

"We might as well wait until Iva and Cherry get over here—I can see them heading across the street. Apparently, everyone in town is going to the book signing."

"Damn right. TMJ Mack, she's one of the biggest writers we ever got coming in here to sign books—except maybe that fine piece of ass Dr. Ethan Murphy," Maxine said, looking around as if to sight said fine piece of ass. "He ain't a medical doctor like you, though—he's got some degrees in—"

"It's TJ Mack, you *loco*," said Juanita. "And Ethan Murphy isn't going to give you a second look when he's got that gorgeous Diana warming his bed."

"Well, a woman can dream, even at my age—"

"Vivien! How are things going at the theater?" asked Cherry, giving Vivien a hug. "I hear there's been some vandalism *and* two murders!" she added in a whisper.

Wow. Vivien had no idea the gossip train traveled that fast in Wicks Hollow. "We literally just left the police station fifteen minutes ago," she said. "How did you hear— Oh, Helga must have told Orbra."

Cherry nodded. She was with a tall, wiry man about her age that she introduced as William Reckless. Vivien concurred that he did, indeed, look a little reckless...while at the same time, somehow, he also seemed very Zen, with an om tattoo on his lower arm and a few rustic strings with charms and beads around his neck. The perfect match for Cherry Wilder.

Vivien filled in Iva (who was accompanied by Hollis Nath), Cherry, Maxine, and Juanita on what they'd discovered about the Nutcracker costumes as they stood just off the sidewalk and out of the way of the people heading to the bookstore.

"I knew it," said Iva. "It was the Sugarplum Fairy who was leading me to the basement—the pit, I mean. She obviously had a lighter, more deliberate touch when it came to communication—unlike the Nutcracker, who was just wild and angry, don't you think, Vivien?"

Vivien could not disagree.

As they stood in line to get into the bookstore—TJ Mack was a very popular draw for the tiny venue—Vivien saw Louise London's brother Benjamin walking down the street, so she waved him over. Trib's didn't open until five on Sundays, but she would have expected Benjamin to already be there prepping things.

"How are things going at the restaurant?" she asked. "I was in there the other day, but you were too busy to come out and say hi."

"It's all good," Benjamin said, grinning. "Trib's a real nice guy. A little picky, you know, but he's a good guy. Thanks again for setting me up with this. I'm learning a lot. Can't wait to get back to New York and find a job at one of the bougie restaurants there."

"Tell your sister hi for me," Vivien said—not that she didn't hear from Louise regularly and insistently (the last communiqué had been along the lines of "when are you moving back to NYC?").

"I will. Thanks—I gotta go. I'm a little late, and Trib's kind of a bear about being on time," he said, and took off at a lope down the street.

"Kid sounds like a stoner," commented Jake. "Wonder how long he'll last."

"He's not a kid—he's probably in his mid-twenties. And anyway, I don't know about that, but Trib didn't seem all that impressed with him when I was in there the other day. But Louise asked me to hook him up here this summer as a favor, so I did. I hope Trib doesn't hold it against me."

"Trib worships you," Cherry said. "I wouldn't worry about it."

They finally got inside to see TJ Mack, who turned out to be an attractive woman in her early thirties. Standing off to her side was a geeky-looking but cute guy with auburn hair who seemed shy and more than a little out of his element, but game nonetheless.

"That's Oscar London," said Maxine in a stage whisper. "He and TMJ Mack—"

"TJ. It's *Tee. Jay*," said Juanita from between gritted teeth.

"But TMJ just *sounds* right," Maxine argued. "Anyway, he and...she just caught a murderer over to the lighthouse up at Stony Cape—"

"They met when she was trying to finish her latest book," said Iva, her eyes starry with appreciation. "The lighthouse got double-booked and neither of them would leave. It's a romcom plot right out of one of her books!"

"I thought she wrote the Sargent Blue thrillers," said Vivien. "Are you saying she does romcoms too?"

"Oh, she's done some very sexy historical romances," said Cherry. "A while ago, and I hope she does more. There's one about a blacksmith, and—"

She got cut off when it was her turn to step forward to get her book signed.

"Oscar London," murmured Jake into Vivien's ear. "Any relation to Louise London?"

She shook her head. "No, hers is a stage name."

They had a brief, very pleasant conversation with TJ (whose real name turned out to be Teddy) in which Vivien learned that the author's cousin was the blacksmith in town—and the father of the teen who'd found the trunk in the orchestra pit. But Vivien didn't fill the thriller writer in on the rest of the plot. She'd save that for another time.

"Oh, hi, Vivien," said Susie Wallaby, whose nephew had been working at the theater the other day. She was standing in line with her hand curled around the arm of an older man who was probably her dentist husband, and they were chatting with Drew Jeffreys, who apparently Jake also knew, about the upcoming football season.

Vivien didn't get any sort of negative vibe from Susie, despite what Helga had told her about the Mean Girls back in high school.

"So nice to see everyone out supporting our local businesses. Isn't Hot Toddy great?" Susie added, looking at the to-go cup Vivien was holding. "We can't wait to come out to support yours too! And make sure you give Gordon a call when you need your teeth cleaned," she added with a wide, sparkling, perfect grin as they inched forward in the line.

"I'll do that," Vivien said, then turned to say hi to Melody Carlson, who was standing in line right behind the Wallabys with a very frail man who could only be her father.

"Dad loves to listen to audiobooks," she said, all friendly and warm. "I thought he'd like a little visit away from the home, get some fresh air, some new scenery. Right, Dad?"

His eyes were dark and a little vague, but he nodded as if prompted. "Yes, my dear."

"Oh, Vivien," said Susie, turning back to them. "I meant to ask if you found a jade bracelet at the theater. I was wearing it the other day when we were out and stopped by to see you, and I lost it sometime during the day. It was Gordon's mother's," she added softly, "and we're leaving to go visit her."

"I haven't seen it, but you're welcome to take a look around," Vivien told her.

"Do you think I could swing by the theater tonight on the way home from here? Would that be terribly inconvenient? We're leaving to go out of town tomorrow for two weeks, and it's going to be really awkward if I don't have it when we visit his parents." Susie gave a pained smile.

"No problem at all. We can wait for you until you're done getting your books, and then we can head over to the theater right away."

"You're a gem, Viv! Thank you so much." Susie turned back to her husband and the coach, chatting vivaciously.

"Well, if it isn't Vivien Savage," came a voice from her other side. "I heard you were back in town."

Vivien turned to see a tall, broad-shouldered man about her age. It took her a moment to place him, then she smiled and laughed as they hugged. "Jesse Prime! It's been a long time since we were driving around in your little Fiero. How are you?"

They were chatting about how things had changed—and she met his darling daughters, who were two and three, and his lovely wife—when Jake's phone rang. He stepped away to take the call, and when he returned, Jesse had gone down the street with his family.

"So that's the guy you let put his hand down your pants in high school, huh?" Jake teased.

"Down my pants? What are you talking about?"

"You said you let him get to third base in his Fiero—the other day when we were talking with Joe Cap about people you knew back in high school."

"Yes, third base—he had a hell of a time figuring out how to get my front-fastening bra undone." She chuckled. "But I didn't let him undo my jeans."

"Up top is second base, sweetheart. Third base is copping a feel in a southerly direction, and, well, you know what a home run is."

"Oh, ha, I guess I had it mixed up. Did I hear you talking to your dad on the phone?"

"Yes. He wants me to bring him some Vernor's and a beef pasty from the market. Like he doesn't have enough food from the Tuesday Ladies." He rolled his eyes. "Which means he's feeling lonely, so I'll sit and chat with him for a while."

"That's all right—I'll just ride over to the theater with Susie and let her look for the bracelet, and then I'll walk back to your house. It won't be dark for hours."

"He'll be disappointed not to see you, but that's probably the best option. We don't want poor Susie to get in trouble with her mother-in-law."

When Susie and Gordon came out of the book signing, Vivien explained the situation.

"I'll text when I'm leaving to walk home," she told Jake, giving him a swift kiss. "Give that to your pop for me, all right?"

"As long as you save a home run for me," he murmured in her ear. "See you in a little bit."

A SHORT WHILE LATER, Vivien unlocked the door to the theater. She had to admit that she was a touch worried the ghost might act up with the Wallabys there, but she was hoping that since she'd figured out what was going on, the ornery ghost would have no reason to do so.

Either way, her plan was to get in and get the Wallabys out—hopefully with the bracelet—in record time.

Dr. Wallaby had a flashlight in his car, and, along with Vivien's, they were able to shine around in all the dark corners of the places where Susie had been until, at last, she pounced with a relieved cry.

"Here! Oh, thank God, Gordy, now I can visit her without worrying about lying," she said.

"That makes two of us. Thanks much, Vivien. I'll look forward to seeing you for a cleaning once you get settled. You do have a beautiful smile," he added as he and his wife went to the door.

"Are you coming now?" Susie asked. "Would you like us to give you a ride wherever? I heard you don't have a car right now."

"Thanks, but no—I've got a couple of things to take care of here, and it's a very short walk to Jake's house. It's not even five o'clock."

Once the Wallabys were gone, Vivien went into the backstage area to see if she could find any other photographs from *The Nutcracker*—and bitterly regretted having thrown away the old playbills and programs. There might have been some clues or information in them, for each actor would have a bio and a photo in the program.

She was digging through a drawer in what would be the stage manager's desk when she thought she heard voices.

"Hello?" she called, and walked out onstage.

"Oh, hello, Vivien," said Melody Carlson. She was helping her father walk down the main aisle. "I'm so sorry—I hope we're not bothering you. Did you find Susie's bracelet?"

"Yes, we did. Can I help you with something?" Vivien asked, feeling a little confused.

"Oh, yes, I'm sorry—it's just that my dad really wanted to see the place again, and I heard you talking with Susie and knew you were going to be here...and since Dad doesn't get to get out much, I thought we'd just stop in so he could look around. Sort of a nostalgia thing."

"Oh, well, that's fine," said Vivien as a prickling swept over the back of her neck. She looked around, hoping the ghost wasn't going to get impatient and start acting up. "I didn't realize your father knew the place."

"Oh, yes, he used to be here all the time, didn't you, Daddy?"

Vivien had stepped off the stage by now, getting close enough to greet them—and close enough to see the way Mr. Carlson's eyes suddenly sharpened with lucidity as he looked around the space.

"This...here..." he said, gripping his daughter's arm tightly.

"Yes, Daddy, I know," she said, giving Vivien an apologetic look. "Why don't you sit down right here in the front row so you can watch the show?"

As Melody helped Mr. Carlson settle uneasily into his seat, Vivien got a good look at him and started. She'd just seen that face—albeit twenty-five years younger—when she was poring over the Nutcracker cast photo...

"You were here," she said without thinking. "During the *Nutcracker* production, the last—"

And then she saw the glint of metal in Melody Carlson's hand.

It was a gun.

And it was pointed at Vivien.

CHAPTER TWENTY-ONE

"IF YOU HAD ONLY TAKEN my warnings seriously and given up the idea of reopening this place," Melody said, moving the muzzle of the gun closer to Vivien. It was only six inches away, and Vivien's knees were trembling so much that she thought they might give out—which would be a sudden movement and not a good idea, all things considered.

"*Go or die.* I was very clear. But you didn't listen, and so now it's going to get a little messy," said Melody. "Now, up onto the stage, if you please. Daddy, stay there and watch just like I did. You won't tell anyone either, will you, Daddy? We'll have another secret to share."

Vivien caught the strange glint in Melody's eyes and decided, for the moment, at least, to comply (if her knees held her upright)...and to try to keep her talking.

Wasn't that what you were supposed to do when confronted by a homicidal maniac? Because clearly she was homicidal—Vivien was guessing it ran in the family—and the creepy look in Melody's blue eyes was definitely maniacal.

"What do you mean, watch like you did?" she asked as she climbed up the five steps onto the stage.

"He didn't know I was here," Melody said. She was talking as if in a dream as she prodded Vivien toward the catwalk ladder. "Up we go, bitch. I never did like you, from the very beginning. The way you came in to school and lorded your celebrity over everyone. Thought you were better than the rest of us just because you'd been on Broadway.

"I was going to be on Broadway too. Daddy promised me. I'd been working hard for so long to be ready...for years and years. It even broke up my marriage—not that I cared when I had Daddy to take care of me. And then he got sick—far too young—and had to go into the home, and I had to take care of him. And he couldn't help me anymore."

Vivien took her time grasping the sides of the ladder and taking the first step up as she tried to follow Melody's convoluted, trancelike speech.

Why was Melody making her climb up? Vivien was afraid she knew, and she didn't like it.

"Your mother—she was the Sugarplum Fairy, wasn't she? In *The Nutcracker* production, the last one here," Vivien said as she stepped up another rung.

If Melody was following her up, she'd have to manage the gun and the climbing. That might give Vivien an opportunity to escape.

"Daddy, don't get upset, all right?" Melody called over to him. "She's not going to tell anyone. I'll make sure of it. Just like I always promised I wouldn't tell either. Up you go, bitch." She jabbed the gun into Vivien's arm, and Vivien climbed.

"What did you see? You had to have been very young,"

Vivien said, trying to climb as slow as possible without upsetting the crazy lady below her.

"He hit them, and then he—he s-stabbed them. The Nutcracker and the Sugarplum Fairy. And then my beautiful, dancing momma went away and I never saw her again. But then it was just Daddy and me, and so then we had a special secret. Didn't we, Daddy?"

Vivien chanced a look out into the audience. Mr. Carlson sat in the front row. Their eyes met, and for a moment, she saw clarity, lucidity, and malevolence in his gaze. The anger and evil there was so shocking and clear and unexpected that she missed a rung and nearly fell.

"She was sleeping with him," came the low, grating voice from the front row. It was surprisingly strong and precise. "The bitch. They were going to run off together. I couldn't have that."

Even Melody seemed surprised by the speech, for she stilled on the ladder below Vivien. "*Daddy.*"

"And then you hid their costumes—why? Why bother?" Vivien asked.

Mr. Carlson shifted in his seat, seeming to grow into his lucidity, to straighten and expand and mature into a stronger, more upright figure as he spoke.

"If they were found here, or if their costumes were found, who would they look at? Me. Had to move them far away, made it look like they were killed way after they left here. I took them to Indiana—made it look like a carjacking." He smiled, and it was a cold, thin, evil smile in his age-spotted face. "She wanted to run away from me...so that's what happened. That's what everyone thought happened, anyway." He laughed, ugly and low.

It was then that Vivien felt (finally!) the air begin to stir. "So you killed your wife and her lover and hid their costumes so no one would connect you—or the theater—to their deaths."

"That's right. Melody and I left for the holidays in Florida. Everyone assumed my wife came with us. It was only later that I told people she'd run off." He laughed again, that horrible, grating laugh, and Vivien felt the air moving a little more sharply. "The police suspected me, of course. When they found her in Indiana with her *lover*. They watched me—oh, they watched me. But they couldn't pin it on me."

"But why did you leave the costumes here, all these years? Knowing they could be found?" Vivien asked.

"Couldn't come back and get them—they were watching me, suspected me from the beginning. Damned mask was too big to carry around—someone might see me. And besides... who would find them, hidden away in this old, abandoned place?"

She looked up, wondering what would happen if she climbed up really fast and took off through the catwalk and left Melody behind. She might be able to get away by climbing along the light cans before Melody got down. It would certainly be harder for her captor to get off a good shot if Vivien was moving among the warren of catwalks and Melody was either below or trying to follow her along the rickety walkway. They always taught in self-defense classes to run if possible for that reason.

But before she had the chance to put her plan into action, Melody jammed the muzzle of the gun into the back of Vivien's calf hard enough to bruise.

"Stop talking and climb. Now. I don't like it in here, Daddy, and I want to go." Her voice sounded very girlish, and that creeped out Vivien even more.

But she climbed. She was more than halfway to the top of the thirty-foot ladder.

"What are you going to do?" she asked, figuring the more she knew, the better she could plan. And why weren't the stupid ghosts acting up *now*—now that their murderer and his accomplice were here?

Wasn't this what the unsettled spirits had been awaiting for twenty-five years? A chance to have revenge?

"You're going to have a little fall," said Melody. "A terrible accident. Everyone knows the catwalk up there nearly fell down the other day. Unfortunately, there's another section that's still a bit loose...and apparently you didn't realize it before you stepped onto it. Oopsie."

Clever. Vivien had to hand that to her. No one would ever think it was more than an unfortunate accident. And Melody would have the perfect alibi—she was with her father, returning him to his assisted living home at the time the murder happened.

"All right, then, up you go, Vivien Leigh *Savage*," spat Melody. "Stop dawdling. This place gives me the creeps." The little-girl voice was gone, replaced by a hard-as-nails avenger. "Go."

"Is that why you didn't just come and take the costumes away?" Vivien asked, even as she began to climb. "Melody?"

"I couldn't find them—Daddy couldn't remember—and this place is *horrible*. Horrible things happened here...lights, wind, noises... I...don't like it here... So awful... I was going to burn the whole place down if you didn't leave—but this will be better. Much better. Less risky. A terrible accident."

Vivien felt the air stirring more now. It was getting cooler, and she could sense the spirits gathering their strength...and she felt Liv, right next to her, telling her to climb.

She got to the top just as all hell broke loose.

If she'd thought the scene Friday when Jake was here was crazy, what happened now was unfathomable—but at least she'd been expecting it.

A loud roaring filled the air, making her wrap her arm around one of the bars of the landing so she could cover both ears with her hands and remain safe.

The roaring swelled, expanding and echoing like a furious freight train, and Vivien heard Melody scream from somewhere below. But she couldn't look, for the shaking had begun, so wildly, so violently, that she was afraid the whole structure was going to collapse.

Lights flashed everywhere, blinking like strobes, blinding her as she clung for her life to the metal rods that held up the ladder and its landing.

The shaking continued, the roaring, the lights, the screaming...and the sudden, frigid wind that made her fingers want to peel away from the burning cold metal she was holding on to.

And then suddenly, everything collapsed. She felt the floor beneath her feet give away, and her ears were filled with screams as she fell.

CHAPTER TWENTY-TWO

LIV WAS THERE.

Vivien saw her sister—her face as she would be now, at thirty-one, and recognized her.

You're safe, said Liv.

And then Vivien felt the ground beneath her.

VIVIEN OPENED HER EYES. She had no idea how long she'd been lying there—in the middle of the stage.

Everything was silent.

Melody Carlson was in a broken heap on stage left at the base of the shattered ladder, the gun still gripped in her fingers.

Mr. Carlson must have stood—or been dragged—from where he'd been sitting, for he was no longer in his chair, or anywhere near it.

Then she saw him—looking no more substantial than a rag doll thrown to the ground, lying on stage right.

She doubted he could have climbed onto the stage, or that he would have done anything but try to run out of the place if he were able.

He looked as if he might have been tossed there.

Shuddering, fighting the urge to puke, Vivien dragged herself to her feet and stood on trembling knees. Good God.

"That was a little too close for comfort," she shouted in a shaky voice to the place at large.

The scaffolding clattered above her, the stage lights flashed on, and then off. Everything quieted.

She guessed—she hoped—that was the pair of unhappy ghosts, turning out the lights and going to their rest at last.

JAKE CAME AS SOON as he got her text, and unfortunately, he had no choice but to bring Pop with him. He didn't want to take the time to argue about it, and his dad wasn't about to stay home.

"Vivien," Jake said as he pulled her into his arms. He was never going to let her go.

Helga and Joe Cap had arrived only moments before him, and so Vivien had to extract herself from his embrace to finish telling her story.

She seemed relatively calm, all things considered.

Jake was also relieved that neither Joe Cap nor Helga seemed the least bit shocked or disbelieving about the story— which, if Jake hadn't been a witness to the ghostly tantrums, he would never have believed...even coming from Vivien.

"I'm certain you'll find that the man standing in the Nutcracker cast photo without a costume is Mr. Carlson, and that one of the little girls who were extras was Melody," Vivien said. "She must have come up to the theater with her mother, and was there when Mr. Carlson murdered his wife and her lover."

"And one would assume, since she was friends with your realtor, that Melody somehow got a copy of the key so she could come in and set up all of her theatrical warnings," Jake said.

"Exactly. She would have known about the sale probably from the beginning, and would have had plenty of time to plan."

"All right, then. So, uh," said Joe Cap, scratching his head and looking up into the rafters. "You said you were up there when all this happened?"

"Yes, when the ghosts started getting wild and violent, I was standing at the top of the ladder on the landing."

Jake looked at the jumble of metal that had been the ladder and landing—which had been thirty feet above the ground—and felt his insides squeeze. "But how... You couldn't have fallen...? Did you?"

"Well, her sister probably helped her down, now, didn't she?" said Pop, pushing his way into the conversation.

Jake stared at him. "What are you saying?"

Vivien put her arm around his dad and hugged him close, whispering something in his ear. Then she looked up and said to Jake, "Liv—I think—caught me. She stopped me from falling and helped me land on the ground."

"And you bitch about your sisters all the time, Elwood," lectured Pop. "Maybe you better be nicer to them—just in case they go first."

"Sure," said Jake, still feeling pretty discombobulated. "I'll...uh...keep that in mind."

"By the way, there's an Elantra in the parking lot. Presumably Melody's," said Helga.

Vivien and Jake were there for another three hours, giving statements and waiting for everything to be cleared away.

"The place is a crime scene," Vivien said sadly. "There's no way we'll be able to open the show on time. But I suppose that's not such a tragedy, because now I have to find a new Elaine Harper. I just got a message—Penny Stern broke her leg and won't be available for three months. Talk about bad juju."

Helga folded her arms over her middle and lifted her brow. "You know you can find someone *very* easily, Vivien. And what crime scene? I don't see any crime scene. Two very unfortunate accidents happened—and everyone knew the catwalk was old and rickety. You tried to warn them, but they were determined to climb up there and look around. For old times' sake." She spread her hands and shrugged. "No crime scene here."

Vivien smiled through a glint of tears. "That sounds about right. Thanks, Helga."

"No reason to thank me. Joe Cap's the one who did the assessment," she said.

And with that last bit of worry cleared from her mind, Vivien smiled and looked around at her place. Her stage. Her theater.

Thanks, Liv.

THE NEXT MORNING, Vivien awoke to the smell of baking bread. She lolled and stretched, enjoying the big, rumpled bed, and smiled.

And he bakes, too.

And he loved her. Still.

Here's to more *better times.*

That was going to be her mantra now—Cherry would be proud of her; she was always promoting meditation and mantras to help with her anxiety—and with that thought, Vivien swung out of bed and made good use of the steam shower.

When she came out to the kitchen, Jake was sitting at his laptop wearing a pair of dark-framed glasses that immediately made her lady parts sit up and take notice (as if they hadn't already been working hard for the last two days anyway).

With his glasses on, Jake looked like an Italian Clark Kent —all studious and a little geeky with his hair combed back. He was wearing a button-down shirt...and boxers, she saw when she came around behind him.

She hid a chuckle when she realized he was on a videoconference call and had dressed for the part—at least, the top half of him. He gave her a brief smile then went back to his call. She poured herself a mug of coffee (noting that he didn't use those environmentally-not-friendly pods; Cherry would be delighted for the second time this morning).

The fresh bread Vivien had smelled was sitting on a rack and made her mouth water, but she didn't dare cut into it until she knew it was fair game. He might be taking it to Orbra's.

She went out onto the patio with her coffee and sat down to look out over the lake. If she'd been up earlier, she might have seen the morning fog rolling off its gorgeous blues, but it was after nine, and that had happened more than an hour ago.

After all, she'd had one hell of a weekend, nearly dying and all.

Still, she could see the seagulls darting above and a red hawk diving for a fish in the water. There was a freighter on the horizon—probably heading to Chicago or the Soo Locks at Sault Ste Marie; she'd watch for a minute to see which way it was going.

To her amazement, a bald eagle flew just a few yards in front of her—so close she could see its prey still wriggling, dangling from its talons.

It would be very easy to get used to this.

A gentle hand on her shoulder made her start, and she looked up and behind to see Jake, still in boxers and button-down shirt. And glasses. *Yum.*

"It makes me very happy to see you sitting here," he said, and dropped a kiss on her cheek. "There's fresh bread inside —I made a loaf with cinnamon and raisins this morning— *Oof!*"

She'd thrown herself into his arms, knocking his glasses askew. "I thought I smelled cinnamon. Oh, man, with butter...hot and fresh from the oven...Jake...I think I'm going to marry you!" she teased, then smacked a kiss on his cheek.

When she would have pulled away, she realized he had her by the arm. "I wish you would," he said, shocking her to the core.

"Jake, really, I was just kidding," she said, her stomach dumping to her toes.

"I'm not." His eyes searched hers. "I told you...I've never

stopped loving you, Vivien. There's been no one else—not really, not long enough to matter—for ten years.

"I didn't realize it until I found you again, but I've been waiting for you, waiting for you to come back. I was waiting for you to call me again, to use the number you never deleted from your phone."

She swallowed around the lump in her throat. "Jake..."

He pulled her close, dropping a kiss on her forehead, then ducked to whisper in her ear. "I want you forever, Vivien...and I'll even take Liv too, ghostly presence and all. As long as she doesn't critique my technique."

She looked up at him through damp eyes. "That's a deal," she managed, smiling through the sudden tears. "But you have to let me flirt with your pop whenever I want, all right?"

"I think I can handle that."

He cuddled her close, and she closed her eyes, resting her head on his chest.

The song she couldn't help but hum was "I Can Hear the Bells."

CHAPTER TWENTY-THREE

Six Weeks Later

VIVIEN LOOKED out from the wings and clasped her hands together, fighting back the rush of happy tears.

We did it, Liv.

We actually did it.

The Olivia Dee Theater was packed on opening night—every brand-new seat filled with an expectant, clapping, cheering audience member—and Maxine and Juanita were taking their final bows.

They'd been adorable and brilliant, as Vivien had hoped and anticipated, and the audience—many of whom knew the old ladies personally—had eaten up their performances, enjoying their sometimes-improvised banter.

Sometimes a little *too* much improvisation, Vivien thought with a grin, but somehow the ladies knew when enough was enough...at least while onstage.

Roger Hatchard got wild applause and a lengthy run of hoots and cheers, and so did Michael Wold—but the audience saved the standing ovation for Maxine, Juanita, and Baxter, who'd been simply delightful as the discombobulated, earnest Mortimer Brewster.

She felt Jake as he came up behind her, rubbing his hands gently over her shoulders as she waited for her turn to come out from the wings.

"How are you feeling about Vivien Leigh Savage's return to the stage?" he murmured near her ear.

"It was perfect. Absolutely perfect," she replied, leaning back against him a little. She'd let Maxine and Juanita bask in their glory a few moments longer.

"Susie Wallaby was also perfect as Elaine Harper," Jake said. "Good call on that."

"She was better than I expected," Vivien said. "And she sold a ton of tickets for this weekend and next weekend to her husband's dentist friends and her sorority."

"Everyone thought you'd step in to play Elaine Harper," he said, nuzzling her a little, and sending delicious shivers down her spine.

"I know, but that would have been just a little too on the nose, you know? My cameo role was perfect—and the best way for me to get back onstage. I had no lines, no makeup, not much of a costume..."

He chuckled in her ear. "You were the best dead body in the window seat anyone's ever seen."

When Vivien stepped out onto the stage—wearing the same men's clothing she'd worn for her "role," but now with her hair down—she was greeted with thunderous applause and cheers that brought down the house. The rest of the cast moved upstage, leaving her alone at the edge of the stage as the cheering and clapping went on and on.

Her eyes stung and she blinked rapidly, glad she was too far away for anyone to see.

And then she felt Liv, coming to stand next to her. She reached for her twin's hand and felt solidness as their fingers curled together—just for an instant—and then the sensation was gone.

They were onstage together again.

They were home.

A NOTE FROM THE AUTHOR

I HAD A PARTICULARLY fun time writing *Sinister Stage* because my husband, children, and I are a "theater family." We've acted, sung, played music, and/or directed in and seen a number of musical theater productions over the years in school as well as community theater, and I met my husband, aka MusicMan, while doing *Oliver!* far too many years ago to count.

Although I did some theatrical shows in high school, my debut on the community theater stage (just after college) was as the dead body in *Arsenic and Old Lace,* and so it was fun to have Vivien make her return to the stage in a similar way. I probably have a picture of me dressed as the dead guy somewhere in my stuff—if I find it, I'll send it out with my newsletter (are you a subscriber? You should be! Go here to subscribe: http://cgbks.com/news).

I also wanted to mention that I knew a family who lived in a house with an actual tree growing in the middle of it— just as described in Jake's house. They recently sold the house, and I'm not gonna lie—I'm trying to figure out a way to meet the new neighbors so I can see if the tree is still there.

I'm also excited to tell you that I'm working on recording all of the Wicks Hollow books, making them available as audiobooks—with *me* as the narrator! I'm not a professional actor (so don't compare me to Jim Dale or Jayne Entwistle, who, by the way, does an amazing job narrating my Stoker and Holmes series), but I'm told the books are quite listenable. You can find me reading *Sinister Summer* (with more to come) anywhere audiobooks are available.

Finally, I want to thank my son and Erin Wolfe in particular for helping me with some of the musical theater references. It was nice to have two more heads thinking about other-than-the-obvious songs I could use. I've created a playlist with all of the songs mentioned in the book, and I'll be making the list public on Spotify and Apple Music for anyone to listen to—in case you're curious or want a backdrop while you're reading. I'll be posting the information about how to find the playlists on my website and social media accounts soon.

Thank you for reading the Wicks Hollow series. I have so much fun writing it, and I can't tell you how happy I am that so many readers are enjoying my particular blend of ghosts, murder, and romance.

— Colleen Gleason

August 2020

Prefer not to get messages in your email?
Sign up for SMS/Text messages and help keep your inbox clear!

Just type in 38470 for the phone number,
and then type COLLEEN in the message space!

ALSO BY COLLEEN GLEASON

The Gardella Vampire Hunters

Victoria

The Rest Falls Away

Rises the Night

The Bleeding Dusk

When Twilight Burns

As Shadows Fade

Macey/Max Denton

Roaring Midnight

Raging Dawn

Roaring Shadows

Raging Winter

Roaring Dawn

The Draculia Vampires

Dark Rogue: The Vampire Voss

Dark Saint: The Vampire Dimitri

Dark Vixen: The Vampire Narcise

Vampire at Sea: Tales from the Draculia Vampires

Wicks Hollow Series

Ghost Story Romance & Mystery

Sinister Summer

Sinister Secrets

Sinister Shadows

Sinister Sanctuary

Sinister Stage

Stoker & Holmes Books

(for ages 12-adult)

The Clockwork Scarab

The Spiritglass Charade

The Chess Queen Enigma

The Carnelian Crow

The Zeppelin Deception

The Castle Garden Series

Lavender Vows

A Whisper of Rosemary

Sanctuary of Roses

A Lily on the Heath

The Heroes of New Vegas

Beyond the Night

Embrace the Night

Abandon the Night

Night Beckons

Night Forbidden

Night Resurrected

Tempted by the Night (only available to newsletter subscribers; sign up here: http://cgbks.com/news)

The Lincoln's White House Mystery Series

(writing as C. M. Gleason)

Murder in the Lincoln White House

Murder in the Oval Library

Murder at the Capitol

The Marina Alexander Adventure Novels

(writing as C. M. Gleason)

Siberian Treasure

Amazon Roulette

Writing as Alex Mandon

The Belle-Époque Mystery series

Murder on the Champs-Élysées

Colleen Gleason is an award-winning, New York Times and USA Today best-selling author. She's written more than forty novels in a variety of genres—truly, something for everyone!

She loves to hear from readers, so feel free to find her online.

Get SMS/Text alerts for any
New Releases or **Promotions!**

Text: **COLLEEN** to **38470**

(You will only receive a single message when Colleen has a new release or title on sale. *We promise.*)

If you would like SMS/Text alerts for any **Events** or book signings Colleen is attending,
Text: **MEET** to **38470**

Subscribe to Colleen's non-spam newsletter for other updates, news, sneak peeks, and special offers!
http://cgbks.com/news

Connect with Colleen online:
www.colleengleason.com
books@colleengleason.com

www.ingramcontent.com/pod-product-compliance
Lightning Source LLC
Chambersburg PA
CBHW070830190726
48292CB00006B/2175